RAG DOLL BONES

A NORTHERN MICHIGAN ASYLUM NOVEL

J.R. ERICKSON

AUTHOR'S NOTE

Thanks so much for picking up a Northern Michigan Asylum Novel. I want to offer a disclaimer before you dive into the story. This is an entirely fictional novel. Although there was once a real place known as The Northern Michigan Asylum - which inspired me to write these books - it is in no way depicted within them. Although my story takes place there, the characters in this story are not based on any real people who worked at this asylum or were patients; any resemblance to individuals, living or dead, is entirely coincidental. Likewise, the events which take place in the novel are not based on real events, and any resemblance to real events is also coincidental.

In truth, nearly every book I have read about the asylum, later known as the Traverse City State Hospital, was positive. This holds true for the stories of many of the staff who worked there as well. I live in the Traverse City area and regularly visit the grounds of the former asylum. It's now known as The Village at Grand Traverse Commons. It was purchased in 2000 by Ray Minervini and the Minervini Group who have been restoring it since that time. Today, it's a mixed-use space of boutiques, restaurants and condominiums If you ever visit the area, I encourage you to visit The Village at Grand Traverse Commons. You can experience first-hand the asylums - both old and new - and walk the sprawling grounds.

DEDICATION

To Karen and Ron who help care for the Honey Beast so the books can actually get finished.

*J*une 1983
Ashley fell out of the tree and landed with a thud inches from Carl Lee's rock.

She scrambled away, watching the boulder as if Carl's blood might still stain the marbled surface. It didn't, though she saw a line of ants march studiously up the rock's face and disappear into a fissure at the top.

Carl Lee had blown his brains out while sitting on the rock three years before. Her neighbor, Norm Smarts, had found him and said there was nothing left of Carl's head except a glob of red and gray mush splattered across the rock.

Now the rock held the mystery associated with haunted houses and creepy dead forests. Kids dared each other to run over and touch it. Sometimes they snuck out to the rock at night and ran home screaming, sure they'd heard Carl bustling through the trees after them.

Ashley didn't like the rock and yet often walked to it when she played in the woods, as if it had some kind of pull. What Mr. Ferndale called a gravitational force, which was interesting enough until he started to drone on about newtons and mass and calculations, at which point Ashley wanted to crawl under her desk and take a nap. She liked science well enough, but Mr. Ferndale made even interesting subjects boring.

During their flame-resistant paper experiment the week before, Harvey Nelson had fallen asleep on his desk. They'd been using Bunsen Burners for Pete's sake! But Ferndale still managed to put a kid out cold.

She left the boulder and started toward home, halting at an odd little chirping sound, like wind through a flapping umbrella. Squatting close to the ground, she listened to see if she could tell where the sound was emanating from.

It took her several minutes of walking in ever-widening circles. She paused next to a dead ash tree. The upper half lay fallen and decaying on the forest floor. At the bottom of the tree, she noticed a dark hollow. She squatted and peered into the opening.

There, wriggling in the tree's empty belly, three tiny raccoons crawled and chirped, their miniature paws like sharp little hands.

Ashley smiled and cooed. She reached into the hole, ignoring the silent voice of Grandma Patty reminding her that if you touched wild animals, their mother would abandon them.

The raccoons scrambled to her fingers, nipping and sucking at the soft ends. Their noises grew louder and more desperate. One began to crawl up her arm, reaching the edge of the tree's opening and flopping onto the ground. It landed on its back, legs pawing at the air.

"Oh, no, poor little critter. Did you fall out of the tree?"

She scooped him up and stroked his head. He was lighter in color than the other two, the mask over his eyes more brown than black.

"I guess you're the Alvin out of this bunch, huh?"

She set the raccoon in her lap and reached in for another.

"Simon," she murmured, gazing into his face and imagining two little spectacles over his black eyes.

The third raccoon made a rather perfect Theodore. He was fatter than the other two and slower. He started sucking on her thumb the instant she picked him up.

"You guys are hungry, aren't you?"

Ashley had seen a dead raccoon that morning on her walk to school. She wondered if it had been the mother of the three babies.

"Ash? You out here?" Her best friend, Sid's, voice cut through the trees.

She pushed the babies back inside the tree and jumped up to meet him.

She spotted Sid. He was still wearing the dreadful powder blue polo shirt his mother had forced him to wear to school that day. It made him look like a forty-year-old banker instead of a thirteen-year-old seventh grader. Ash kept her mouth shut about the shirt. Sid got enough teasing without adding his best friend's voice to the mix.

"Sid," she yelled, waving her arms wildly. "Look what I found!"

Sid hurried over, his face flushed.

Ashley led him to the tree and squatted down.

He got on his knees and peered into the hole.

"Whoa," he murmured. "They're so little."

"I know, and I think the mom died. They seem really hungry."

Sid used the end of his shirt to wipe off his thick glasses and then returned them to his nose, leaning in closer.

Ashley reached a hand in and scooped out Alvin.

Sid recoiled and shook his head.

"Maybe you shouldn't touch them, Ash."

"Well, it's too late now. Plus, this one practically jumped into my lap. I'm telling you, they're starving. If we don't help them, they'll die."

Sid sighed, a sound Ashley knew well. The sigh marked his surrender to Ashley's plan despite his obvious desire not to.

"What do you think they eat? Like bugs?" Sid asked.

Ashley rolled her eyes.

"They eat milk, stupid. They're babies."

"Oh, and what? You're a raccoon expert now?"

Ashley cuddled Alvin against her chest.

"We need a bottle."

"A baby bottle?" Sid asked, scratching his chin. "Who do we know with a baby?"

Ashley bit her lip.

"The Potter's have a new baby, but I don't think they'd offer a bottle up for the raccoons," she thought out loud. "A medicine dropper!" she announced, imagining the tray of medicines that had stood next to Grandma Patty's bedside for the last six months of her life. Ashley's mother had bought medicine droppers by the dozen. Not only had Grandma Patty needed them for medicine; near the end of her life, she'd also taken water and bits of meal replacement shakes through the droppers as well.

Ash put Alvin back into the tree. "Okay, medicine dropper and milk. Anything else?"

Sid shrugged. "A blanket? It might get cold in there at night."

Ashley nodded in agreement. "Yeah, good idea. Dang," she paused. "We might be out of milk."

"We only have skim," Sid told her, rolling his eyes. "My mom won't buy anything unless it says low fat."

Ashley wrinkled her nose. "Skim tastes like white water."

"I know," Sid grumbled.

Ashley stood and waved at Sid to get up. "Okay, let's go."

They hurried through the woods, and Ashley forced her legs to slow as they walked through the neighborhood back to her house. She wanted to sprint home, grab the milk and medicine dropper, and return to the woods. But if Sid did so much as a single jumping jack, he'd start sweating buckets, and then his mom would throw a hissy fit because he'd soiled his new shirt.

"Yes!" Ashley cheered, when she opened the refrigerator. A new gallon of whole milk sat on the top shelf. "My mom must have gone to the grocery store before work."

Sid opened the freezer door.

"Fudge pops too," he said, his eyes gleaming.

"I hope she got Ding Dongs," Ashley said, glancing toward the pantry. "Last time she bought Twinkies. Those taste like cream filled cardboard."

Sid got a faraway look in his eyes. "I love Ding Dongs and Twinkies."

"I know you do," Ashley said, filling a glass jar with milk and sticking two medicine droppers in her back pocket. She pulled an old blanket from the hall closet. "Grab us a couple fudge pops and let's go."

When they returned to the woods, the raccoons were where they'd left them, still scrambling around and making their little mewling-chirping sounds.

Ashley opened the jar of milk and nestled it between two large sticks on the ground. She filled her dropper with milk and plucked Alvin from the tree.

Sid held two fudge pops in his hands. His own, mostly eaten and Ash's half-eaten one, which she'd given to him as soon as she spotted the tree.

She held the tip of the dropper near the raccoon's mouth and depressed the rubber ball sending a trickle of milk over his little black nose.

"Open up," she whispered, nudging the dropper against his muzzle.

It took a few tries, but when Alvin opened his mouth, he hungrily bit at the dropper. Some milk went into his mouth, but most of it streamed down his face into the grass.

7

Sid finished Ashley's fudge pop and set the sticks on the ground. He filled up a medicine dropper and reached into the hollow of the tree.

"That's Theodore," Ash told him.

"You named them after Alvin and the Chipmunks?" Sid asked, grimacing as the little raccoon pawed against his hand. "Their claws are sharp," he complained.

"Because they're hungry," Ashley told him.

"I'm pretty sure they'd be sharp even if they weren't hungry," Sid retorted.

"Quit talking and feed him," Ashley said.

After several minutes, Ashley returned a damp Alvin to the tree. She pulled out Simon.

She glanced toward Sid and her mouth dropped open. He held Theodore cradled in his palm. The little raccoon clutched the dropper with both hands, and he drank the milk as if it were a bottle."

"How'd you do that?" she asked.

Sid shook his head.

"I didn't do anything. He did it. I guess he was hungry."

They put a blanket in the tree and nestled the raccoons in before heading for home.

"Shit," Sid sputtered, staring down at his shirt.

A smear of chocolate lay in the center of his chest.

"Dang, you're in for it now," Ashley agreed.

She left him at his road and walked another block to her own house.

She read the note her mom had left on the kitchen table.

Sandwich stuff in the fridge. I'll be home late. Love you -Mom

Ashley flopped on the worn sofa, searching in the dusty cavern beneath for her copy of *Interview with the Vampire*, which was on loan from Sid, who had stolen it off his father's forbidden bookshelf the week before.

Sid's dad insisted he was too young to read horror novels.

Little did Sid's dad know, the kids in town had an entire network of books, magazines, and VHS tapes they passed between them, most of which came from Sid's dad's very own bookshelf.

Ash found her page, eager to find out if the child vampire, Claudia, had truly killed Lestat.

Wednesday afternoon idled by the same as most afternoons. Her mother was waiting tables at The Rainbow Trout Grill. She'd pop in to change her clothes and then head to Sunny Meadows, an elderly care home downtown, where she'd work the midnight to eight am shift emptying bed pans, wiping wrinkled, old asses (Ash called them that, not her mom), and mopping piss from the sticky linoleum floors.

Ash ate toast for dinner, gulped a glass of milk for her mother's sake, and gazed out the window into the warm, almost summer, evening.

In two weeks, school would let out for the summer, and Ash had never been so ready to pound down those cement steps outside Winterbury Middle School. It had been a rough year.

A few of the girls in her grade had gotten their periods, almost all of them had started wearing bras, and Ashley, ever-flat chested and frankly not interested in colored lip gloss and hair permanents, walked into school each day feeling like a daddy long-legs spider in a field of monarch butterflies.

She'd also gotten stuck with Ms. Fleming, the seventh grade teacher referred to as Ms. Flem-face, who gave demerits if you walked into class seconds after the bell rang. She lectured in a steady drone, putting you to sleep within two minutes of sitting at your desk. She only smiled on days when she was giving a pop quiz. Students of Flem-face knew if their teacher looked happy, they should not.

Ash had liked elementary school. She'd shared classes with Sid, her best friend. The teachers had been nice. Kids in elementary school went out for recess, had snack time, celebrated holidays with decorations and cupcakes. Middle school was a slap in the face after elementary.

Now they spent all day every day staring in dull contemplation at the white words chalked across the blackboard. Algebra and Shakespeare and the Civil War.

Each night when her mother came home from work, Ash offered a lie about her day, and her mother absently patted her head before falling into bed to sleep until the following morning.

Ash laid back on the couch, propping her feet on the end.

"But now we have raccoons," she murmured, smiling. "Raccoons and summer vacation."

2

"*H*i, Mr. Wolf," Tara Hanson called, peeking her head into his classroom. Her girlfriend, Kim, followed by Debbie, also stuck their heads through the doorway.

"Hi girls," he said, offering them a distracted smile as he graded the last of the day's five question quizzes. He put the quiz out every Wednesday. Four questions related to the coursework, which that week included an analysis of chapter seven in *Jane Eyre*, and one question was for fun. Today he'd opted for *What are you afraid of?*

"The Swirly Cone is doing two for one ice creams until Saturday for the last week of school," Tara went on.

"That so?" Max asked, chuckling at Donnie Cleppinger's answer: My ma's undies.

"Yeah and their flavor of the week is cherry. That's my favorite," Tara added.

Her friends giggled, and Max looked up to find all three girls blushing.

He set his pen aside and wondered what he could say to send the girls skedaddling. They were nice girls, sure, but he had ten papers left in the stack beneath him, and over his dead body was

11

he taking the damn things home to grade when he already had to appear at his mother's Wednesday night dinner. On top of that, he'd rented *Poltergeist* the night before and he still had an hour left and wanted to watch it before the video store tapped him for another night at two dollars a pop.

"I'm a chocolate guy myself," he admitted, glancing at the clock. It was going on four o'clock. He had exactly one hour until he had to be pulling out the chair at his mother's dining room table and sitting his butt down. Maria Wolfenstein did not suffer late arrivals at her dinners, especially her own children. "Sorry to run you off girls, but I'm up against it here." He lifted his pencil and tapped the pages.

The girls giggled again.

"Maybe we'll see you around," Tara said, giving him a huge smile so white it almost glowed.

The girls disappeared back into the hall and Max focused on Betty Rogers' answers, though he could still hear the voices and the distant pronouncement, "He's so hot," by who he guessed was Tara.

The visiting girls were not a rarity for Max Wolfenstein, known to the kids as Mr. Wolf, since his first day at Winterberry Middle School two years before. In part, the kids loved Max because he was young and fresh-faced. He looked more like their older brothers than their fathers.

He also drove a motorcycle, had the laid-back attitude of a surfer dude rather than an uppity English teacher, and struck a decent resemblance to Rob Lowe, who had starred in *The Outsiders,* which had released earlier in the year and had all the boys and girls talking. Rob Lowe, known as Sodapop in the movie, was a tough street kid.

Max shared little else in common with Sodapop. He taught English after all, and if his students could have seen him a decade before when he was walking in their shoes, they would have caught sight of a scrawny kid with a bad bowl cut who often resembled a turtle struggling down the hallway with an over-sized shell on its back. By high school he'd had a spurt, shot up to nearly six feet by his senior year, and joined the basketball team. He ended his high school years as Wolf instead of Wolfy, his boyhood nickname, and had more than a handful of admirers who, a few years earlier, had pointed and laughed when he'd walked down the hallway.

Despite time's helpful encouragements, Max related more to the loners and oddballs in his classes than he ever would the blond cheerleaders like Tara or the square-shaped jocks who, at thirteen, already had arms the size of small gorillas.

"Speaking of," he muttered, pulling out Sid Putnam's paper.

Sid was a pudgy little fellow with giant glasses forever sliding down his small pointed nose. His front teeth were too big for his face, but stayed mostly hidden behind large fleshy lips. He laughed in a spasmodic hyena pitch, and though he tried to contain the sound by never laughing at all, he was rarely successful. Mostly because he sat next to Ashley Shepherd, his seeming best friend with a sharp sense of humor and a tendency to talk during class.

Ashley was whip smart with a dry, rather adult humor that often surprised Max. She was also pretty. Someday she'd be a knockout Max thought. She had long thick black hair and tanned skin, not from the sun, but a heritage he guessed came from Spain or Mexico. There was no father in Ashley's life as far as Max knew. Her mother, when she could make it, attended conferences alone and had the distracted, frazzled look of a woman who worked too much and slept too little. Ashley was a latchkey kid who Max imagined spent most of her afternoons eating cereal and running wild in the woods.

He'd seen her several times walking alone down by the railroad tracks that ran through downtown or riding her bicycle on the country roads. Sometimes Sid was with her, but Sid's parents kept a much closer eye on their youngest child.

Sid had answered all the questions correctly, but when Max's eyes trailed over the last question, Sid's answer gave him pause. What are you afraid of? the question asked. Sid had written in his tiny chicken scratch: The boy in the woods.

Max shuddered, his red pen leaving a squiggle next to Sid's answer.

"Well, that's creepy, isn't it?" he asked the room, which had grown oddly quiet.

Through the windows, he saw most of the students had ambled away from the sidewalk. No cars or buses occupied the circular driveway. The American flag hung limply in the still sky.

"An imaginary boy?" Max jotted next to Sid's answer with a smiley face that didn't feel all that jovial.

He graded the last of the papers, pausing a final time to read Ashley's answer to the final question.

Her response was not unexpected, 'nothing,' she'd written, and Max almost believed her.

MAX STEPPED into the hallway at the sound of raised voices.

A woman's hysterical cry rang out. "No one saw him? How could that be, Principal Hagerty? Someone must have seen him. They must have." The woman's voice grew shrill, and the man beside her wrapped a protective arm around her back.

Max saw the principal's face drained of color, and his eyes big and bulging as he tried to reassure the couple before him.

"He's a young man. He's of the age-"

"No!" It was the man who spoke now, or bellowed might better describe it. "Simon did not wander off to sow his wild oats or whatever you're trying to imply, Principal Hagerty. I want an announcement. I want permission to post fliers. We've called the police."

Something touched Max's elbow, and he jumped, sending his papers fluttering into the air like a dozen white butterflies. They floated down and settled on the shining floor.

"Mr. Wolfenstein, I apologize," Brenda Cutler told him, blushing.

Miss Cutler taught Home Economics. She was a short, round woman with a mop of frizzy black hair. She was forever donning an apron splashed with cocoa powder or flour. The aroma of cookies followed her, and when she walked, she bounced as if skipping across balloons.

Max grinned and blew out a breath.

"It's okay, Miss Cutler. You caught me eavesdropping."

"Worrisome to be sure," Miss Cutler said, inclining her head toward the couple.

"What's that?" he asked.

"Simon Frank," she whispered, her eyes going wide. "He's been missing since last week. Both his parents work. They don't even know when he went missing. He never came out for breakfast Friday morning, but they figured he got an early start.

Sometimes he arrived to school early to play boardgames in the cafeteria with a few other boys. Both his parents worked late Friday, and his bedroom door was closed when they got home. It wasn't until about noon on Saturday, his mother looked in on him. Bed was made, not a sign of him."

"Simon Frank," Max murmured. He'd had him for sixth grade English the year before. Simon was a nice kid, skinny and freckled with a loud laugh that carried from room to room. Max had heard Simon's laugh more than once as it echoed from the art room across the hall from Max's own English class.

"He lives by the old train depot," Brenda added.

"No chance he's just playing hooky? Took off with some friends?"

"Not likely," Brenda answered. "Simon's chummy with Jon Hastings and Benjamin Rite. Both were in school yesterday and today. In fact, both boys asked Mr. Ludgin, the social studies teacher, where Simon was. The three had plans to play dodge-ball after school today. Not long after, Simon's parents called and sounded the alarm."

Max frowned. "They seem really upset."

"Sure, sure. Though I'd say that's at least partially on account of little Vern Ripley. He's been missing for six months now. Not a trace of him found."

"I'm sorry, who?"

"Vern Ripley," Brenda repeated," looking at him with surprise. "Oh my, I forget you don't make the rounds with all the kids like some of us do. Vern was an eighth grader this year. A few days after the new year, he walked off with a sled and never came home."

"Vern Ripley?" Max repeated, trying to place the boy, but he was unable to conjure an image.

3

*M*ax thought of the two missing boys as he drove to his parents' house for supper.

Few crimes happened in Roscommon. He occasionally heard rumors about drunk and disorderlies at the town bar, and several years before a girl had been killed in a hit and run, but Max couldn't remember a single murder in all his years in the little town and definitely not any missing kids.

He parked his motorcycle behind his brother's car and hurried into the house, aware he was showing up fifteen minutes late for dinner.

His mother greeted him at the door, tapping her watch before she threw her arms around him and planted a kiss on his cheek.

"Nice to see you too, Mom," he told her.

"Max, I wish you'd call if you're going to be late. At five minutes passed, I started to imagine your motorcycle wrapped around that big beech tree on Kinley Road."

Max's mother stood fussing with his hair like he'd regressed to eight years old. She licked her fingers and patted the dark cowlick on the back of his head.

"Mom, it's fine, please, hands off."

She continued as if he'd said nothing.

"Mom!" He took her shoulders in his hands and gently pushed her away.

"Aww, is Maxy Waxy getting his bath?" his older brother, Jake, asked, striding into the front hall and folding his hand like a kitten as he pretended to lick his paw.

Max flipped him off behind his mother's back.

Jake rubbed his hand over his hair and made loud purring sounds.

"You're next, Jakey," Marie Wolfenstein told her oldest child as she made a last grab at Max, straightening the collar of his shirt.

Max skipped away, running into the dining room where his father had already taken his seat at the head of the table.

Jake's wife sat to his right, her pregnant belly pressing against the table's edge.

"Get behind his ears," Eleanor called, laughing.

"How are you feeling, Eleanor?" Max asked, sitting in his chair with a huff and pulling on his shirt to skew his mother's straightening job.

"Well, my ankles are the size of oak limbs, and I have heartburn so bad I'm lucky to sleep for two solid hours every night, but other than that, I'm peachy!" She laughed and winced, putting her hands on either side of her belly to steady its quaking.

"I had heartburn the entire second and third trimester with Jake," Maria announced, bustling into the dining room with a platter of sausage, Jake on her heels. "Heartburn, morning sickness, and afterward I had stretch marks six inches long." Maria patted her wide hips and shot a disapproving look at Jake, who'd bent to kiss the top of his wife's head.

"My little Maximilian, on the other hand," she continued, looking adoringly at her younger son, "was like carrying a peaceful little cloud. He never kicked, let me eat anything I wanted, and slid into the world with hardly a peep."

"I always knew I was your favorite," Max told her, sticking his tongue out at Jake.

Jake laughed and cast his blue eyes toward his mother.

"Mom, don't try to make him feel better. You prefer me. It's okay. We inevitably love most what we work for, right? If it gets handed to you, who wants it?" Jake winked at Max.

"Enough out of you two," their father announced, clinking his fork against his glass so hard Max feared it might shatter.

Their father was big, much like his sons, but where Max was muscular and wiry, their father was barrel chested with big hands and feet.

He smiled, his dark eyes crinkling with joy.

"Maria dreamed of an eagle last night! Jake and Eleanor are having a baby boy!" he announced.

Eleanor's eyes popped wide, and she shot a questioning glance at Jake, who grinned.

"Dad," Max started, but Maria cut him off.

"In our family, Eleanor, our children appear in dreams long before they arrive in the world. I dreamed of eagles before Max and Jake were born. My sister, who gave birth to three daughters, dreamed of butterflies during each of her pregnancies."

"Wow, that-" Eleanor started, but Marie interrupted her.

"My mother dreamed of a beautiful black and gold butterfly before I was born. Two months before she gave birth to my brother, Sigmund, she dreamed of an eagle swooping toward the sea and plucking a fish from the water."

"It's all very scientific," Max offered with a laugh.

Max's father pointed his fork at him.

"Doubt is the opposite of faith, my son. There is more to this life than your books."

Max nodded.

"Still, you'd think if dreams could divine the sex of babies, our German grandmothers would have made a fortune."

"You bite your tongue," Maria chastised, her eyes sparkling. "We don't impart our wisdom for silver and gold. Such dreams are meant for our children." She reached over to Eleanor and rested a hand on her daughter-in-law's belly. "Do you hear that young man? There is eagle in your blood."

Eleanor giggled, and Jake draped an arm around his wife, leaning in to kiss her cheek.

"I'd like to tell you the weirdness will end when the baby is born, but we both know I'd be lying."

Max, Eleanor, and Jake suppressed their laughter as Maria gave them dirty looks, and their father began heaping his plate with food, whistling a happy tune beneath his breath.

"I made sauerbraten," Maria said, scooping a ladle of the pot roast onto Eleanor's dish. "The vinegar will help with your heartburn."

Eleanor smiled, but Max saw her hesitation.

"You sure it won't make it worse," Max asked, smelling the pungent vinegar.

Maria glowered at him.

"How many years have I cooked for you, Maximilian?"

"Twenty-seven," he told her. "Well, maybe twenty-six considering I didn't have teeth the first year."

"And have you ever-" she started.

But he cut her off. "And I've never gone to bed hungry." He laughed. "I'm just trying to look out for my brother's lovely wife."

He winked at Eleanor, who offered him a thankful smile, though they both knew she'd eat the sauerbraten. Maria had a way of convincing you she'd prepared the perfect antidote for what ailed you. For most of his young life, Max had believed schnitzel cured the common cold.

"How's school going?" Jake asked, taking a sloppy bite of sauerbraten.

"The usual. Last two weeks of school insanity. The kids are practically eating the wallpaper, and I suddenly have six months' worth of papers to grade."

Jake laughed.

"And that's why," he started, tilting his glass of wine toward his younger brother, "I'm in the insurance business."

"And a fine insurance man you are!" Herman beamed, leaning forward and slapping his son on the back. "I'm proud of both my sons."

"Don't we know it," Max murmured. "Oh, Mom," Max laughed as he saw Maria's eyes well with tears.

"Such good boys you are," she agreed, exchanging delighted faces with her husband across the table.

Max grinned and shook his head. Since he and his brother had moved out of the house, their parents had become increasingly sentimental. Every week during Wednesday night dinner, they lavished their sons with praise, and one of them often cried.

They were not typical German parents. Max had met his mother and father's siblings and their children, his cousins. A cool detachment seemed to reside in the houses of their extended family.

The Wolfenstein residence had no such separation. Max could not recall a time in his life when his parents weren't hugging and praising him. Their joy at the loss of his first tooth was as dramatic as his high school graduation.

"Sidney Mitchel Putnam, what have you gotten on your brand new polo shirt?"

Sid looked up to find his mother waiting for him on the

front porch, hands on her narrow hips, brow so creased it looked like waves of sand on a windblown beach.

He peered at the splotch of chocolate goo on his shirt from the fudge pop he'd eaten with Ashley. A strictly off-limits fudge pop as far as his mother was concerned, who allowed Sid one treat a day, always after dinner and always some healthy version of the popular treats - sugar free cookies for instance.

"Um, uh, in art class we-"

"Save it," she snapped, marching down the porch and prodding him inside the house. "Into the tub."

She pulled the shirt over his head and held it to her nose, her mouth pinching into a little angry bud.

"Art class," she huffed, shaking her head. "Do you want pimples like Zach? That's where chocolate gets you."

Sid's older brother, Zach, suffered from such terrible acne; their mother had started putting makeup on his face every morning before school. Their father had scoffed at this, but then shut his mouth after a look from his wife that could have melted the polar ice caps.

"Okay, Mom," Sid said, annoyed. "I can take it from here."

He stood naked except for his underwear in the little bathroom as the bathtub filled with water.

His mother shook her head, already rubbing at the blotted stain as she walked out the door.

"Believe you me, Sidney Mitchell, I've seen it all before."

Sid rolled his eyes and locked the door behind his mother. He settled into the bath, preferring not to imagine what exactly his mother, a nurse at Frankfurt Emergency, had seen. He'd overheard her on more than one occasion telling his father about wounds leaking puss and a guy who nearly chopped his arm off trying to chainsaw a tree branch while standing on his roof.

Sid's father would moan and beg his wife to spare him the gory details. His dad loved horror novels, but when it came to real life, he preferred the sugarcoated version. Which was why Sid couldn't understand his dad's choice to become a volunteer firefighter.

"Parents," he grumbled. They were more like aliens than real people.

Sid loved creepy tales, but recently had discovered he had more in common with his dad than he'd originally believed.

The realization had come the week before, on the night when Sid nearly died.

It had been an ordinary night.

He'd left Ashley's house to walk home just before dusk. If he didn't step foot across the threshold of his front door before nightfall, he'd get a lecture from both his parents. Five blocks from his house, he'd broken into a sloppy run. He wasn't a runner. The extra pounds combined with an overlong torso and too short legs made running a chore more loathsome than scrubbing toilets.

He'd glanced at the patch of woods that offered a direct path to his backyard. He walked in the woods all the time. He'd found his salamander, Captain, named after Captain Kangaroo, though he kept that part to himself, under a fallen maple tree.

The problem was he rarely went in the woods at night unless he was with Ashley. She wouldn't hesitate to stride into the trees and cut three minutes off her time, but Sid had paused, gasping for breath and studying the outline of the dark leafy branches.

Lily-liver. His brother's voice had taunted from within his mind.

"Am not," he'd muttered out loud before he'd turned into the woods.

The near-dark became full dark as soon as he'd stepped into the dense forest.

His sneakers had crunched over branches, and he'd squinted toward the path beneath him. It had become almost impossible to see in the overgrown ferns. He'd taken his glasses off, blown a halo of breath onto each lens, and then wiped them on his t-shirt. When he'd put them back on his face, the path hadn't looked any clearer.

Sid had then stumbled over a root and balked when he fell full-face into a wall of cobwebs. Clamping his lips closed, he had swiped and pulled at the fine gossamer webbing. He'd wanted to scream, but he'd bit back the bellow of surprise for fear a huge hairy spider would crawl right into his mouth.

He'd continued walking, pulling the web from his eyebrows and hair, half considering returning to the street. The lamps had already come on. The sidewalks would've been washed with warm yellow light. He'd have been able to see the blue glow of televisions from peoples' living rooms. It had seemed like a world away from where he stood in the black forest, his face a mask of gauzy strands.

The Six Million Dollar Man wouldn't have been afraid in the woods. Sid had imagined the man striding and leaping with his great bionic legs. He'd picked up speed then, dodging around a tree and laughing as he'd spun away from it, suddenly feeling graceful and fast.

He'd leapt over a pile of sticks, likely gathered by some kids attempting to build a fort that hadn't come to pass. He had landed smoothly with a thwack and crunch and had reached low, grabbing a stick and swiping at the air in front of him like a samurai. He had whipped the stick against the tree and crouched, slicing it back through the air as if it were a silver blade sharp enough to cut glass. Realizing he'd slowed, he'd thrown the stick aside and again picked up his pace.

Behind him a twig had snapped, and Sid had stopped walking. He glanced back, and already the beat of his heart had quickened. The throbbing had pulsed out to his fingers and down to his toes.

He'd turned in a slow circle, squinted into the darkness, and searched for movement. He'd seen nothing, but the shadows were dark and deep. A man or worse, a monster, could've been standing five feet away and Sid would've been none the wiser.

Sid had turned back to the invisible path and forged on. He'd gone only a few feet when another twig snapped, and leaves crunched underfoot.

He'd started to run, and his lungs had screamed in instant protest. His breath had whistled out, and he'd put his hands in front of him to bat away the branches that blocked his path.

He'd twisted around, needing to see what chased him, but only the thick impenetrable darkness had unfolded behind him.

When his foot had hit the log, he'd had only a second to flail and panic before his upper body had heaved forward and he'd sprawled onto the forest floor. The sleeve of his shirt had gotten caught on a sharp branch jutting from a tree. He'd felt the branch jab into his shoulder and heard the sharp tear of fabric as his shirt ripped. He hadn't even thought of his mother's exasperated sigh when she saw the shirt. His only thought had been to run, get back up and run, run or whatever was in the woods would drag him back into the darkness.

He'd pressed his hands down and felt the sharp prick of a thorn in the flesh of his palm.

Suddenly a hand had clamped onto his ankle.

Sid had screamed and tried to wrench his leg away, but he'd only managed to fall forward on his face. He'd sputtered in the grass, jerked his leg, and rolled onto his back.

The creature behind him had leered from a face as pale as the moon. Dark sunken eyes had glared out from its hideous face.

Sid had kicked out, and his sneaker caught the thing in the chest, sending it sprawling backward.

Sid had lunged away, pushing up to his hands and knees, and then finally to his feet.

He had then run faster than he'd ever run in his life. His legs had seemed to be propelled by a force that couldn't have possibly come from him. The thing his father called the survival instinct, the superhuman power that arrived when death loomed.

Death.

The word had exploded in his mind, and somehow, he'd run even faster. When he'd broken from the trees, the glow of evening had barely registered. His feet had slapped the pavement in loud reverberating thuds.

He hadn't dared to slow, to turn back, hadn't even thought of his burning legs and aching lungs. He'd run until his feet hit his driveway, and even then, he'd raced to the door, pulled it open, before crashing into the foyer.

His brother looked up, startled. Headphones had covered his ears, and he'd been rifling through his bookbag.

He'd looked from Sid's face to his shirt and then back to his face. Without taking off his headphones, he'd shaken his head and laughed. "Mom's going to freak when she sees your shirt." He'd traipsed out of the room without another word.

Sid had collapsed onto the rug and pressed his face against the welcome mat.

He'd made it. He'd survived.

A loud rapping sounded on the bathroom door, and Sid sat up, his heart pounding. He'd sunken low into the water, lost in his memory of that terrifying night. The water had grown lukewarm.

"You okay, Sidney?" his mother called.

"I'm good, Mom," he told her, pulling himself up and stepping out of the bathtub.

His feet and hands had pruned. He stared at the puckered flesh and flashed again to that monster in the woods. Its skin had also looked wrinkled.

He'd told Ashley the story the very next morning on their

walk to school. She'd listened, her dark eyes big and believing. That's what he loved about Ashley. She always believed him.

If he'd told his parents, they would have scolded him for watching scary movies with Ashley and insisted he'd imagined it. His older brother would have laughed and come up with a new degrading nickname like wussy or namby-pamby.

Ashley did none of those things. Instead, she probed for more information. What did the monster look like, smell like, sound like? Were its hands more like claws? Did it seem hungry? Did it have sharp teeth?

That afternoon, they'd even gone back to that stretch of woods and searched for evidence of the creature. They'd found nothing, but Ashley still hadn't doubted his story.

Sid toweled off and pulled on his brown Chewbacca bathrobe. He hurried down the hall to his room, slipping quietly past Zach's closed door. Zach loved to pester him about the robe. Sid's parents had offered to buy him a new, more adult robe, but Sid had refused. They wore itchy looking terrycloth robes that were bor-ing! He liked his bathrobe just fine - thank you very much.

4

"Help ya?" the man who sat behind the reception desk looked up as Max walked into the police station.

"I hope so. I was wondering if I could talk to whoever's working the case involving the missing kids."

The man crinkled his brow. "Missing kids?"

"Yeah, Vern Ripley and Simon Frank."

The man scratched at his raw looking chin. He'd likely shaved that morning according to the little red bumps dotting his skin.

He picked up his phone and hit a number.

"Someone here wanting to talk about some missing kids. Yeah, sure. I'll send him back."

The man cranked around in his seat and pointed to an open door.

"Detective Welch has a few minutes."

Max thanked him and walked toward the open door.

The man behind the desk had a pockmarked face and salt and pepper hair. His large neck sat atop square shoulders. He looked like a jock, an aged high school football player who needed to continue his winning streak off the field.

Though he smiled at Max, it was a cold appraising smile that put Max on edge.

"Name?" the detective asked.

"Max Wolfenstein."

"You related to Jake and Herman?"

"My brother and father."

The detective smiled and nodded.

"Good folks. They insure my house. My wife thinks your brother's a hoot. That baby come along yet?"

"Anytime now."

"You in the insurance business too?"

Max shook his head.

"I'm a teacher at Winterberry Middle School."

"Oh, yeah? Well convenient you came in. We were fixin' to make our way around to the teachers next week. You know Simon Frank?"

"I had him in my English class last year."

"English?" The detective looked at him as if he might be joking.

"Yes. Books?"

The detective offered a humorless chuckle.

"Sure, I'm familiar with books. But all of my English teachers were ladies. You just caught me off guard there."

Max gritted his teeth and tried not to retort with a quote from *The Adventures of Huckleberry Finn* that Simon Frank himself had been fond of quoting the year before, *Well, Ben Rogers, if I was as ignorant as you, I wouldn't let on.* "Stereotypes rarely serve us," he replied instead.

The detective laughed as if they'd shared a joke. "Ever hear Simon Frank talk of running off? Did he ever skip class, that sort of thing?"

Max looked at the detective, surprised. "Are you assuming he's a runaway?"

"Assuming?" The detective leaned back in his chair and

surveyed Max with a less friendly eye. "You know what people say about that word. So no, assuming I am not. Simply throwing mud at the wall to see what sticks."

"I wouldn't peg Simon as a runaway. What concerns me is he's not the only kid to go missing. Vern Ripley disappeared in January."

"Whoa, pull back on the reins there, partner," the detective told him, sitting forward and planting two large hands on a stack of papers as thick as a brick. "In my business, I'd call what you're doing right now fishing. Are you a deep sea man, Mr. Wolfenstein? Because you're clearly trying to hook a sea monster, and I'm here to tell you they don't exist."

Max blinked at the man and almost laughed. The absurdity of his comment brought another immediate memory of Simon Frank from the year before, when they'd been reading *Moby Dick* in second period English. At one point, he'd slapped his book and groaned. "They seriously never catch the whale? This book bites!" The memory sobered him and his smile fell away.

"I don't think connecting two missing kids is akin to hunting for monsters at all, Detective Welch. They were around the same age and attended the same school. From the little I've heard, they disappeared without a trace. That doesn't sit right with me. I'm not a detective, but-"

"Exactly," Welch punctuated the air with a single meaty index finger. "And I've been a detective for twenty years, Mr. Wolfenstein. I'm sure in your line of work, reading all that mumbo-jumbo, flights of fancy are a regular pastime for you. In my line of work, flights of fancy get people killed. Capiche?"

Max left the station feeling like he'd just been reprimanded by the principal. He climbed on his motorcycle and pulled onto the road, needing to put some distance between himself and Detective Welch.

～

ASHLEY HADN'T SEEN the boys, but Sid had. His feet slowed to a plod until he'd nearly stopped.

They'd set up makeshift ramps in the parking lot that bordered Wildwood Park. Sid watched as the boys bounded across the asphalt on skateboards, their low sneakers slapping the hard surface as they bent low and struck the plywood boards propped on paint cans.

Shane Savage, who Sid hated based on his cool name alone, did a kick-flip, landed on his board, and then rolled to a stop. He glanced up and even from across the field he saw Shane struck dumb as he spotted Ash.

Ashley was still half-turned, watching the park behind them where a guy was getting dragged from tree to tree by his huge Siberian husky. He called out, "Heel, heel, damn you, Fluffy," but the dog only continued dragging him forward.

Ashley laughed, and when she finally turned forward, Sid had come to a full stop, a deep groove between his eyebrows.

"Ah, shit, the Thrashers," she groaned.

Sid didn't know where the gang of boys had gotten their name. Probably their leader, Travis Barron, had coined it and then thumped anyone who called them anything different.

"Let's go back," Sid whispered.

Travis had just attempted the same ramp as Shane, but he'd landed with his board wheels up. Sid heard him cursing from across the field.

"Hey, Trav, it's Butterball Four-Eyes," one of the other boys called out.

Sid's eyes, magnified by his owl-eyed spectacles, slid over to Warren Leach, who stood a foot taller than every other boy in the seventh grade. Warren's size was a two-parter. He was supposed to be in the ninth grade, but he'd been held back twice. He also came from a family of big beefy guys with thick necks and angry red faces.

"No way," Ashley hissed. "It will take us an extra ten minutes to go the long way. I'm not scared of those ass bags."

Sid grabbed for Ashley's arm, but she'd already begun to stride purposefully toward the parking lot.

"Butterball Putnam and his spic girlfriend. My, what a fine pair you make," Travis jeered, snapping his foot down on his skateboard so the end kicked up. He caught it in his hand.

Ashley faltered at the term spic. She'd heard it before, Sid knew. He'd been standing beside her on more than one occasion and usually the mouth that uttered it belonged to Travis Barron or one of his bonehead friends.

"I'd rather be a spic than a poser," Ash retorted. "I've seen dogs ride a board better than you."

Sid had caught up to Ashley and grabbed the back of her t-shirt just as Travis threw his skateboard down.

"I'm going to rearrange your face, bitch," Travis shouted, red climbing up his neck.

Nothing enraged Travis Barron more than being called a poser. He fancied himself a future skate-pro, but in reality, he could barely ride switch. His daddy's money got him the clothes and the board and all the skater videos he could watch, but he still sucked.

"Get 'em," Travis yelled.

Warren took off first, his big body lumbering with surprising speed. Two other boys followed, but not Shane. Shane watched the scene unfold, his mouth a grim line.

Ashley turned on her heel, grabbing Sid's hand and yanking him along.

"Go to the hole," Ashley spat," shoving Sid toward the pond at the edge of the park.

She could outrun the boys. Sid could not.

He took her advice and raced to the right, panting as he came upon the small patch of woods bordering the pond. He tripped over a root, managed to keep his feet beneath him, and then slid down the hill that edged the pond. The hill dipped inward, creating a little mushy cave blanketed in moss and stinking of wet. They called it the hole.

Sid crawled inside and tucked himself into an awkward little ball, wheezing as he tried to get air into his constricted diaphragm.

The wet grass beneath him soaked through his shorts, and he hoped there weren't any leeches in the pond.

"Damn you, Ash," he muttered, listening as one boy called out, "She went that way."

After that, the park went silent except for the frogs and crickets chattering from the cattails and reeds edging the pond.

Sid stared at his *Star Wars* watch, counting the minutes. After more than an hour, he heard a rustling above him. Sid shrank further into the cave, pulling his legs tight to his belly and holding his breath.

A pair of feet hopped down to the grassy bank before him.

5

$\mathcal{H}$e recognized Ashley's tattered blue sneakers with purple laces.

"Hmph." Sid let out a little groan and a whoosh of breath.

"I thought it was Warren for a minute there," he grumbled, crawling out on his hands and knees. His feet had fallen asleep and sharp prickles tittered in his feet. "Ouch."

Ashley offered him a hand, and when he stood, Sid saw scrapes on her arms and leaves in her hair.

"You climbed the English Vermillion?" Sid asked.

"Yep. Warren couldn't pull his big ass up that tree with a ladder."

Sid snorted.

The English Vermillion was a huge oak tree on the opposite end of the park. In autumn, the tree turned a dazzling pink-red, which Ashley had commented looked the exact shade as the crayon color named English Vermillion. The name had stuck, and Sid rather liked the way they could whisper the word and know what the other referred to while the rest of the world did not. Their own secret code.

"Sorry," Ashley told him, as they climbed back up the hill.

They stuck to the wooded part of the park as they headed out. "I should have listened to you."

Sid shrugged.

"They'd already seen us. They would have come after us anyhow. I'm sorry they called you that name."

Ashley's face darkened, but she waved his comment away.

"I don't care what he calls me. Travis is a waste of space."

Ashley had guts of steel, but Sid knew the insult upset her. Travis was a dirtbag, but he had money, and other kids listened to him. Though he was a year ahead of them, Travis had singled Sid and Ashley out in elementary school. He'd been picking on them both since the third grade. In a way, Travis's cruelty had brought them together.

It had been Ashley who had stood up for Sid when Travis had knocked him down in the hallway four years before, sending his book bag flying and his books scattering across the slick linoleum floor.

"What d'you do that for, jerk?" Ashley had shouted, and though she'd stood six inches shorter than Travis, she'd shoved him.

Travis had cursed and pushed Ashley as hard as he could. She'd hit the racks of metal coat hooks, one of them jabbing into her armpit.

A teacher had witnessed the incident, and the principal had suspended Travis for three days.

After that, Travis made it his life's work to torture them. Their shared enemy had bound them together, and now Sid couldn't imagine a world without Ashley.

"Does your dad have *Hell House*? I heard a teacher talking about how ghastly it was. I'm dying to read it," Ashley asked, as they turned onto Ash's street.

Sid frowned and imagined the books lining the top shelf in his father's bedroom. "I'm pretty sure, yeah. You already finished *Interview with the Vampire*?"

"Yep, last night. It was awesome," Ash told him, leaning over to grab a penny she'd spotted on the pavement.

"Tails up, I wouldn't-" Sid started, but she'd already grabbed it and stuffed it in her pocket.

"Heads-schmeads," she said. "I'm saving for a new bike. I'm taking everything I can get."

"The Huffy Pro Thunder?" Sid asked.

He didn't have to ask. He'd visited the bike shop with Ashley half a dozen times. She'd sit on the bike, trace her finger over the silver spokes and grip the handlebars.

"I only need twenty-two dollars and it's mine," Ash said, a faraway gleam in her eye.

They had decided in school that morning to walk to The Crawford House to get wood for a raccoon den.

The Crawford House sat in an isolated stretch of woods about a quarter mile from the pit. Long before they'd been born, the house had served as the town's funeral parlor.

Sid didn't like the house, not that there was much to like. It had been abandoned for well over fifty years, and for whatever reason, the townspeople had never cleaned it out after the owners had died.

Sid had heard rumors of coffins still sitting in the basement and a hearse in the garage where the roof had collapsed and smashed the windshield. He and Ashley had crept around the house a few times. Mostly they went there to scavenge wood for their forts.

"Here, look at this," Ashley said.

She unfolded a piece of paper and thrust it into Sid's hands.

He looked at a makeshift raccoon hut complete with a steepled roof and a little archway for the raccoons to crawl in and out.

It appeared to be suspended from a tree.

"Why isn't it sitting on the ground?" he asked.

"Because other animals might eat the babies," Ashley said, as if it were obvious, and when he thought about it, it kind of was.

"But how will we get it to stay in a tree?"

Ashley pointed a finger at the tree in her picture. "We'll put it in that fat oak tree by Carl Lee's rock. The one with the low branches. That way we can reach it, but it will be sturdy enough to hold the hut. And I brought some rope from my garage."

"What kind of rope?" he asked.

Ashley shrugged. "I don't know. It looked like an old ski rope. My mom hasn't water-skied ever, so I'm pretty sure she won't miss it."

Sid nodded. "But what if the babies fall out?"

"They won't," Ashley insisted. "Look at the drawing. We'll build a little gate in front of the door, like a foot high. They won't be able to climb over it."

Sid nodded, though he wondered if Ashley's design wasn't a little beyond the scope of their capabilities.

He'd brought a hammer and ten nails from his dad's toolbox, a roll of duct tape, and an old blanket, but other than that, their supplies were limited.

As they stepped into the clearing where The Crawford house stood, Sid's breath hitched.

Solemn fear swept over him in a wave as he gazed at the withering, derelict house.

The windows that were still intact were grimy. Some of them were smeared with graffiti while others were nearly hidden by vines. The tall nearly flat roof supported layers of fuzzy green mold, the type his own father tackled every summer with a spray bottle of bleach and the garden hose. In the center of the roof stood a cupola, the windows gone, black voids in their place.

The front of the house was flat and square, but a huge crumbling stone porch and stairs protruded beneath a double front door that Sid knew was wide to allow hordes of people through during funerals.

Sid had only been to one funeral in his life. His Grandpa Quinn had died several years before. They had held his service in a modern church with chairs instead of pews and a coffee station next to the glass doors that opened into the viewing area. He'd walked to the casket with his brother, their parents standing behind them.

As Sid had leaned down to kiss his grandfather's powdered cheek, he'd heard the croaking sound of 'help me.' Sid had stood up so quickly, he'd stepped on his mother's toes, probably already pinched in her black high heels and she'd cried out in pain. Zach had snickered as their parents led them to their seats, and Sid realized it had not been the disembodied voice of his Grandpa Quinn, but his maggot brother playing yet another shitty joke on him.

The house before him held no resemblance to the church he'd attended.

Everything about The Crawford House whispered doom and dread. He tried to imagine the house as it had been: pale green brick, windows shining, pots of flowers on the wide stone porch, but in his mind the flowers moldered to black. In every window, ghoulish faces appeared, some white and wispy, others with flapping skin and jowls hanging.

"That house is haunted," Sid murmured, eyes darting from window to window, sure at any moment, a face would peer out. As he stood, he realized it was not any face he searched for, but the pale face of the boy in the woods.

The face of the monster.

"Help me with this," Ashly grunted.

She'd gone to the shed, which had mostly collapsed. She tugged at a board still nailed to the frame.

"Let's just use these," Sid said, kicking at a pile of boards that had already fallen away.

"Those are rotted," she said. "These are still in good shape."

He frowned and grabbed the edge of the board. Together they yanked and twisted until it pulled free.

"Do you think there are ghosts in there?" Sid asked, after he caught his breath,

Ashley glanced at the house.

"Yeah, definitely. But that's why we're out here. They're probably trapped inside."

Sid nodded. Ashley always said things with such confidence that he simply accepted them at face value. Sure, she believed in ghosts, but she wasn't scared because they were trapped in the house.

A bit of his fear subsided as they tackled the next board and then the next until they'd ripped ten from the shed.

"This is enough," she said, hoisting seven of the boards into her arms.

"I can carry more than three," Sid complained.

"You've got the back-pack," Ashley said, starting into the woods without him.

He quickly snatched up the remaining three boards and followed her.

As they walked away from the house, Sid tried to ignore the sense that eyes followed them.

6

"Maxy," Jake said, giving his younger brother a loving rub on the head. Max slapped his hand away and their mother tisked. "Frank Welch came to see me yesterday. He said you were down at the station a few days back shouting conspiracy theories like a madman."

"What?" Max and his father blurted at the same time.

Jake grinned. "His words not mine."

"That guy's a Neanderthal," Max huffed, taking a plate of potato salad from his mother and setting it on the table. She'd added Sunday night dinners to their schedule as Eleanor's due date approached. Max's mother wanted to ensure they made up the future missed dinners ahead of time.

"Why were you at the police station, Maximilian?" their father asked, looking somber.

"Because we've had two students disappear from Winterberry Middle School in six months. Two!" He held up his fingers as if his brother and father might not understand the number. "I wondered if they were following any theories. It seemed strange to me that nothing has been posted. I haven't seen an article in the newspaper. There are no safety precautions being offered to kids or parents."

He looked at his brother and father with indignation, growing furious all over again at Detective Welch.

Herman Wolfenstein frowned. Jake cocked his head sideways.

"Any chance you're making it bigger than it seems? Welch implied they're runaways, no connection at all. And Max, you can't save everyone."

"Jake," Max spat, "they're kids. No money, no resources. One of them has been missing for months!"

"Okay, yeah. That's pretty suspicious," Jake agreed.

"And what do you think is going on, Maximillian?" Herman asked.

"Honestly, I don't have a clue. But there are people who take kids. That's what scares me. Is there a bad man in our town and the police are keeping it all hush meanwhile the kids are out on summer break in two days? They'll be roaming the streets, the woods. If there is someone taking them, hurting them, whatever. The town should be aware of it."

"That is terrifying," Maria said, grimacing as she put a tray of roasted beets on the table. "I'll pray for those children tonight."

"Yeah, do that, but also tell your friends. Let people know there are kids missing and to keep a closer eye on their own kids and grandkids."

"Lot of good that'll do," Herman grumbled. "Remember you boys at twelve, thirteen. It would have been easier to cage wolves."

"Exactly," Max agreed. "But that's why kids need to be aware. If someone approaches them, they need to run like hell."

ASHLEY SAT on her back porch and gazed at the sky.

"Werewolf moon," she said to no one.

Her mom had picked up a second shift and wouldn't be home until midnight.

Ashley had watched a show, eaten some cereal, and decided it was too warm out for bed.

It was actually only about sixty degrees, but the first summer nights enchanted her. The air hung with the fragrance of cut grass and the perfume of blossoming flowers. Their yard backed up to the woods, and already the foliage burst forth and trickled over the lawn.

In the peak of summer, she and her mother would tackle the overgrowth with huge gardening sheers, but for now it reigned free.

Fireflies began to prick the darkness, their yellow lights like fairytale glitter in the aromatic twilight.

She used to catch them with Grandma Patty. Her Grandma would supply the jar, and Ashley would run barefoot, giggling, as her grandmother yelled out, "ooh, that one, he looks like an all-night burner. Oh, jump high, little Pan, there's one racing for the clouds."

Grandma Patty chose Ashley's nickname for her long pelt of glossy black hair. According to Grandma Patty, she knew Ashley was a panther even before her hair grew in. Only Grandma Patty used the nickname, and she continued to call Ashley Pan until the end of her life.

On her deathbed, a year and a half before, she'd clutched Ashley's hands in her own, which were so frail and soft they felt like they might turn to dust and blow away.

"Pan, take care of your mama, okay? She will need your panther spirit in the years to come. It's not an easy thing to lose a mother."

Ashley had wanted to tell her it wasn't an easy thing to lose a grandmother either, but she'd only nodded, tears pouring down her cheeks. She'd watched her grandma slip into the coma that would be the final sleep of her cancer-riddled body. Ashley's mother wept from a chair in the corner of the room.

When the doctor came in, he told Ashley's mother that perhaps the girl should leave, wait in the hall, and Ashley had shrieked and clung to her grandma's hand.

"You'll have to drag me out," she'd snarled.

Her mother had waved the doctor away.

"Leave us in peace," she'd told him, the irritation at his suggestion clear on her face.

Together, Ashley and Rebecca had stood, arms wrapped tightly around each other as if they, too, might slip away into the underworld. Given the choice, Ashley probably would have.

The thought of waking up all the days of the rest of her life without Grandma Patty made her stomach twist into a rubber band ball.

A firefly lit only inches from Ashley's face, and she reached out a hand, catching it in the cup of her palm. She opened her hand and gazed at the dark little bug, his butt glowing fiercely and then extinguishing once more. He took flight, his wings tiny whirring blurs in the dusk.

Hopping from the porch, she got a running start and did a cartwheel, her long dark hair twirling through the grass and then fanning up high before settling back on her shoulders. She did another and then another until the darkness and the stars and the forest all blurred together.

She laughed and dropped onto her butt in the downy grass, lying back.

Wisps of pale cloud drifted in front of the bright moon.

"Werewolf Moon," she said again, using Grandma Patty's name for the full moon when the funny, almost see-through, clouds surrounded it.

She shuddered, glancing at the dense forest and remembering the werewolves from the movie *The Howling* she'd rented with Sid the previous summer. In particular, she thought of the serial killer who transformed into a werewolf, and left her creeped out for days afterward. She'd taken to locking her bedroom window each night when she went to bed.

Sid's nightmares had lasted for weeks after the film, and his mother had refused to let him watch movies at Ashley's house for a month.

The vision sucked the magic from the night, and she rolled over and stood up, brushing off the back of her shorts.

As she walked back to the house, a rustling sounded behind her.

She paused and squinted toward the trees.

"Kermit?" she asked.

Her neighbor, Mrs. Lincoln, owned a stout little bulldog named Kermit that frequented Ashley's and every other neighbor's yard despite its owners' best efforts to keep him contained.

The rustling grew louder, as if Kermit were digging furiously at branches and bushes.

She made it halfway across the lawn before the hideous face of Eddie, the werewolf in *The Howling*, rose back to her mind like a song she couldn't stop humming.

Ash paused and stared into the trees.

"Kermit?" she repeated, but the dog didn't come trotting out to greet her, and that was unusual.

Kermit loved attention. If you so much as coughed near him, he hurried over and offered his backside for petting.

Backing up, she trained her eyes on the outline of trees. The rustling stopped, but a shadow momentarily blotted out the moon's glow on the grass. She glanced up to find large birds, vultures she thought, soaring above her. They circled over the trees, making eerie figure eights in the moonlight.

She'd never seen vultures at night.

Curiosity still trumping fear, she stood in place and studied the trees.

Something white appeared briefly within the dense branches, a flash of a face that she couldn't quite make out.

"Who's there?" she yelled, expecting a kid from the neighborhood to jump out and yell, "Boo!"

Instead, silence greeted her.

The face had disappeared into the shadows, but a moment later, a branch cracked, closer to the edge of the yard.

She took a step back and then another, her eyes still focused on the dark foliage, unable to turn away because somehow her back toward the thing would make it worse.

Her heart hammered in her chest, and her mouth grew dry.

Another branch cracked, and again she saw the flash of something pale, a face, but it moved quickly, as if trying to stay concealed.

She backed up, and her legs hit the porch with force, sending her thumping hard to her butt on the edge of the wooden stairs.

The face stepped from the woods, crouched down as if he were not a person, but an animal.

Hollow black eyes stared from pale skin stretched over the sharp bones of its face.

Ashley tried to scream, but only a gasp sputtered from her lips.

The thing's eyes locked on hers; its pale lips parted to reveal a yawning black hole.

It darted from the forest.

Ashley turned and scrambled on hands and knees, wincing as a splinter lodged in the flesh of her palm. Adrenaline coursed through her as she lunged to her feet, yanking open the back door and diving inside. Gasping for breath, she snapped the deadbolt into place, collapsing to the floor and heaving for breath against the door.

Just as her breath began to settle, something scratched at the door.

Ashley froze, eyes bulging from their sockets as she bit her teeth together and tried not to scream.

For more than an hour, she sat perfectly still, counting the passing minutes on the clock over the refrigerator and silently praying her mother would walk through the door, released early from her shift.

Eventually, her butt became so numb she could no longer feel it. Ashley scooted away from the door, staying low out of fear the monster would be watching through the open blinds.

She crawled on her hands and knees into the living room and then stood and ran to her bedroom, slamming and locking the door behind her.

She grabbed her aluminum baseball bat and crawled beneath her comforter, wishing her mother hadn't picked up the second shift.

7

*A*rmed with a gardening fork and a can of bee repellent, Ashley headed into the woods behind her house. Her weapons were meager, but she didn't actually want to encounter the monster, just find evidence that he'd been there. And she needed to check on the raccoons.

After walking for five minutes, she spotted a person through the trees.

Ashley ducked behind the fat beech tree she and Sid called The Walrus.

Shane Savage was sitting on Carl Lee's rock, his legs dangling over the side, his eyes gazing into a space of trampled grass. For several minutes he didn't move, barely blinked, and Ashley grew antsy behind the tree.

Finally, she stepped out and planted her hands on her hips. "What are you doing here?" she demanded.

"This your rock?" he asked, cocking an eyebrow.

A sheaf of blond hair fell over one half of his forehead. If it got much longer, it would obscure his left eye.

"No, it's Carl Lee's rock. So why are you sitting on it?"

Shane laughed. "Carl Lee's dead."

The blunt way he said the words knocked Ashley off kilter. She searched for a witty comeback. "Exactly," she said at last. "You don't live over here."

"So?"

"So, maybe you should go back to your own woods."

Shane lived several miles away in a stretch of barren fields called Sycamore Mobile Home Park. Warren lived there too.

"My cousin lives over here. I was looking for her."

Ashley frowned. "Who?" she demanded.

"Ask me nice and I'll tell ya."

Ashley huffed and started to turn away. "Why don't you like me?" he retorted. "I've never done anything to you."

"Your friends have done plenty," she barked, turning back around to face him. She would not run away from her own woods. If anyone should leave, it was Shane Savage.

"The Thrashers aren't my friends," he told her. "I skate with them sometimes. That's it. They're a bunch of shit eaters."

Ashley spurted laughter, and Shane's own face broke into a smile.

"Total shit eaters," she agreed.

Shane stood on the rock, stretching his arms overhead with a loud yawn. He hopped down and turned back to gaze at it.

"Weird isn't it? Someone died right there on that rock."

Ashley nodded.

It was weird. Sometimes she sat on the rock and had those exact thoughts. She wondered if animals crept up to Carl Lee's body and sniffed it, and if police found the tracks of birds in the blood that coated the surface of the rock.

"My dad knew him," Shane continued. "Carl Lee. He was a Vietnam Vet. On Independence Day every year, he flew a black flag from his porch."

"My mom knew him too," Ashley admitted. She'd bugged her mom into telling her details about Carl Lee on more than one occasion, but Rebecca Shepherd rarely complied. "They went to high school together. I think she might have dated him when they were kids."

Shane whistled. "That's far out. He wasn't like your dad or anything?"

Ashley glared at him, and his eyes shot wide.

"Shit, what? Not cool? I just know you don't have a dad, so..."

Ashley stuffed her hands in her pockets.

"I do have a dad, dickweed," she spat. "In case you didn't notice, I'm not exactly white. My dad lives in Mexico."

Shane nodded as if that were cool, though she wasn't sure what part he found cool, her absentee dad or her non-whiteness.

"My dad's a dick," Shane admitted. "My mom's cool, though. Why's your dad in Mexico?"

Ashley shrugged.

"My mom met him there on vacation and got pregnant when she was nineteen. The rest is history."

"So, he's never been around?"

Ashley sighed, kicking at a clump of leaves.

"Why do you care?"

"Why not?" he asked. "Have somewhere better to be?"

Ashley considered the possibilities. She could go home, eat a bowl of cocoa puffs and flip through the channels. Or she could continue down her original path, searching the woods for clues of the boy or the monster or whatever he was.

"No, he's never been around. I've never met him. I talked to him on the phone a few times when I was little. He and my mom talked about making a go of things, but..." she trailed off. There wasn't much more to tell.

"That must suck for your mom. I mean doing it all on her own."

Ashley nodded.

"Yeah, probably. I had my Grandma Patty until a year and a half ago. She lived with us."

"Your mom's mom."

"Yeah."

Grandma Patty's small bedroom remained in the back of the house. Ashley's mom had tucked her coral print comforter into the creases of the bed and stacked her pile of pillows, crocheted with little sayings like 'This house is a home,' near the headboard. Ashley went in sometimes and curled up on the bed.

The room no longer smelled like her grandmother. The residual odors of the medicine and the lotion that had consumed her final days remained. It stank of the disinfectant cleaner her mother used to wipe down the rocking chair and the dresser after Grandma Patty went into the ground.

"No grandpa?" Shane asked.

Ashley shook her head. "He died when I was like five. I have a few memories with him. He drove a big truck for a living. Had a massive heart attack on the road one day, and his truck just drifted into a guardrail."

Shane grimaced. "Damn, at least he didn't take out like a school bus of little kids or anything."

"Yeah."

Grandma Patty said Grandpa died doing what he loved, chugging down the road, watching the trees whip by as the sun rose over a new horizon.

"So, why do you come out here?" Shane asked, leaning back against the rock. He wore a black t-shirt displaying the band AC/DC over jean shorts. A chain ran from his wallet to one of his belt loops.

Despite going to the same school, Ashley had rarely spoken to Shane Savage. They'd shared only a few classes, and he tended toward the punk-rock cool kids while Ashley's group included Sid and a handful of other kids from her neighborhood who liked to watch horror movies and build forts in the woods.

"I like the woods," she said. "And..." The story of the boy in the forest pushed to the tip of her tongue and there she stopped it, clamping her teeth together.

Shane hung out with the Thrashers. Maybe he didn't call them friends, but how much would he love to take Ashley's crazy tale of a boy in the woods back to those jerks. The Thrashers would have new material to torture her and Sid with for the summer.

"And that's it. I like the woods," she finished.

Shane frowned, and Ashley wondered if he'd push for more. Instead, he shrugged.

"Me too. Though this spot gives me the creeps." He leaned a hand on Carl Lee's rock and then pulled it away as if burned. He barked an embarrassed laugh. "Do you think he haunts this place?"

Ashley glanced at the rock and then the dense forest beyond Shane.

"I've never seen him out here," she said.

When Sid had arrived at her house the following day, grumbling about spending the day before at his Aunt Gretchen's house, Ashley filled him in on the monster boy in her backyard.

Sid sat at the kitchen table, finishing a bowl of cocoa puffs, an off-limits food in his house. He pushed his bowl away and glanced at the kitchen door.

"Do you think it's like a zombie or something?" Sid asked, tilting his bowl and drinking the brown milk.

"Could be," Ashley said. "It wanted to kill me. I can tell you that much."

Sid nodded.

"Me too. Whatever it is. It's bad."

"I tried to find it yesterday," Ashley said, not mentioning her encounter in the woods with Shane. "But I didn't see anything."

Sid grimaced.

"You tried to find it? That's crazy."

"I didn't want to find the monster, just proof it had been there."

Sid fidgeted in his chair and picked at a scab on his arm.

"Because you thought I was making it up too?" he asked.

Ashley glowered at him.

"No. I didn't say that, did I?"

Sid shrugged.

"Did you check on the raccoons?"

"Yeah, I fed them later in the day. They're okay."

"Should we tell someone?" Sid asked, imagining his parents' faces if he and Ashley sat them down and revealed their near-deaths by zombie-forest boy.

Before she answered, he shook his head. "I'll never be allowed to watch another scary movie as long as I live. My mom already took away all my horror comics after I had those nightmares about *The Howling*."

"No adults would believe us," Ashley agreed. "If we could get proof, but even then..."

"Like what? A photograph?" Sid stood and put his bowl in the sink.

Ashley leaned against the counter and chewed the side of her thumbnail.

"We'd almost have to trap it."

"No way," Sid shook his head from side to side so hard it made him dizzy.

"I need to think about it more," she said.

Sid swallowed the lump in his throat, hopeful she'd abandon the idea all-together.

"Want to go to the pit?" Ashley asked. "It's going to be like ninety degrees today."

"Do you think it's safe?"

"Well, we've only seen it at night, right? It probably isn't out during the day. Maybe it sleeps in the day like a vampire."

"Yeah," Sid agreed, rinsing his bowl. "I bet sunlight hurts it or something."

Sid rushed home and put on his swimsuit, meeting Ashley back at her garage.

"Damn my tire's flat again," Ashley roared, kicking her bike.

Her bike was old, a hand-me-down that a neighbor had given her mother years before. The tires went flat at least twice a month.

Sid squatted down and touched it.

"It's the rim."

"I know it's the rim," she grumbled.

"Just ride on my hubs," Sid suggested, delighted at the prospect. He loved when Ash rode on the back of his bike, hands on his shoulders laughing in his ear if he hit a bump.

"All the way to the pit?" she asked, squinting toward the midday sun, a fiery ball that seemed to swallow the cool blue sky in a single gulp.

It was gonna be a hot one and the pit would be their only respite.

Other kids in town had pools. Some of them swam at Higgins Lake, but most of those kids had boats. Ash and Sid would be stuck on the packed beach patrolled by Deputy Dingleberry. Technically, he wasn't a deputy, just a park ranger who made it his sole duty to ruin everyone's summer by yelling at kids who swam past the buoys or played chicken in the water.

Sid rarely went to the beach, and when he did go, his family accompanied him. His mother forced him beneath a giant umbrella and insisted he slather white zinc from forehead to toes. He looked like the Pillsbury doughboy.

The pit, a rock quarry abandoned decades before, was a kid only kind of place.

Sid's dad had told him that fifty years before, a section of the forest had been cleared so trucks could travel in and out of the quarry carrying away huge chunks of gravel and limestone, but eventually the town had closed the quarry down. Nature had taken back the forest except for where the kids had borne footpaths through the weeds and created their own rugged oasis deep in the woods.

One side of the pit was rock and sandstone rising fifty feet high. The rock sloped down to a weedy ledge.

The water looked black year-round, though Sid knew it was only because the water ran deep, deeper than any of them could ever swim. It was a game he'd watched other kids play. They plugged their noses or held their breath and ducked beneath the dark surface. Down and down they'd swim, only to pop up twenty seconds later, gasping for breath and shrieking that it felt colder than a freezer down there.

Sid had never tried himself.

He preferred to stay in the deceptively warm layer at the top, floating on his back and gazing at the never-ending sky. When he imagined the same infinite space beneath him, his heart would beat faster, and he'd paddle to the shore to warm up. Really, he just needed to get out of the abyss, the space where monsters might hide, where something ancient might slumber in the icy quarry bed.

"Earth to Sid," Ashly said. "Are we going to go or what?"

Sid nodded and hopped on his bike, waiting for Ash to climb onto the metal knobs jutting from the back tire. When her hands clasped his shoulders, he pushed away from the curb, standing as he peddled until he gained his balance.

There was no designated trail to the quarry, and Sid and Ashley had created their own. Sid stashed his bike beneath high ferns and followed Ashley into the trees.

They each picked up a stick. Ashley carried one in case the Thrashers showed up and for walking. Sid liked to pretend his was a sword, and he periodically sliced it against dead trees, which he and Ashley then pushed over.

Beneath the trees, the temperature was cooler, but the bugs descended like a flock of end-of-the-world locusts. They buzzed in their ears, landed on their bare arms and legs, and feasted on their young blood. The part of the woods they walked through had a swampy area, which inevitably gave rise to a horde of insects.

"Damn blood-suckers," Ashley hissed, slapping a large one on her bicep and leaving a bloody smear in its place.

Sid swatted his ear where another had been trying to burrow into his skull. They ran the last few yards, breaking from trees into the hot noon sun.

8

*T*he quarry stood empty. Not surprising, as most of the kids opted for the lake or pools, and it was early enough in the summer that the icy water held little appeal. Sid lacked bravery in most instances, but he prided himself on being one of the first kids in the water every year.

No road went to the quarry. You had to walk in. In summer, teenagers frequented the pit at night, building bonfires on the high cliff and smoking grass or drinking beer they'd scammed from their parents' garage refrigerator.

Ash and Sid still had a few years before they'd be into such activities, but they often saw the charred remains left from the previous night's gatherings: beer cans smashed and burned, a snack bag or two, cigarette butts.

Ash would swear and kick at the dirt, gathering up the garbage and putting it in a neat little pile. She hated litter bugs.

Sid hated them too, because Ashley did.

Ashley took off her tank top and tennis shoes, then her shorts, not hesitating as she ran down the high embankment of the quarry. Halfway down she cannon-balled off the cliff.

The jumping spot was only ten feet above the water, but Sid

still cringed when her bare feet left the hard sand and pull in close to her body. She sailed, a little ball of dark skin and hair and hit the water with a black splash. She disappeared, and Sid paused at the rock ledge, breath held until she broke back through the surface.

He took a shaky breath and smiled when she waved.

"You gonna jump today?" she asked, waving him in.

She asked him every time they swam at the quarry. And like every other time, he shook his head no.

She didn't respond, just flipped over and started a long breaststroke deeper into the quarry.

She never pressured him to jump, not like other kids did. Their other friends would goad and dare him. They'd try to drag him to the edge and threaten to throw him off until Ash ripped them in two with some insult that left them defending themselves and Sid forgotten on the sidelines.

He walked until the water was flush with the rock, then he sat down and removed his high-top Reebok tennis shoes followed by his mid-calf white socks with the blue piping. He'd worn his swim shorts, so they stayed put, and he glanced toward Ashley, ensuring she didn't notice as he pulled his Batman shirt over his head and dropped it on the ground, hurrying into the water before she saw his pale fleshy belly.

Despite his mother's insistence he was perfect just the way he was, Sid understood that he was fat. Not fat like the guys who had to sit in wheelchairs because their feet didn't fit into shoes fat, but fat enough that people noticed his weight before they commented on his sparkling personality.

His father had tried to get him into running. Sid's dad ran three miles every day first thing in the morning, after one cup of coffee, but before his oatmeal. Sid had tried it a handful of times, but he'd barely made it three blocks before dropping to his knees and vomiting on the sidewalk.

It was a strange physical reaction because he ran with Ashley all the time. They ran through the woods playing tag, and they ran in dodge ball. He got winded then too, but nothing like he did with his dad. When he ran with his dad, his heart had started thumping before he'd even finished tying his shoes.

The icy water took his breath away, and he dunked under, knowing if he hesitated, he'd be tempted to crawl back out and bake in the sun like a lizard.

He doggy paddled out to Ashley as she dove and popped her head above the water again and again, like a mermaid he thought. And he an awkward little crab struggling to keep up with her.

"Want to swim a story?" she asked.

Their favorite game at the quarry was to swim a story. They took turns weaving a tale as they swam through the dark waters, briefly transporting them both to another realm as they paddled in the midst of the northern Michigan woods.

"Yeah," he said, flipping onto his back. "You start."

"Once upon a time, there were two explorers, Sapphire and Stone."

"I better be Stone," he told her.

She splashed him. "Sapphire and Stone had traveled the world searching for the Lost Kingdom of the Dark Prince. The Prince could only live in total darkness. The sunlight caused him excruciating pain."

Ashley stopped and waited for Sid to pick up the story.

Sid scissored his legs beneath him.

"In daylight, the Dark Prince was hideous," he said. "Big and pale with white amphibian eyes. But in total darkness, he transformed. He became the most handsome man in the world. Stories were told of his beauty, but only the cat people had ever seen him. You see, the cat people had eyes that could penetrate complete darkness."

Ashley grinned and made big lazy circles with her hands on the surface of the water.

"Though Sapphire was a regular person," she said. "Stone was a cat person, but it was a great secret. Not even his closest friend, Sapphire, knew the truth. Sapphire had become obsessed with finding the Dark Prince because only the Prince grew black violets. Black violets were flowers that bloomed only in deep dark water. In places so black and so cold, no mortal could reach their depths."

Sid shuddered, looked into the water beneath him, and continued the story.

"Stone feared Sapphire's obsession with the Dark Prince for he knew if he laid eyes on the Dark Prince, he would know the Prince's true beauty. In Stone's eyes, Sapphire would see the truth of the Dark Prince and she might leave him forever to live in the darkness with the Prince."

Ashley snorted.

"Stone didn't realize Sapphire had no interest in living with the Dark Prince. She only wanted the black violet because she, too, had a secret. She had been stricken with a terrible illness and would die within the year. The only remedy was a tea made from the petals of the black violet."

Sid dunked under the water and popped back up, shifting again to his back as his legs had begun to grow achy from treading water.

"They scoured lands far and wide," Sid continued, watching the cliffs of the quarry, particularly the Witch's Cave, a black hollow named years earlier for a group of high school girls who'd been caught having a seance in it. They'd been attempting to resurrect their friend who'd fallen from the cliffs to her death a year earlier.

It was a tragic tale, and it had closed the pit for a time, but soon kids had started ignoring the no trespassing signs, and within a year, they'd returned to the quarry with an added fervor thanks to the untimely death of one of their own.

"Despite their search," he continued, "they found no trace of the Dark Prince until one rainy afternoon…"

Ash followed Sid's gaze to the cave, a gleam in her eye.

"They sought shelter from the storm in the Witch's Cave on the jagged cliffs deep in the Shadow Forest. It was a perilous journey to the cave, and they clung to the rock, terrified of the bottomless black sea beneath it."

Sid turned over, legs kicking beneath him. He glanced down at the dark water, wishing he'd forced the story in a less creepy direction. Of course, that was the point. They always wove the pit into the story, and they always dragged themselves out afterward, feeling as if they'd been courting death during their swim.

"As they plunged into the cave," Ashley continued, "they spotted the purple flames of a fairy sage. The woman was not your typical fairy. She was old and wrinkled with black eyes and flimsy gray wings that looked like they'd been woven from spiderwebs. 'Why have you come, she croaked?'"

Sid dipped his face in the water struck through with tendrils of sunlight. Through his blurred vision, he saw the gaping nothingness beneath them.

When he emerged, Ashley watched him expectantly, arms treading the water.

"We've come for the black violet, Stone told the fairy sage," Sid began. "The fairy cackled and rolled her big black eyes. Her tongue darted out and licked her papery lips. Then you've come to the right place." Sid's breath had caught as he told the story and again, he pushed onto his back, contemplating the blue sky, embarrassed that he always ended up winded and panting before they finished the story.

"'The Dark Prince is down there,' the sage shrieked," Ashley announced in a gravelly voice. "And she pointed at the black water where no creature dared venture. It was known to be filled with ghosts and demons, monsters who preyed on the weak and innocent and the strong too. Sapphire blinked into the storm and knew she had no choice."

Sid cleared his throat, calmer on his back. "Halfway down the cliff, Stone caught Sapphire. 'It's too risky, Sapphire. The violet isn't worth it,' he told her. But when their eyes locked, the truth passed between them. He understood that without the violet, Sapphire would die. Stone was terrified of the dark water, terrified of what would happen if he met the Dark Prince, but he understood he was the only one who could save Sapphire. 'Go back to the cave,' he yelled." As Sid spoke the words, both he and Ashley's eyes drifted up to the cave and above it to the top of the rocky cliff where Shane Savage stood pulling off his t-shirt.

9

---

*T*he suspense of the story deflated between them. Sid imagined it like a little black balloon popping and drifting down into the murky depths.

"What's he doing here?" Sid hissed.

Ashley lifted a hand from the water and waved.

"Don't wave at him," Sid said, trying to push her arm down.

Ash looked at him surprised. "He's cool. I talked to him."

"What? When?"

"I ran into him by Carl Lee's rock yesterday."

"Why was he there?" Sid demanded.

"He's got a cousin who lives on our side of town."

"Well, I don't like him," Sid said.

"Who said you had to?" Ashley asked.

Sid frowned, frustrated Ashley didn't offer to drop Shane Savage then and there. Shane - with his stupid blond hair and his stupid skateboard covered in stupid stickers.

"The Thrashers are probably behind him. Are we going to be friends with them now too?" he complained.

"Take a chill pill," she told him, splashing water his way. "He doesn't even like those guys. Let's get out and warm up."

"What about the story?" he asked, hating how whiny his voice sounded.

"We'll finish it next time."

Sid scowled as he paddled behind Ashley to the shore. She reached it before him, climbing the rocks lithely. He realized she should have been the cat in their story. As he struggled up the rocks, he figured he made a better walrus.

Ashley sat on a flat rock.

Shane made his way down the sloping cliff that surrounded the pit.

"Hey," he said, waving. "You guys swim out here too?"

"Doesn't everyone?" Sid muttered under his breath.

Ashley shot him an annoyed look. "Yeah. Beach is too crowded," Ashley explained.

"For me too," Shane agreed.

He didn't pause to chat, but plunged off the rocks into the cool water. He disappeared, and when his head popped above the surface, he was several yards into the quarry.

"Show off," Sid grumbled too quietly for Ashley to hear.

Shane's arms sliced through the water in long clean strokes. He tilted his head as he swam, appearing as if he took no breaths at all, but merely kept his head down. Sid had seen adults swim that way, but never kids.

He saw Ashley's eyes follow Shane and thought he spotted a tinge of pink in her cheeks.

Shane returned and climbed the rocks, jumping from one to the next, already showing muscles in places Sid doubted he'd ever have any.

Shane dropped next to them, stretching his legs long.

"It's so hot," he announced.

"We noticed," Sid griped, picking at a group of weeds poking through a crack in the rock.

"Super-hot," Ashley agreed.

"Did you jump?" Shane asked gesturing to the cliff, not the

top of the cliff, but the halfway point where the rock ledge jutted out and offered a less stomach-dropping option.

Ashley nodded.

"First thing I do every time. I saw you opted for the sissy jump," she gestured to the space before them.

It wasn't lost on Sid that he too had done the sissy jump.

"That's my warm-up," Shane said, springing to his feet and running up the rock.

He 'supermanned' off the outcropping, tucking himself into a ball just before he hit the water.

Sid too tucked himself into a ball, pulling his legs in close and resting his chin on his knees.

Shane returned a minute later, dripping, a huge grin on his face.

"Superman, huh? I've seen toddlers do that trick," Ashley told him.

Shane laughed and shook his wet hair at Ashley, spraying her with cold drops. A few of the droplets hit Sid's legs, and he bared his teeth, which he'd clamped together to keep from speaking the rolling list of snide comments parading through his mind.

"I'd like to see you do better," Shane challenged. "In fact, I dare you to do a flip."

Ashley said nothing, just stood, wrung out her long dark hair and marched up the rock. She stepped to the edge, and Sid stared at her dark feet, toes relaxed.

If Sid stood on the ledge, his toes would grab the rock like talons and his eyes would be screwed shut.

A part of him wanted to cry out for Ashley not to jump. A stupid thing that might cause her to slip and make things worse. Not to mention he'd watched her jump a hundred times, but his eye had wandered to the Witch's Cave and to the tumble of rocks that lay at the bottom of that steep drop. He tried not to think of the crumpled body of the girl who'd died on those rocks, her blood steadily washing into the dark water.

Ashley jumped, curling into a ball and flipping. She landed on her back, still curled up and disappeared into an explosion of sparkling water.

Shane whistled from the rock ledge.

"You're up," she called to him, "but I dare you to do a back-flip."

Shane's eyes widened a bit.

Sid saw the first hint of fear, and he relished the look, though it disappeared too quickly for him to truly enjoy it.

Shane bit his lip, turned to face the trees, and stepped to the edge.

Again, Sid wanted to yell out. He wasn't Shane's friend. What did he care if he fell? But he couldn't do anything to help the fear instinct, a hot bubbling in his gut that made him want to demand they stop acting so crazy.

The same sensation made him want to cry at his own cowardice.

Ashley climbed from the water; her eyes glued to Shane.

Sid could have been invisible.

Shane leaped backward, contorting his body, but as his head started to roll back, he faltered. He fell to the water with his arms and legs splayed, hitting the surface with a crack.

"Back-smacker," Ashley announced, clapping.

Shane's face was red when he climbed out on the rocks, but he continued to smile. He shrugged.

"Backflips are freaky," he admitted.

Sid expected Ashley to taunt him, but she didn't. She sat back on the ground beside Sid.

"Yeah, I usually spaz at the last second too," she admitted.

Sid sighed, a tad disappointed Ashley didn't razz Shane for his flop, but grateful they seemed to have tired of the game.

"I've got a Dr. Pepper," Shane said. He trotted to his clothes and pulled a bottle of the dark fizzy pop from the deep pocket of his shorts.

Sid eyed it thirstily.

Shane twisted off the cap and handed it to Ashley. She took a long drink, burped at the end, and gave it to Shane. He swallowed a gulp of the pop and then offered it to Sid.

Sid gazed at the soda, his mother's 'sugar will rot your teeth' reminders floated through his mind, but mostly he thought of his lips touching the bottle where Ash's lips had touched and Shane's too. It felt like a deal, a pact of friendship if he drank from the bottle, an agreement that Shane was one of them.

He shook his head, eyes watering at the fizzy bubbles beneath his nose. He handed the bottle back to Shane.

"No thanks," he said, forcing his chin lower into his knees.

Ashley's eyes lingered on him, but she didn't ask why he skipped the drink.

Shane didn't seem to notice. He took another drink and then handed the bottle back to Ashley. They went back and forth that way until the last of the dark liquid disappeared.

Another group of kids showed up. They took turns jumping off the rock ledge. In the water they laughed and yelled and splashed each other. Sid pretended to watch them, but mostly he listened to Ashley and Shane talk about how bad Mr. Ferndale's science lab sucked and how they both thought the new gym teacher rocked.

Sid had his own opinion about both teachers, opinions at odds with Ash and Shane. He loved Mr. Ferndale, who had given him special projects to work on at home, like making a volcano in a plastic bottle with vinegar, baking soda, and dish soap.

The new gym teacher, Mr. Curry, always smiled and laughed and slapped Sid on the back, encouraging him to run faster, put both hands together to hit the volleyball, or take part in some other way that left Sid panting and red-faced. Sid thought the teacher secretly hated him. He didn't have any reason for his beliefs, but they plagued him just the same.

He dreaded gym class as much as social studies, a class Ashley wasn't in, but Travis Barron was.

His favorite class was English with Mr. Wolf. It was Ashley's favorite class too. Mr. Wolf could make anything they read interesting from *Romeo and Juliet* to *Call of the Wild*. Both of which Sid had enjoyed immensely.

The kids in the lake looked like high school kids, though they were likely not old enough to drive.

One girl shrieked as a boy picked her up off the cliff's edge and jumped, holding her wriggling in his arms. Sid cringed as they fell toward the water.

Shane and Ashley didn't seem to notice.

Sid's butt started to tingle and grow numb. He stretched his legs out. They looked pale and soft, almost glowing in the sunlight. Ashley's legs were dark. Her right knee was skinned where she'd fallen on the sidewalk the previous week when they'd been running home after school.

Shane's legs were pale, but somehow they looked more like a man's legs than Sid's. Fine golden hairs coated his calves. Hair had appeared on Sid's legs, but it grew in odd little patches, prickly and so white blond it looked the color of cat whiskers.

From his mother's magazines, Sid had gathered he had an issue with self esteem But for the life of him, he couldn't figure out how he'd ever feel better about his body when guys like Shane Savage existed in the world.

Shane got up to pee in the woods.

Ashley leaned close to Sid.

"Let's show him the raccoons," she said.

Sid's mouth dropped open as if Ashley had kicked him in the gut.

"What?" she asked, her expression so clueless he wanted to cry.

And he knew she really didn't get it.

The raccoons belonged to them. Sid and Ashley. If they shared them with Shane, well... it would change everything.

"I don't feel so hot. I think I'm just going to go home. You can show him the raccoons if you want." Sid stood up and hastily pulled on his t-shirt.

"What? No. I thought we would work on their den some more. I thought-"

"Just call me later. Okay?" He started toward the trees.

Sid felt Ashley's gaze follow him, but he couldn't turn back. Tears had begun to well behind his eyes, and the moment he stepped into the woods they poured hot and fierce over his cheeks.

10

*M*ax drove his motorcycle to a ramshackle house on the north end of town. It was the cutoff point for the school district, a desolate stretch of road the bus drivers grumbled about having to cover, especially during February and March when the snow drifts reached chest high levels and billowy days further reduced visibility to mere centimeters beyond the windshield.

In June, the spread of country road was anything but barren. The forest crowded in on either side of the baking concrete. Vines and weeds reached out, leaving their snaky entrails, smashed by pick-up trucks, smeared across the road.

Patches of farmland lay between the forests, the crops reeking of the latest fertilizer dump so potently in some areas, Max's eyes watered beneath his helmet.

He found Vern Ripley's house easily enough. It was the lone house on a large, desolate lot. The dilapidated farmhouse leaned heavily to the right where an oak tree, with a trunk roughly the size of a small car, stood as if patiently waiting to catch the falling house.

The yard was choked and littered with the kind of debris

that revealed Vern's stepfather as a tinkerer who rarely finished projects. Cars on blocks, whole engines, and a sprinkling of tools and automotive parts lay strewn along the gravel path.

Max climbed off his bike as the screen door swung out, and a woman stepped onto the porch.

She held her hand up to block the sun. A little girl in a paint streaked t-shirt and ratty cloth shorts followed on her heels.

"Mrs. Ripley?" Max asked, taking a few steps toward the house and holding up his hands as if telling her, 'please don't shoot.'

She stood in the half open doorway, blocking her daughter, who rammed herself into her mother's arm like a rabid animal who'd spotted a weakness in the bars of its cage.

She didn't respond, instead shifting her gaze to the child. She forced the child, not unkindly, back into the house and pulled the heavier interior door shut.

"Yes, I'm Goldie Ripley," she said, pausing at the top of the porch stairs.

She wore brown overalls with a white tank top. Her feet were bare, and her short curly hair stuck up wildly as if she'd only recently woken up.

"I'm Max Wolfenstein. The kids call me Mr. Wolf. I teach at Winterberry Middle School."

"Okay," she said, as if preferring he get on with it.

"Have you heard from Vern?" he asked, abandoning his earlier plan to admit to the woman he didn't really know Vern.

She raised her eyebrows.

"You seen him?" she asked.

He glanced at the window where the little girl had peeled back the curtain. She didn't peek coyly at him, but rather stood with her face pressed to the glass. She held up a bag of potato chips and waved it as if it were a distress call. A large gray cat hopped onto the windowsill beside her, and she broke her gaze with Max to pet the cat instead.

"No, I haven't seen him. I only just heard he was missing. I hoped to ask you a few questions."

"The police already asked a few questions, and I ain't got any new answers. Vern run off just after Christmas, likely mad at me and his daddy for not buying him the video player he wanted."

Max watched the woman rifle in her pockets and pull out a pack of cigarettes. She knocked the box against her thigh and retrieved one, propping it on her lip and lighting it with a pink lighter.

"You believe Vern ran away, then?"

Something flashed across Goldie's face, and she took a long drag on her cigarette, replacing the look with indifference.

"Vern's a real independent boy, always has been. He used to take apart radios and car engines with Darwin. He's real smart. If anyone can make it out there on his own, it's Vern."

Max understood Goldie didn't think Vern had run away, but she needed to convince herself he had. If he'd run away, he might come back.

"Is Darwin Vern's biological father?"

Goldie glared at him.

"I don't know what that has to do with nothin. Darwin raised Vern from diapers. Vern's *real daddy*, if you can call a man who ain't ever bought him a single birthday present a real daddy, was in Alaska last I heard, workin' the pipeline. Course, we ain't ever seen a dime of all that pipeline money."

Max wanted to probe Darwin and Vern's relationship, but sensed he'd stepped on a hornet's nest bringing it up. Best not to spray the bees too.

"I'd like to hear about the day Vern went missing, if you've got a few minutes to chat," Max said.

Goldie had stepped back to the door as if a sixth sense told her, her daughter was preparing to burst through it. Sure enough, the child barreled out, the large gray cat clutched in her skinny arms.

"Put that cat down. Good lord, Lacy. One of these days you're going to get your eyes clawed out of your head."

Lacy dropped the cat, and he ambled into a patch of sunlight, flopping on his side.

Goldie caught her daughter by the shoulder as she started toward the stairs.

"You stay in the yard. I don't want to see you go past the swing set."

Goldie gestured at the swing set that included a metal slide on one end. An old tractor tire turned sandbox rested beside it.

"But I want to play in Vern's fort!" The girl gestured to a tree near the road.

About fifteen feet in the air, Max spotted a piece of plywood positioned on two large branches. A black tarp hung over the platform, holey and flapping in the warm breeze. It looked abandoned, forlorn, sinister even, and Max jerked his eyes from the eerie treehouse.

"You're not to go near that fort. You hear me?" Goldie grabbed her daughter's arm.

The girl cried out and jerked away. She jumped off the porch, skipping down three steps before running to the swings.

She stuck her tongue out at Max as she passed.

Goldie shook her head as if eternally perplexed by the child. She sat down on the top step of the porch and gestured to the space beside her.

"You're welcome to sit."

Max walked to the bottom of the stairs, but he didn't sit down.

"Vern left on January fourth," Goldie explained. "We had one of those winter storms and got about two feet of snow overnight. They called school off, which Darwin was all pissy about because Joe brings his three kids into the garage and they run like wild animals. Vern and Lacy slept in.

Vern came down around nine and said he was going sledding. I told him to take his mittens because his gloves are the thin kind that get all wet. He didn't take them. I know because I saw them lying in his bedroom later that day.

Lacy and I," she paused and gestured at her daughter. "That's my daughter, Lacy. We baked most of the day. Joe's Autobody was having their Christmas Party that next weekend. He does it in January every year, and I'd offered to bring Christmas cookies. We baked until about two o'clock. I thought it strange Vern hadn't come home, but he'd been sulking since Christmas. He wanted one of those handheld video game thingies all the kids have. Well, we just couldn't afford it. Last year wasn't a great year for us, and we were lucky to get food on the table let alone little video games you can carry in your backpack."

Goldie finished her cigarette and stubbed it on the porch, tucking the butt in the pocket of her overalls.

"If I'd have known it meant so much to him, I would have found a way," she said, lifting a hand to study her fingernails.

Max noticed the same color paint he'd seen on Lacy's shirt in the cuticles of Goldie's nails.

"By the time Darwin got home with the truck, I was worried sick. Night comes early in January, and by five pm, there was nothing but dark out there." She gestured at the dense forest edging their property.

"We loaded up Lacy and drove for hours. We went all over town, stopped at his friends' houses. Nothing, not a peep. We called the police the next morning and filed a report, but Darwin found a note in Vern's room. It didn't look like a note to me, just the scribblings of a kid, but the police seemed to consider it proof he'd run away."

"What did the note say?" Max asked, his eye flitting involuntarily back to the treehouse and the black tarp above it.

He'd drawn a picture of a boy flying in the clouds, just a little sketch. Vern had written *flying south for the winter* underneath the figure of the boy. He loved to draw and was good at it too."

Max alerted to Goldie's use of the past tense and considered mentioning it, but swallowed the words.

"The police considered a kid's drawing a note?"

Detective Welch's smug face rose in Max's mind, and he flexed his fists unconsciously.

Goldie nodded, took out her cigarettes, and opened the top. She counted the cigarettes, touching each one before sighing and putting the box back in her pocket.

"That's it. Not a peep out of the police since then and nothing from Vern, not even a phone call."

---

11

*A*shley almost told Shane about the raccoons, but changed her mind at the last moment.

Shane had stashed his skateboard in a pile of brush near the woods. He grabbed it and they headed for town.

"Want to go to the skate park?" he asked Ashley. "I've been trying to grind on the rail over there."

She shrugged. She didn't have anything else to do, and she could always feed the raccoons on her own later.

"Sure."

Shane pushed along beside Ashley, one foot planted on the board, the other pushing off the road.

Ashley crossed her fingers and let out a sigh of relief when she saw the skate park was empty. She'd thought the Thrashers might be there, at which point she would have abruptly turned and walked home.

Shane pushed off hard and jumped his board onto a long metal rail a foot off the ground. He hit the side, his board skidding, but only made it a few feet when he jumped off and let the board clatter to the pavement. He tried a second time.

"So, why's your dad a dick?" Ashley asked, as Shane rode his board up the curve of a ramp.

"Huh?" he asked, glancing at her.

"The other day you said your dad was a dick," she explained. She didn't know why she asked the question, to fill the silence maybe.

Shane tucked his hair behind his ears and bit his lip as he tipped the skateboard over the edge of the ramp and cruised gracefully down, bending his legs and jumping up before landing back on the board with both feet and drifting to a stop.

He put one foot down and kicked back to where Ashley stood.

"I guess he wasn't when I was little. It's hard to remember now, but I think he was decent for a while."

"And then what?"

"And then my sister killed herself."

Ashley's mouth fell open.

"Catching flies?" he asked.

She closed her mouth.

"I didn't know you had a sister."

Shane shrugged, pushed off hard on his board and sailed away, curving around in a circle and coming back.

"Most people don't. She died before we moved here. We lived in Saginaw until I was seven. My sister had ten years on me. She was born before my parents graduated from high school. It was a big scandal my mom said. My mom's family had money, my dad's didn't. Typical bullshit."

"What was her name?"

"Annabelle. Everyone called her Belle. I called her Belly. Not in a mean way," he added hastily. "Like in a kid way, you know?"

Ashley nodded.

"I was crazy about her," he laughed and squinted at the pavement. "But it's getting harder to see her in my mind. Every year she fades a little more. But my mom keeps an album in her closet and we pull it out a few times a year when dad's gone. He won't talk about her. If we talk about her, he gets all pissy and stomps out the door."

"Why?"

"Beats me. My mom says he never learned to process his feelings - whatever that means."

"Why did she do it?"

Shane walked up to the highest ramp, dropped his board and set one foot in the center. He kicked off and sped down the drop, curving up and catching air. He flipped the board and again landed easily in the center, not even a wobble in his knees.

Ashley whistled, impressed.

She'd tried skating a few times, but couldn't get a feel for the board beneath her. She'd always ended up flat on her butt with skinned elbows to show for her efforts.

"She left a note," he explained. "She said she was sorry, it was better this way, not to be mad at her. She said she wanted me to have her cassette player and her tapes." Shane laughed, but no smile accompanied the sound.

"You've read it?"

"My mom keeps it in the album. It's on the very last page. I used to sneak it out and read It over and over again. Like maybe if I read it enough times, I would know why she did it. But there's nothing there. There's no *why*."

Ashley searched for words. When someone died, her mother would tell the family I'm praying for you or you have my sympathies, but Ashley didn't find those words comforting. Plus they'd sound strange coming from her lips.

"That really bites," she offered.

Shane looked at the sky, tilting his head so far back, his blond hair brushed his shoulders.

Blazin', Hot, Stud. That's what the girls at school called Shane. But the word that came to Ashley's mind as she watched him was beautiful. She could practically hear the other kids ribbing her for such a thought. Guys weren't beautiful. And yet... Shane Savage kind of was.

She felt warmth rise into her cheeks and looked away.

"If you look high enough, like put your head so far back you can't see the ground, there's only sky. There could be nothing but sky right now," he said. "She jumped off the roof of her high school. It was a pretty high building, like three stories."

He pulled his head down and blinked at the ground.

"Makes me dizzy," he murmured.

Ashley tried to imagine his sister, Belle. Maybe she looked like him, beautiful with golden hair billowing out behind her as she stepped to the edge of the roof at her high school.

Did she look at the sky or the ground?

"The janitor found her. She did it in the afternoon. I still remember the day, weird how days get stuck in your mind. I can't remember the first time I fell off a board, but I can remember that day vividly. My mom was cooking chili. It was October, one of those cold, blustery days where you look out the window and see the wind shaking down all the trees. I wanted to play in the leaves, but my mom wanted me to wait for Belle to get home from school so she could keep an eye on me. It was sunny. A sky like today with those huge clouds, *marshmallow fluff,* Belle called them. And later on, I thought about that. It wasn't a kill yourself kind of day. Didn't people kill themselves when it was raining or gray? Who kills themselves when the sun is shining?"

He bent down and picked at a skull decal peeling off his board. He ripped it off, but only a corner pulled free, leaving a one-eyed skeleton gazing up at him.

"By the time the cops showed up, the sun had set and my dad was home from work. We ate chili at the table and my mom kept glancing at the door. Every few minutes she'd say an excuse like maybe the girls went for sodas or Belle's been working so hard on her history paper so she probably stayed after for help. We saw the cop car pull into the driveway and my dad stood up so fast his chili knocked over. I remember my mom scrambling to clean it up. She started to cry, these big gasping sobs, and I thought it was because the chili was dripping onto the carpet. I kept saying, 'It's okay, Mom,' and trying to sop up the chili with my stuffed bear. Now, I understand she somehow knew."

"That your sister had killed herself?"

Shane ripped another strip off the skeleton.

"That Belle was dead. When the cops came in, one of them took off his hat and held it to his chest. My mom collapsed. She curled into a little ball and started wailing. My dad told me to go to my room, but he wasn't paying attention, so I just stayed right there.

"We're sorry to inform you that your daughter is dead. That's how I remember it. I'm not sure if that's right, though. That part of my memory is more like watching a film. I might have taken those words from a movie, for all I know."

Ashley frowned, her mouth dry and her heart thudding softly against her breastbone. The world seemed fuller suddenly, bright and aching and hard to take in. In her mind, she could see a seven-year-old Shane watching his mother on the floor, chili dripping from the table as two policemen took their entire world and crushed it into a little ball and then threw it in the trash.

"I don't know if she died instantly or lay there on the concrete, everything broken, blood leaking out of her. I remember the casket was closed at her funeral. There were hundreds of kids, like teenagers, kids her age. The girls were crying and falling into each other, and the boys stood shoulder to shoulder, eyes all screwed up and confused. My mom had to be carried out after the service. My uncle Joe carried her because my dad had to help carry the casket."

Ashley wanted to speak. She searched again for the right

words and managed only a little puff that sounded a bit like 'sorry.'

Shane sat heavily on his board, pulling his legs in and resting his elbows on his knees.

"I guess that's why my dad's a dick."

Ashley sat down too, crossed her legs, and pulled at her t-shirt, wishing she had gum or some poppers to explode, anything to focus on other than Shane's solemn face.

His eyes didn't water, but they'd gone a few shades paler as he spoke, the navy irises fading to match the sky.

"She'd be twenty-six now. We celebrate her birthday every year. Mom and me. My dad would go ape-shit if he knew. But we go out to a restaurant and get a piece of cake and put a candle on it. Her birthday is in September. She'd had her seventeenth birthday just a few weeks before she did it. My parents had given her a new pair of roller skates for her birthday. She loved to roller skate. There was a rink a few miles from our house, and she went there with her girlfriends every Friday night."

"Do you have any other brothers and sisters?" It was a stupid question. They attended the same school. She knew he didn't have other brothers and sisters.

He shook his head and then looked up, offering her a wry smile.

"Want to go get ice cream? Swirly Cone still has two for one."

Surprised at the abrupt shift in conversation, she nodded.

Shane hopped up, dropped his board, and pushed toward the road, looking back as she hurried to keep up.

1 2

"*D*id you see his eyes?" Ashley whispered as Warren passed her and Sid in the hallway.

To both their surprise, he didn't reach over a meaty hand to knock Sid's books from his arms.

Sid twisted around, but Warren had already shuffled around the corner.

"What was wrong with them?" Sid asked, stopping at his locker and hoisting his books under one arm while he fumbled with the lock.

One by one the books slipped and fell, and Ashely caught each one before nudging Sid out of the way and putting his combination in for him.

"What if I'm sick one of these days, Sid? How will you ever get your math homework?"

Sid laughed and held up his thick fingers. "My mom says I'm all thumbs."

"I hate to agree with a parent, but she might be right," she said.

Ashely swung open his locker, and a tumble of papers flew out followed by his *Star Wars* lunchbox. Ashley rolled her eyes at the box, choosing not to mention for the hundredth time that he'd get made fun of less in the cafeteria if he brought a brown bag like she did.

"Meet you here before lunch?" Sid asked.

"Yep." Ashley nodded and walked off.

Sid didn't need to ask. They met at his locker before lunch every day and then ate their food at choking speed before rushing outside for twenty-three minutes of recess before returning to the building for their final two periods of the day.

Ashley had almost forgotten all about Warren's strange appearance until she spotted Travis Barron and Warren outside the side entrance to Winterberry Middle School. Travis's head shook from side to side and his cheeks flared red as if he were yelling at his large friend. Warren seemed unmoved by the display, his shoulders hunch forward. After another minute of yelling, Travis threw up his hands and stomped back through the doors of the school.

Ashley ducked into the empty science room and flattened herself against the wall.

She slid over to the window and peeked out.

Warren lumbered away from the school, slow and heavy, his head bowed as if walking into a stiff wind, though Ashley didn't notice any rustling in the trees.

The bell for lunch rang and classroom doors swung open. Feet pounded down the hall as other middle schoolers stampeded toward the lunchroom.

She was wasting precious minutes of her lunch period, but couldn't tear herself from the window. Warren walked to the end of the sidewalk and turned onto the grassy trail that would take him through the woods beside the middle school.

In the sky above the woods, Ashley saw birds. She pressed her face against the glass and watched as vultures, a dozen or more, circled in the blue sky.

∼

ASHLEY ATE her peanut butter and grape jelly sandwich in three bites and slurped the last of her orange juice.

Sid ate with one knee propped on the bench, chewing vigorously, and poised to flee the lunchroom as quickly as possible. He stuffed the remnants of a tinfoil-wrapped veggie lasagna into his empty *Star Wars* container.

"No salad today?" Ashley asked.

Sid's lunch always included a salad in some form, the extra gross kind with slimy purple beets and hunks of impossible to swallow broccoli.

"Last week of school," he said, smiling to reveal bits of green stuff in his teeth. "And she said the lettuce at the grocery looked wilty."

Sid snapped his lunch pail closed, and they hurried to stash it in his locker before bursting onto the playground. They speed-walked to their group of friends at the back of the playground. They'd already gathered and were shuffling books and videotapes between them.

"I saw Warren skip out," Ashley said. "It looked like he and Travis had a fight."

"Good," Sid muttered. "He won't be in science class, then."

"Ash, do you have *Interview with the Vampire*?" Darren Mound called, as they approached.

She pulled the paperback from the back of her shorts where she'd tucked it into the waistband.

Sid held up a VHS tape of *Rosemary's Baby*. "I've got *Rosemary's Baby*," he announced, and several of their friends held up their own tapes. Sid selected *The Evil Dead*.

"You're going to watch that at my house, right?" Ashley asked him as she exchanged books with Darren, who then traded *Interview with the Vampire* for a tattered copy of *The Godsend* with another girl.

J.R. ERICKSON

"Obviously," Sid said. "My mom would probably give our TV away if she caught me watching it at our house."

"Mine too," their friend Rita said, as she swapped a VHS of *The Shining* for a rented copy of *The Fog*. "My mom thinks horror movies make kids do drugs." She laughed and shook her head. "Parents are seriously clueless."

Their group met twice a week on the playground to swap horror books and movies. In the summer, they'd made plans to have a weekly meet up at the arcade.

The screams began as they were trailing toward the building.

The bell to end lunch would ring any minute, and Ashley and Sid started back toward the double doors.

The scream tore across the play yard and halted Ashley and Sid mid-stride.

Heads shot up and running slowed to a stop. Ashley saw a sixth-grade girl trip over the asphalt ridge by the basketball courts and go down on her hands and knees. Ashely cringed. She knew the sharp sting of such a fall. That girl would spend her afternoon classes picking stones from her palms.

"Where'd that come from?" Sid started, but the scream came again, piercing the air and now punctuated by voices.

Ashley ran to the side of the school. Other kids did the same. They crowded around her, and they all watched in stunned silence at the teacher screaming and clutching her throat as Mr. Curry, the gym teacher, carried a body from the woods.

Simon Frank laid long and limp in the teacher's arms. Curry struggled to carry the boy. His knees dipped low with each bend, and Ashley expected Simon's body to slip free and land with a thud on the grass. It didn't.

As more teachers surrounded the boy, ushering Mr. Curry and the screaming teacher through the doors, Ashley heard the first sirens in the distance.

MAX HAD DIALED 9-1-1. He didn't understand why until Mr. Curry struggled through the double glass doors with a dead child in his arms.

Max didn't realize in those first seconds that the child was dead, but as he rushed forward to assist the winded teacher, he saw Simon Frank and gasped, almost dropping the kid before he'd relieved Mr. Curry of the burden.

Miss Bluhm was still screaming, and Max wanted to tell her to shut up. It was too much - the screams and the face of the boy beneath him. Max looked away as he carried Simon, heavier than he could have imagined, down the hall.

He wasn't only heavy, he was gruesome. Simon stank of decay, his body felt swollen and doughy. The boy was dead, beyond dead, and Max knew he was doing it all wrong. Mr. Curry should not have picked the child up. They should have left him in the forest for the police and the coroner. He didn't know much, but he knew that.

The bell shrilled, and Max tensed, ready for an explosion of children at opposite ends of the hallway, but to his relief, no curious faces and stamping feet appeared. Other teachers rallied. They blocked the doors, organizing the kids into rows outside.

"Bring him in here," Mrs. Pollister, the school nurse, insisted, grabbing Max's elbow and ushering him into the nurse's station.

Max laid Frank on the little padded table that stood against the wall. White medical paper crinkled beneath him. The smell of rot filled the little room.

Max continued to look away from the boy, but he didn't miss Mrs. Pollister's shocked expression as she leaned over him.

"My God," she breathed. "He's dead."

Max nodded his head numbly as Mr. Curry and several other teachers crowded into the little carpeted nurse's room.

Somewhere down the hall, Max heard Miss Bluhm's screams shrinking to sobs.

"Miss Bluhm and I were walking in the woods and found him," Mr. Curry explained, his face crimson as he spoke.

Mrs. Pollister's hands went to Simon's neck as if to search for a pulse, but then her fingers curled in and she shrank away.

Simon's neck had been torn open, soft, dark tissue lay exposed beneath the flaps of skin. Maggots squirmed in the wound.

Max stared at Simon's t-shirt. It displayed a roaring lion bursting forward with teeth bared. It was a Van Halen shirt. Max had noticed Simon wearing the shirt a few months before. Max himself had seen Van Halen in concert two years earlier. He'd asked Simon if he'd ever seen them live. Now the question hung strange and inappropriate in the center of his skull - live, live, live....

"Good Lord," another voice rang out.

Max saw Principal Hagerty in the doorway, his hands rushed up to cover his mouth.

Max's gaze shifted back to Simon, and his stomach clenched as if he might spew.

The boy's eyes were wide open, wider than seemed possible. Usually a dull brown, Simon's eyes were glazed with tiny red veins and so bulging, they looked like they might fall out. His lips were pulled away from his teeth in a grimace of terror.

Simon had been terrified when he died, and his final expression was plastered on his face like the ghoulish rubber masks the five and dime stores sold around Halloween.

The sound of sirens grew louder, deafening. And soon official sounding voices crowded the halls of the school.

Paramedics shouted for the teachers to make room.

Max stumbled into the hallway, pressing his hands into the cool brick walls as he fumbled to the boys' bathroom. He shoved through the door, burst into the largest stall, and dropped to his knees to retch.

"*W*hat did you mean earlier," Sid blurted, as they walked home.

They'd passed the video store, and Ashley had glanced in. She'd planned to check if they'd gotten *Frightmare* in yet, but the desire had vanished.

The screams of the teachers continued to echo through her head.

She knew Simon had gone missing. She'd heard a few other kids talking about it in the cafeteria earlier in the week. Ashley figured he'd gotten mad at his parents and was hiding out at a friend's house, punishing them for withholding his allowance or refusing to get him a new video game. It never crossed her mind something bad happened to him.

"About what?" Ashley asked, shoving her hands into the pockets of her jean shorts.

"You asked me if I saw Warren's eyes." Sid explained, shifting his backpack from one shoulder to the other and then back again. The heavy bag caused the entire left side of Sid's upper body to droop, but no one wore their bag full-on, not unless you were a supreme dork. And Sid wasn't adding dork to his already loathsome nickname, Butterball.

"I forgot," Ashley murmured, still trying to wrap her mind around Simon, one of their own, being dead. "They were kind of yellow and shiny looking. I don't really know how to explain it."

"Like he was sick?" Sid asked, a hopeful tinge in his voice.

Ashley frowned, though she understood why Sid hoped Warren was sick. Warren delighted in torturing Sid, and as summer approached, a sick Warren would give him a brief respite.

"Maybe," Ash said, though sick hadn't been the word she'd thought of when she'd noticed Warren earlier.

She stopped walking, struck by a disturbing thought.

Sid looked back at her.

"What?" he asked.

"What if Warren killed Simon?" she said.

Sid's eyes widened, and he glanced toward the woods running along the opposite side of the road.

"Warren's a jerk, but... I don't know, Ash."

Ashley struggled to imagine it as well. Warren doing what exactly? Stabbing Simon? Beating him with something?

Simon was a quiet kid. He and his few friends mostly stayed out of the way of the Thrashers. Ashley had never seen him get his lunch tray dumped in his lap or watched his books skid across the floor because Warren had slapped them out of his hands.

"If he did," Sid muttered. "I hope they find out soon. If Warren wants to kill anyone, it's probably me."

Ashley resumed walking, not wanting to agree out loud with Sid. Warren already didn't like him, but the day before, Sid had gotten Warren in trouble during math class.

Paula George had complained to the teacher that her Walkman had disappeared from her desk. Sid pointed out the headphone wire, noticeably pink, hanging from Warren's desk. When the teacher wrenched open Warren's desk, the boy had turned bright red and glared at Sid until Mr. Crisp told him to go to the principal's office.

"Could it have been Warren, Sid? In the woods?"

"The monster?" Sid asked.

"Yeah." Ashley bobbed her head up and down.

"I didn't really see him. It was dark, but maybe if he were wearing a mask."

"Yeah," Ashley agreed. "That's what I think. If he had one of those ghoul masks on, it totally could have been him."

Sid shuddered and glanced behind them. Ashley glanced back too, but the road stood empty.

"Are you going to visit the raccoons tonight?" Sid asked as they turned onto his street.

Ashley shook her head.

"Better not. If my mom hears about Simon, she'll try to call. I don't want to freak her out."

"Yeah," Sid agreed. "My mom's already wearing a path in the driveway."

Ashley followed Sid's gaze to his driveway where his mother walked back and forth, her long blue skirt billowing like a 'come home this instant' flag.

"See you in the morning," she told him, turning onto her own street and leaving him to walk the last half block on his own.

MAX HEARD his front door open. He leaned forward on the sofa and saw his mother's gray sedan parked in his driveway.

"Hi, Mom," he called as the door clicked shut.

She peeked her head into the room and then produced a tinfoil covered pie.

He imagined the soft give of Simon's flesh, as if his organs and bones were merely pie filling beneath his skin. He frowned and shook his head.

Maria gave him a sympathetic glance, and she walked past him, depositing the pie in the kitchen before she returned to the living room.

She sat next to him on the couch and rested a hand on his leg. "Linda called me from the school. She told me what happened today."

Max snorted.

His mother sounded as she had a dozen times in his youth when a teacher or the principal had called home to say Max had been teased or Max had been stuffed in a locker after gym class or the time Max had taken a cleat and smacked Kurt, the school bully, on the back of the head for tripping Max during his timed mile.

For a moment, the memories startled him, and he marveled at his choice to become a teacher.

"I'm sorry, honey. That must have been terrible for you."

He leaned back and sighed, avoiding looking at his mother because her kind face might bring him to tears.

He'd been avoiding the thought of Simon since he'd climbed on his motorcycle after school and sped away, and yet in truth, he'd thought of nothing else.

"It was bad," he admitted. "And we made it worse. Now that detective will really hate my guts."

The word guts left a filmy aftertaste on his tongue, and he stood, hurrying to the kitchen for a glass of water.

"The boy was dead," Maria said, walking in behind him a moment later. "Sometimes it's too late."

Max closed his eyes.

"I know it was too late, Mom. But we messed up the scene, contaminated it or whatever. Mr. Curry shouldn't have picked him up. I touched him too. I carried him." Max shuddered at the memory of the soft bloated body and felt shame at his disgust.

"You're teachers, Max. It goes against your being to leave a child in the woods, cold and alone."

~

WARREN WAS NOT in school the next day, nor the day after.

The teachers were subdued, many red-eyed, and there'd been rumors the last two days of school would be cancelled. Instead, things went on as usual with the added air of mystery and obvious sadness.

Ashley watched the gym doors after she'd changed into her shorts and t-shirt. Other kids shot hoops, and a few had dodge-balls, hoping Mr. Curry would give them free days for the last few gym sessions before summer.

Curry walked in wearing his signature navy blue Winter-berry t-shirt and white shorts.

Ashley remembered the dark smears on his white shorts the day he'd stumbled from the woods with a dead Simon clutched in his arms.

He blew his whistle before quickly taking attendance. Several kids were missing, noticeably absent were Simon's two best friends, Jon Hastings and Benjamin Rite. Ashley guessed they'd be out for the rest of the week.

When Mr. Curry reached Warren's name, Ashley looked around the room, searching for the boy's square head in the crowd.

Sid shuffled over, pulling on his Batman t-shirt. On the other side of the room, Travis and two other friends stood whispering, their heads close together.

"Warren Leach?" Mr. Curry repeated.

He put a mark on his clipboard and blew his whistle a second time.

"Basketball today. Groups of five. Line up on the wall," he shouted.

"We're not going outside?" Melanie Dunlop asked. Melanie had a Madonna obsession. Even during PE, she refused to take off the dozen bracelets encircling her wrists. Large fake gold hoop earrings hung from her ears. She liked to go outside so she and her friends could sit on the bleachers and giggle about the boys.

"No," Mr. Curry told her.

He didn't elaborate, but Ashley knew why. There had been long yellow tape streaming along the edge of the sidewalks, blocking not only the woods near Winterberry Middle School, but the playground as well.

"Warren's gone again today," Ashley whispered.

"Yeah, I noticed in science class," Sid told her.

AFTER SCHOOL they walked into town.

Sid had gotten his allowance the day before and he bought them each a Dr. Pepper and a chocolate chip cookie from the Seven Eleven store.

Afterward, they cut through the laundromat and climbed onto the building's roof.

Sid finished his cookie in two bites and then walked the perimeter of the roof, looking over the edge. When he rounded the front of the building, he jumped back.

"What?" Ashley asked.

Sid put a finger to his lips and pointed over the side.

Ashley walked to the edge and peeked over. Travis and three of his goons stood by a park bench, their skateboards beneath them.

Ashley laid on her belly and scooted to the edge, peeking her head over the side and tilting her ear to listen. Sid did the same.

"Dude, he's totally planning something wicked," Travis boasted. He pulled out his knife, flipped it open and flung it toward a patch of daisies. The knife stabbed through a daisy and into the ground.

"I don't know, Travis," one of his friends said. The friend, Gary, was taller than Travis with long skinny legs and arms and a stringy mop of hair that looked like he hadn't washed it in a week. "My ma said his parents are flipping out. They think somebody kidnapped him."

Travis chuckled and retrieved his knife. "That's what Warren wants them to think, dumbass."

The other two friends grinned and nodded their approval, but Gary didn't seem to buy it. He closed his mouth, though, and Ashley knew why. If he challenged their leader, he'd soon find himself the hunted instead of the hunter.

"Then where is he?" Gary finally said, tipping his skateboard on its edge and spinning it around.

"I know where he is," Travis boasted.

Sid's eyes popped wide and Ashley grinned.

But instead of saying the words out loud, Travis leaned close to his friends and whispered it.

Ashley and Sid couldn't hear them.

Sid leaned further over the roof. Ashley darted a hand out as Sid's glasses slid from his face. Her thumb brushed one lens, and Sid's own arms shot out as he scrambled to catch them, but it was too late.

The spectacles landed with a crack at Travis's feet.

14

*A*ll four boys looked up.

Travis's face contorted in a snarl.

"You're dead," he yelled, pointing a finger at them. Then he glanced down, his scowl replaced with a mean grin.

"And now you'll be easy to catch too."

Travis lifted a foot and slammed his shoe onto the glasses.

Sid squinted toward the boys, cringing when his glasses cracked, but Ashley knew he couldn't see the glasses or even Travis's face. The boys would be a blur against the sidewalk below.

"Bloody hell," she snapped, grabbing Sid's arm and pulling him up. "Just move your feet," she hissed.

The Thrashers would run through the laundromat to the service door that led up the stairs and eventually opened onto the roof. Every kid in town knew how to get there, but not every kid knew about the old dumbwaiter in the fourth-floor hallway. It was their only chance.

Sid bumped along behind her, breath wheezing between his teeth. She tugged him forward.

"Stairs," she told. "Grab the rail."

He took the rail in one hand, holding hers in the other.

Below them, Ashley heard the heavy laundromat door crash open and the slap of tennis shoes on the cement steps.

Sid groaned, but Ashley didn't allow the vision of the boys pounding up the stairs to frighten her.

She jerked Sid down the hallway, nearly tripping when he stepped on her heel.

"The dumbwaiter," she whispered, shoving the metal door open with a shriek.

Sid planted his hands on the edge, his face a mask of terror, but he didn't complain as he hoisted himself into the dark opening. She gave him a little push, and he tucked into the back corner of the metal box. She crawled in behind him, crushing against him, and pulling her legs against her chest.

If the boys made it to fourth floor as she closed the door, they'd hear it, and she and Sid would be stuck in the tiny, claustrophobic space.

She momentarily flashed on the boys lowering the waiter halfway so that they'd be trapped inside the wall in perpetual darkness. For half a second, she wanted to jump out and take her chances with the Thrashers. Instead, she gritted her teeth and yanked the door closed, sealing them in darkness.

Sid's breath came out in raspy huffs, and she could feel him trying to slow down his breath. Even she found it difficult to breathe in the space. The air was stale and warm, and the darkness seemed thicker than the air outside the dumbwaiter.

Her right leg and arm were pressed against the cool metal door. Footsteps smacked down the hallway.

"They're not on the roof," one boy shouted.

Behind her, Sid made little gurgling sound in his throat.

More footsteps thumped down the hall.

Travis's voice rang out. "Well, they didn't jump," he snarled.

"Third floor," Gary announced. "The window at the end opens up to the fire escape."

J.R. ERICKSON

"Shit! Come on," Travis shouted.

Shoes pounded away.

Sid started to move, as if ready to plow into the metal door and force his way into the light.

"Not yet," Ash warned.

Several minutes passed in silence.

She wondered if oxygen had become scarce in the little enclosure. Every breath seemed smaller than the last. Soon they'd be sipping air, and after that, they'd open their mouths, but their lungs would hang empty and deflated behind their ribs.

Just as the words *let's go* formed on her tongue, she heard the soft plod of a footstep in the hall. It was a muted sound. The person walking didn't want to be heard.

Ashley shrank back, listening for another footstep.

Instead, she heard the metallic ting as someone's hands clutched the door to the dumbwaiter.

As the door flew open, both she and Sid screamed.

A woman wearing a gray cleaning uniform lurched back, her own scream erupting from her thin lips. She clutched her chest, her head shaking from side to side and sending her gray hair flopping back and forth on her head.

"What are you kids doing in there?" She fumed. "Get out this instant. Good Lord, you nearly gave me a heart attack. Damn kids," she continued, still wide eyed.

"It's not them?" Sid whispered.

"No, no, a cleaning lady."

Ashley climbed out and tugged Sid's hand to follow. He half fell out of the dumbwaiter, struggling as Ashley tried to keep him from tottering over completely.

The cleaning lady glared at them furiously.

"Sorry, ma'am," Sid said, squinting at the woman.

"Yeah, sorry," Ashley offered, pulling Sid down the hall.

They took the stairs slowly, stopping often to listen for any sound of the Thrashers. When they reached the laundromat, the coast was clear.

Outside Sid's glasses had been crushed into a dozen pieces.

"My mom's going to kill me," he grumbled, as Ashley placed the pieces in his hands so he could feel the damage for himself.

"Yeah," Ashley agreed. "But better they destroyed your glasses than your face."

"It'd probably be an improvement," Sid grumbled.

Ash elbowed him.

"Oh, come off it, Sid Putnam. I'll pity you for your glasses, but that's where it ends. There's nothing wrong with your face."

"Except it's attached to my body." He waved at his thick middle.

Ashley never knew how to respond when Sid went down the long winding road of 'I'm fat.'

"Nobody likes me, everybody hates me, I think I'll go eat worms," she started singing.

Sid stuck his tongue out at her and then picked up the second verse.

"Big fat juicy ones. Eensie weensy squeensy ones. See how they wiggle and squirm!"

They sang the song together as they walked the last few blocks to Sid's house.

"My mom's running errands," he said, relieved when he stepped out of his house wearing an old pair of spectacles. "And look what she got!"

He held up a box of Spokey Dokeys. "Glow in the dark," he added.

"Cool," Ash said, following Sid as he pushed his bike out of the garage.

He sat down and started trying to attach the little plastic beads to his spokes.

Ashley walked to the side of the house and gazed into the woods. If only they'd picked up what Travis had said to his friends. Clearly, he'd whispered the location of Warren's hideout. She tried to imagine where someone like Warren would disappear to, where any kid in Roscommon would.

She wandered back to Sid, watching absently as he fumbled with the beads. He squinted through his glasses and bit his lower lip as he worked. His face reminded her of similar expressions from several days before. He'd been prising at a board, a grim look of determination in his eyes.

"The Crawford House," Ash blurted, startling Sid as he attempted for the third time to attach a neon green Spokey Dokey to the spokes of his Huffy bicycle. The plastic bead bounced on the pavement and disappeared into the grass.

His old glasses, with duct tape on the bridge, slid down his nose.

"Gosh damn-it," he fumed, kicking the plastic package and sending the rest of the spoke beads flying. His mouth fell as he watched the beads disappear, and he bit his bottom lip. Ashley saw tears sparkling in his eyes, and she grabbed his shoulder.

"Hey, it's okay. Here." Ashley bent and scooped up a handful of the scattered spokeys. She knelt down and quickly attached five to his spokes.

Sid sat heavily on the curb, picking up the remainder of the beads and dropping them into the plastic package with a frustrated plunk.

"What about The Crawford House?" he asked finally.

"Someone could hide there. Live there even."

Sid wrinkled his nose. "If they want to die from the plague."

"You don't get plagues from dingy houses, stupid," Ashley told him, rolling her eyes.

"I don't follow, Ash."

"If Warren's the boy in the woods, he might be hiding out at The Crawford House? It would be the perfect place."

Sid shuddered. As if to do something ordinary, he took off his glasses and picked at a little smudge on one lens. "In an old funeral home?" Sid asked, shaking his head.

"I bet you anything that's what Travis was talking about," she continued.

"I don't know," he replied.

"Have any better ideas?"

She watched Sid's forehead crease, and he stared at the line of cracks in the pavement beneath him.

"Maybe we dreamed it. Maybe there is no boy in the woods or Warren or whatever it is."

"Come on," Ashley hollered.

"Okay, okay." He held up his hands. "We didn't dream it. But what's he up to then? Stalking other kids from Winterberry? Was he trying to kill us?"

"I don't know, but... I think he got Simon and the other kid too, Vern," Ashley said, remembering again the image of Simon's lifeless body as they carried him from the woods.

15

"Listen," Max announced, "Quiet, hush. You're mine for five more minutes, so hush up."

The din in the room quieted except for Ashley and Sid. Max gave them a pointed look, and they both clamped their mouths shut.

"I don't want to alarm any of you, but I'm sure you realize multiple kids have gone missing over the last six months," Max started. "And what happened to Simon Frank is just, well, it's a terrible tragedy."

"Who else?" one girl piped up.

"Vern Ripley, dummy," a boy across the room shouted. "He's been gone for like six months!"

"He went to live with his dad," another boy stated matter of factly. "His stepdad's a total prick."

"No, he didn't," another girl argued. "I live next door to his mom. She said his dad is working on the pipeline in Alaska. No one knows what happened to him."

"Okay, hold on," Max said, trying to talk over the voices.

"My brother said Warren probably got eaten by the same bear as Simon. Last year we saw three black bears in the woods."

"Black bears don't eat people, dummy," yet another boy chimed in.

"I saw Warren like two days ago," another boy said. "He's not missing!"

"Quiet," Max yelled, finally silencing the group once more. "Warren's parents have reported him missing. Vern Ripley's parents have reported him missing, and Simon Frank's parents had reported him missing. I don't know what happened to these kids, and I don't know if any of them are connected."

"What do you mean, connected?" Jessica Blanchard, a straight A student who also played several sports and was president of the debate club, asked.

"He means a kid killer," Travis Barron hissed, smiling cruelly at Sid and Ashley, who looked quickly away from him.

Max stared at the kid, unnerved by his tone, but then continued. "I am saying be careful this summer. When you go out to play, go together. Don't let your friends walk home alone, especially at night."

"Like the buddy system?" another girl asked.

"Yeah, exactly."

"Forget buddies, carry a knife," Travis said, patting his side pocket and offering the other students another cold smile.

"That's a good way to get hurt," Max told him. "Just be on the lookout," Max finished. "And tell your parents what's going on. They need to be aware. We all need to be more aware."

The bell rang, and the kids jumped from their seats.

Only Ashley and Sid seemed to take their time, and though they weren't talking, the significant glances that had passed between them as he spoke were not lost on Max.

"We're free!" Ashley shouted as she and Sid fled down the steps.

They'd been careful to blend into the crowd of middle schoolers, knowing the Thrashers might try to single them out after school.

"That was pretty weird, what Mr. Wolf said," Sid mused.

Ashley nodded. "I didn't know Vern Ripley was missing. I thought he'd moved away," she admitted.

"I didn't either. My dad said the cops believe Simon got attacked by a wolf or something."

Ashley frowned. "No way. Have you ever heard of a wolf around here?"

Sid shook his head. "No, but maybe it's just a fluke - what happened to us and Simon. Maybe it's not connected at all," he said hopefully.

Ashley sighed in exasperation. "I'm going to Mr. Sampson's Bike Shop," she said. "Wanna go?"

Sid hung his head. "Mandatory last day of school dinner at Charlie Kang's."

Ashley laughed.

Charlie Kang's was a Chinese restaurant a few towns over. The food was delicious, but every year Sid's parents took him and his brother on the last day of school to spend the evening planning what classes and extracurricular activities the boys would enroll in next year.

"Grab me a fortune cookie," Ashley told him, waving goodbye and turning onto the street where the bike shop stood.

"TWENTY-TWO DOLLARS and she's all yours," Mr. Sampson told Ashley, patting the seat on the Huffy Pro Thunder.

Ashley grinned and nodded, still touching one handlebar, not quite ready to walk away from her future wheels.

Mr. Sampson smiled approvingly.

She knew he appreciated her enthusiasm. A lot of kids

walked into Sampson's Bike Shop, and when their parents pulled out a check, the kid barely smiled, let alone offered a thank you.

Ashley had been visiting the bike shop at least twice a week since the previous fall when she first spotted the Huffy Pro Thunder in the store window. There'd been a moment, a long pause where the breath seemed pulled from her lungs as she gazed at the purple and gold bike. This was *her* bike. She knew it in her guts.

That day, she'd walked in and handed the dollar-fifty she'd stuck in the pocket of her coat meant for a candy bar and the arcade to Mr. Sampson. He put the bike on layaway, and though she knew other kids and parents had tried to purchase the bike, he'd always refused. She'd watched him do it more than once.

As Ashley walked home, floating on the fumes of being near her future bike, she gazed at the cloudless sky and felt the overwhelming joy of impending summer. The air smelled like freshly cut grass and the sweet intoxication of the Swirly Cone baking fresh cone bowls. A group of kids hooted and laughed from the baseball diamond as they played an early evening game.

Not even the strangeness of the previous week could get her down.

As she turned onto her road, she saw the birds. They circled in the distance, several blocks away. She counted ten, maybe eleven, buzzards flying in a slow circle above the woods.

She walked toward them, her legs simply pushing along despite her mind's bumbling protests. As she passed in front of her own house, not even bothering to glance at it, her mother's voice rang out.

"Ash! Where are you going?"

Ashley turned, surprised to see her mother standing next to her car, balancing a grocery sack on one hip and a pizza box in her raised hand.

"I got out early!" She grinned. "Pepperoni and mushroom."

Ashley faltered, her mind blank, and then she trotted over to her mother.

"Yes, pizza!" She took the box from her mother's hand.

"And cookies." Her mother held up the paper bag.

As Ashley followed her mother into the house, she remembered the birds. She glanced back at the sky, saw them lazily drifting in the distance and shrugged it off.

THE FOLLOWING MORNING, Ashley woke with the fervor of the first day of summer. She climbed out of bed, sun already peeking through her curtains, and stretched.

Ashley heard her mother's worried voice "Oh dear."

She finished pulling her hair into a ponytail and walked to the living room where her mother stood in a bathrobe, her hair still wet from the shower, watching the news.

"What is it?" Ashley asked, plopping on the sofa and searching for her tennis shoes in the dark cavern beneath it. "Sweet," she announced when she pulled out her cassette tape of Joan Jett and the Blackhearts singing "I love Rock and Roll." "I've been looking everywhere for this."

Her mother didn't respond, and when Ashley looked up, she saw her gaze still glued to the television.

"Wait, is that our woods?" Ashley asked, scooting down to the carpeted floor and crawling closer to the screen. She leaned forward and turned up the volume.

Technically, the woods weren't theirs, but they ran along the back of their neighborhood and the kids had claimed them. Each section of town seemed to have its own set of woods, and the kids who lived closest declared ownership over them.

"Melanie Dunlop was last seen walking into these woods

yesterday afternoon by her brother." The reporter gestured at the woods behind her.

"I have gym class with Melanie," Ashley murmured, picturing the girl who favored brightly colored tights and poufy, teased hair framing her heart-shaped face in a halo of blonde frizz.

"You do?" Deep grooves marred Rebecca's face as she frowned at the television. Ashley saw her Grandma Patty in her mother's face.

"I mean, maybe she just got lost," Ashley murmured, but a memory was surfacing.

The birds circling over the woods yesterday afternoon as Ashley walked home. When had she seen those birds before? Just days earlier at the school when Warren had disappeared into the forest shortly before they'd found Simon's dead body.

"It's terrible," her mom murmured, walking backward to the sofa and sinking down. "You haven't seen anyone, Ashley? Anyone unusual hanging around? My boss at the nursing home mentioned they found a boy dead outside the school. It hasn't even been in the papers."

"Simon Frank," Ashley told her.

"Was he sick?"

"I don't think so."

"Don't play in the woods, honey. Okay? Not until the police find that girl."

Ashley didn't mention the other missing kids or the warning Mr. Wolf had given his students the day before.

Through the living room window, Ashley spotted Sid walking up the driveway.

She hurried out to meet him.

"Did you hear about Melanie?" Ashley asked, rushing down the driveway.

Sid nodded. "My mom's having a cow."

"Mine too," Ashley said, looking back and waving at her mother who watched them from the living room window.

"Hi, Ms. Shepherd," Sid called.

Rebecca waved at the kids and then stepped from the window, letting the curtain fall back into place.

"Do you think he got her?" Sid asked, polishing an apple on his t-shirt and taking a bite.

Ashley considered the day before when she'd almost walked into the woods herself. What was the significance of the birds?

"The night I saw the monster," Ashley said, "or Warren, whatever it was, there were birds in the sky. Big buzzards. I've never seen buzzards at night."

"Me either," Sid said.

"And I saw them again when Warren walked in the woods."

"Probably because Simon's body was in the woods," Sid offered.

"Yeah, but then I saw them again yesterday on my way home from the bike shop. They were flying over our woods, the woods Melanie walked into yesterday."

Sid chewed his apple thoughtfully. "But what does that mean?"

"I think it's a warning," Ashley said, growing excited. "It's a way for us to know where the monster is at."

Sid looked at her skeptically. "I get that Warren stinks and all, but buzzards following him around?" He laughed, waiting for Ashley to do the same.

Ashley sighed and shook her head. "We really need to work on your jokes, Sid."

*M*ax saw Ashley and Sid sitting at a picnic table outside the Swirly Cone. He pulled his motorcycle to the curb and climbed off, hanging his helmet on the handlebar.

"Hi guys," he called, waving at the kids.

"Mind if I join you?"

Sid grinned and nodded. "Sure, yeah."

A man standing at the window, turned and waved at Max. He knew the man from the martial arts studio he practiced at several times a week.

"See ya on Friday, Wolf?" the man called as he walked backward, holding a chocolate ice cream cone.

"Yeah, I'll be there," Max told him.

"Did he call you Wolf?" Sid asked, impressed.

Max grinned and nodded. "Yep, beats Wolfenstein that's for sure."

"Your real name is Wolfenstein?" Ashley asked, picking a peanut off her ice cream sundae and flicking it to a seagull that had landed nearby. "Why does the school call you Mr. Wolf?"

"I asked them to shorten it when I started. For the kids'

sakes. But yeah, my full name is Maximilian Wolfenstein," Max admitted with a laugh. "People started calling me Wolf in high school. It stuck."

"People call me Butterball," Sid complained, arranging his spoon with equal parts ice cream and hot fudge. "I sure hope it doesn't stick."

"How about you Ashley? Any nicknames other than Ash?" Max asked.

Ashley shrugged. "I like Ash. Seems fitting. I'm what's left after the fire."

Max lifted an eyebrow, but Ashley didn't elaborate.

"How's summer vacation going?" Max asked. "I heard the sheriff is kicking around the idea of a curfew on account of the missing kids. I've always wondered if kids actually abide by those."

Sid's head shot up and a significant look passed between him and Ashley. Neither of them responded until Ash kicked Sid beneath the table.

Sid grunted. "It's good."

"Curfews are a joke," Ashley said. "Whatever's snatching kids is not likely to stop just because they're indoors."

"You mean whoever is snatching kids?" Max corrected.

"Yeah, sure." Ashley directed her gaze at the table where a glob of ice cream, likely from the patron before them, melted into a blue puddle.

Max steepled his hands on the table and then, seeing how adult-ish it looked, he pulled them back down.

"Anything interesting going on?" Max asked.

Ashley's eyes bored into Sid's as if commanding his silence. "Nope," she said, taking a bite of her sundae.

"Oh, come on. Nothing? You guys haven't been sneaking into the gravel pit out on Marsh Road to swim? No scamming Paulie Goldman for free tokens at the arcade? I can't remember a summer I didn't do those things."

Both the kids' faces brightened as if his revelations put them at ease, but Ashley remained tight-lipped.

"I scored a hundred and two thousand on *Donkey Kong* last week," Sid offered, holding up his hands as if he were manning the controls and mashing buttons.

Max whistled. "Impressive. Never did much *Donkey Kong*, but I used to kill it on *Death Race*. I held the highest score for two years. Finally got knocked off by my brother of all people."

"That's so cool," Sid said.

"Your brother's the insurance guy?" Ashley asked, and Max noticed a thoughtful look on her face.

"Yep. He and my dad are the Wolfensteins behind Wolfenstein and Son."

"And they sell like insurance for houses, right?"

"Yeah," Max confirmed, wondering where she was headed with her questions.

Sid looked equally confused.

"Do you know who owns The Crawford House?"

Max wrinkled his forehead. "The old funeral home?"

Ashley nodded, and Sid's face lost some of its color, his mouth turning down at the corners.

"Not off-hand. The heir died in the house as I'm sure you both know. Ever been in it?" Max gave them a conspiratorial smile.

He shouldn't condone them visiting the old abandoned house, but it was a rite of passage of sorts in their small town. All the kids did it despite their parents' protestations that it was dangerous. And it was. The house was filled with rotted floorboards, old rusted embalming equipment, and whatever bacteria cropped up in a place like that after so many years in ruin. Still, if he took the high-handed approach, he'd never get a peep out of either of them.

Sid watched Ashley, but Ashley gazed at Max with unwavering, and somewhat unnerving, eyes After a moment, she nodded.

"We've been out there a few times."

"Ever been inside?"

Ashley glanced away and shrugged. "I ran into the foyer on a dare last year and grabbed a piece of peeling wallpaper. Scored a Kit Kat too, because Norm Phillips was too chicken to go in."

Max nodded at her respectfully. "I went in once, all the way in," he told them.

"All the way?" Sid gasped. "Like to where the coffins are?"

Max nodded as a shudder crept up his spine. He bit his teeth together to keep from making it visible. He hadn't thought of that day in years, and now as he spoke of it, the terror that had gripped him slipped back in like an old unwelcome friend.

He laughed and glanced at the ice cream window, empty for the first time since he'd arrived.

"Let me grab a cone. Scary stories are better with a little sweetness. My mom used to tell me that."

Both kids nodded, and the moment he stepped away, Max saw their heads move together and their lips start moving.

"Chocolate and vanilla twist," he told the girl behind the counter.

As he waited for his cone, he remembered more than a decade before when he'd gone into The Crawford House. He'd been camping in his backyard with his two best friends, Andy Hayes and Jerry Cavanaugh. They'd been sitting around their little bonfire, built fastidiously by Herman Wolfenstein, who'd given them a veritable Boy Scout lesson before he allowed Max to handle the matches.

As they sat and told spooky stories, Max's older brother Jake showed up. As the oldest amongst them and one of the coolest guys in the tenth grade, they'd listened raptly as he'd told them the story of the man who'd died in The Crawford House, the only son of the man who'd built it.

"Blane Crawford was your typical rich kid," Jake had started. *Daddy owned the local funeral parlor, and in those days with plagues and farm accidents and a million other ways to die, business was good, real good. And in true rich kid form, Blane moved off and squandered his daddy's money on booze and women. He came home penniless just weeks before his old man keeled over on the john. Course, he could have been just fine - kept the funeral home going and had a nice little life. Except Blane didn't just like to drink. He loved to drink, and he didn't like to work. Instead, he threw big parties at the house.*

Partygoers used coffins for tables, slamming shot glasses onto the polished lids. They slopped beer onto the plush carpet and ashed cigarettes into the sterling silver urns that Blane's daddy had bought for future clients.

Mind you, half the town had said their final goodbyes to the people they loved in that funeral parlor. There was an outcry, for sure, but it was Blane's house. If he wanted to run it down, there wasn't a thing they could do about it.

One day in mid-summer, somebody called up the sheriff and reported Blane missing. We ain't seen him in weeks, they said. A couple day bender was one thing, but weeks? The sheriff went out there and knocked on the door, but nobody answered. Eventually, they busted in.

Later, the sheriff said his guts felt twisted like barbed wire going into that house. He knew something was wrong, but in he went with his deputy, and the smell hit 'em the minute they walked through the door. A rancid, rotted smell, and the flies were so loud they thought Blane had left some piece of embalming equipment turned on.

They covered their noses and walked in. They searched the first floor, disgusted by broken bottles and dishes of molded food everywhere. Both the sheriff and the deputy had been to that house, see. The sheriff's own mother had died not two years before and had her final service there at The Crawford House.

It was the most beautiful house in Roscommon in those days. Edwin Crawford had spared no expense when he'd built it because he had believed in honoring the dead. He called the house his gift to God. But his son, Blane, had practically destroyed it in the year he'd owned it since his father had passed.

Anyway, they searched and searched and couldn't find Blane. It was the deputy who'd said to follow the buzzing sound. They'd been thinking the whole time it was a fan or some other machine they were hearing. They went down the stairs. That's where the embalming room was, in the basement. There were coffins down there too. A room full of them.

They walked into that room full of coffins. At first, the sheriff thought he was staring at a black coffin. He even started to tell his deputy how morbid that seemed, a black coffin. But as he looked, he realized it was moving. The coffin wasn't black at all. It was covered with buzzing, writhing flies.

He and the deputy started waving the flies away. Shoo- shoo. And finally, they got close to it. The smell was so bad, the deputy retched before they even opened the coffin. The sheriff flung up the lid and...

Jake had paused at this moment, moving closer to the fire so his face glowed orange

Blane Crawford's dead, decomposed body was lying inside, but it was so rotted, you could barely make out his face. The skin had slid away, leaving meat and bones, and worst of all were the maggots. Maggots the size of pickles crawling in and out of his eye sockets. Those men turned and ran from that house. They ran like the devil was gonna' crawl outta that coffin and pull them inside.

"You don't know that! How could you know that?" Jerry had demanded, but Max remembered the look on Jerry's face, the terror outlined in the deep groove between his eyebrows. He'd felt a similar expression on his own face.

"Swear it on my life," Jake had said, tapping a finger on his chest. "Mr. Ketchum told me. And he knew. He was alive back then. So anyway," Jake continued, shooting an irritated glance at Jerry for the interruption.

They sent some poor black kid in there to get the body. Nobody else

would touch it, but they paid, and he said he'd do it. It was so rotten, he
had to carry it out in buckets.

The sheriff started looking into Blane's death. They did an
autopsy, but couldn't find anything wrong with him. So, he started
asking around town. Maybe someone killed him. He had more than a
few enemies for sure. Guys he'd scammed out of money, women he'd
screwed and never called - that kind of thing.

They never figured out what happened. The final theory was that
Blane crawled in there himself and got stuck. Maybe he was fixing to
scare someone who was coming over. One of his friends said he'd been
complaining about headaches, so the sheriff though he might have
tried to sleep in there because it was dark and quiet. And then there
were the vampire theories. Nobody loves coffins like a vampire, but
nothing ever came of that.

"Mister, Mister!"

Max looked up to find the girl holding out his ice cream
cone. From the look on her face, she'd been trying to get his
attention for a minute.

"Sorry," he said, taking the cone and quickly licking the ice
cream that had already dripped down the side. "Mind lapse."

She smiled and turned back to the soft serve machine.

Max returned to Ashley and Sid, wishing he hadn't thought
of The Crawford House at all, wishing he'd never offered to tell
the tale that followed.

But at the expectant looks on their faces, he knew he
couldn't back out.

"That's one of my favorites too," Sid said, nodding at Max's
ice cream as he scraped the last of his sundae from the bottom
of the plastic bowl. Ashley still had half of hers left.

"The perfect combo," Max agreed, forcing a smile and half-
considering an excuse to leave.

He dreaded telling the story, though he didn't quite
know why.

Whatever it was, reliving that night in The Crawford House

felt like opening a door, a secret door tucked deep in the cellar where strange black light leaked around the crevices. Where the thing inside wanted you to open the door, but once you opened it, you couldn't close it again. Once you'd seen what was inside, you couldn't unsee it.

"Tell us about going into The Crawford House," Ashley said, handing the rest of her ice cream to Sid.

His eyes lit up. "Thanks, Ash!" Sid took the ice cream and ate it in two bites.

Max sighed and licked his own ice cream.

"I was thirteen," Max started.

"We're both going to be thirteen in the fall," Sid told him, bobbing his head happily.

Ashley shot him a silencing look, and he clamped his mouth shut.

"I'd been camping out with my two buddies," Max continued, "and my brother came out to our bonfire. He told us the story of The Crawford House and of Blane Crawford, who had died there."

From the looks on Ashley and Sid's faces, Max knew they too had heard the story of Blane Crawford's gruesome demise.

"I'd been to the house a few times, but I'd never gone in. Well, that night, Jake started razzing me about being scared. He'd gone in, he'd told us. He'd gone into the embalming room and taken a scalpel. He'd given it to Margo Reeves, and she'd kissed him."

"Margo Reeves?" Sid exclaimed. "She's my next-door neighbor. She has twin girls. They're like this big." He held up his index finger and thumb.

"They're a little bigger than that," Ashley told him, rolling her eyes. "Go on," she said.

Max laughed, realizing he shouldn't have used Margo's name. The last thing he needed was an angry phone call over a kiss that happened a lifetime before.

"I got fed up with Jake's pestering, and I wanted to one-up him. That's the problem with being a younger brother. You do everything second. It starts to piss you off."

"Tell me about it," Sid grumbled.

"I told Jake I wasn't scared. I said I'd go into The Crawford House and spend a half hour and that only a yellow-belly turned and ran out with a scalpel. I boasted that I'd hang out in there – maybe even have a chat with Blane Crawford." Max sighed and rolled his head back. "Man, I regretted that big talk the second we stepped into the woods with our flashlights. I spent the entire walk, and it took us a good twenty minutes, thinking I might puke.

"When we got there, Jake had this look, this laughing, mocking look, and it made me so mad. It was the only thing that got me into that house. Otherwise, I tell you, I'd already come up with a half a dozen excuses for why I wasn't going in. I knew I'd lose face in front of my buddies if I backed out. I could have lived with that, but Jake was my brother. I'd have to deal with his taunting twenty-four hours a day until forever. At least that's what it seemed like at the time. I mustered every ounce of courage in my body and went in."

17

Max paused, wishing he could tell the story without the memory that went with it, but it arrived, unbidden from the darkness of his memories.

"It smelled," he shook his head trying to remember, "like the forest, but it was also dank, and I could smell chemicals. I realized later it was from the embalming stuff that had never been removed. And there was a smell of something dead. I tried not to think of Blane Crawford, but that was next to impossible. I told myself it was just a raccoon stuck in the old chimney or something. I could have stayed on the first floor. I wanted to. But I knew Jake would grill me about the basement. I had to go down there, or they'd know I'd wimped out."

"So, you went?" Ashley asked, her eyes big in her tanned face.

"I went," Max agreed. "I walked down the stairs on legs like Jell-O."

"I love the cherry kind," Sid announced.

Ashley cast him an incredulous look, and he blushed red.

"Me too," Max offered. "But that night I didn't want to think of anything red or jiggly. It was so dark. I had this weak little flashlight that barely lit the path in front of my feet."

"What did you see?" Ashley asked.

Max remembered stepping off those soft groaning stairs into a dark hallway. There were doors open and hanging off their hinges. Through the first door, he saw the embalming room, the tiled floor littered with leaves and dirt. The walls were peeling and the ceiling was a mass of water damage. As he'd shone his flashlight into the room, he'd spotted a huge spiderweb in one corner, and his light lit up a spider who seemed to cast a thousand glowing eyes on him.

"There was a metal table in the embalming room. A tile floor with a drain all clogged with leaves. Spiderwebs everywhere. I saw a sink in the corner filled with a dark liquid-like goo. I don't know what it was. It was probably just water and dirt, but..." Max closed his eyes. "It scared the crap out of me. I left that room and went into the next one. The coffin room."

Now he stopped, realizing his ice cream had begun to melt down his hand and drip onto his shoes.

"Oops." He licked the ice cream off his hand and grabbed a pile of napkins to wipe it from his shoes, before standing and throwing his ice cream in the trash. His appetite for sweets had disappeared.

"There were maybe five coffins. A couple had their lids open. I could see the satin lining inside all spotted with mold. I didn't want to walk around in there, but I did. I kept thinking I'm down here, and Jake's gonna ask how many coffins? What color were they? It was absurd, but I couldn't help it.

"I walked deeper into the room. The carpet was gross, but in one spot, it was black. A long black mark, like a coffin had been there and left a burn mark or... or something, had leaked out of it."

He'd pictured Blane Crawford then, seen him so clearly decaying in that coffin, huge maggots on his face that he'd turned

117

and fled. Max had sprinted full speed into a coffin. The coffin hadn't tipped over, but it had rocked hard on its base, and the impact had hurled Max backward. He'd landed on his back, the wind knocked out of him. His flashlight had skidded across the room.

"It took me a minute to stand up," he continued. "I was seeing stars, and the next day I had a bruise the size of Texas on my chest." He winced, remembering the purple black bruise that had throbbed for days.

"And then?" Ashley asked, her hands gripping the bench beneath her.

Sid, too, sat on the edge of his seat as if poised for flight.

"And then I got the hell out of there," Max said. "I grabbed my flashlight and ran upstairs and out the door."

The flash of disappointment in Ashley's face was undeniable, but Sid grinned, as if relieved there were no more horrors to reveal.

"What?" Max asked Ashley.

"You left something out," she said, crossing her arms over her chest.

A little flutter of fear lit in Max's belly. He grinned and looked away.

"That's my story, and I'm sticking to it."

"Come on. We've seen scary stuff too. If you tell us, we'll tell you," Ashley said.

Sid's mouth dropped open. "Ash, you said-," he started, but Ashley cut him off.

"I know what I said."

Max looked back and forth between them. He didn't want to share the story, largely because, in the fourteen years since he'd walked into The Crawford House, he'd learned to dismiss what he'd seen. He didn't want to remember it. He preferred to believe his brain had been so high on fear and then shock after running into the coffin that he'd simply imagined the next part.

"Tell us," Ashley insisted.

Max chewed his tongue. He shouldn't tell them. Teachers were role models. They reminded kids the boogeyman wasn't real, that monsters didn't exist. He was supposed to say, *Stop doodling werewolves in your notebook. Those aren't real.*

Instead, he opened his mouth and spoke. "After I fell, I had to lay there for a few minutes. It felt like an hour, but it might have been only five seconds. Finally, I rolled over and started to get up. I was looking at the flashlight. It illuminated the floor beneath one of the coffins.

"Suddenly, I heard this horrible creak, like when you push open a door and the hinge is so rusted it screeches like an angry cat. I was on one knee by then, and I froze. I mean froze like my blood turned to ice. I didn't take a breath. I realized it wasn't a door I'd heard but a coffin. In the beam of that light, I saw a foot step down as if someone were climbing out of the coffin above it. And then the other foot came down. The skin on the feet and legs looked rotten, blackened, and kind of curdling."

Sid shook his head from side to side, and Max half expected him to clamp his hands over his ears and start crying. Ashley looked equally horrified, yet strangely unafraid.

"The feet turned as if the thing above them had spotted me across that room. And it had. It was pitch black except the little halo of light from my flashlight. The only thing I could see were those feet, but it could see me. I felt it watching me. I bolted. I jumped up and ran for my life. I still remember running up those stairs."

Max's arms broke out in goosebumps.

"I've never experienced anything like that adrenaline rush since. I could have outrun the fastest kid in the school right then. But I also felt... heavy. As if something were pulling me back. Not touching me, but pulling me just the same."

He stopped and let out a shuddering breath. "The guys

laughed when they saw me come out. I barely acknowledged them. I sprinted home without looking back."

Sid put his hands to his mouth, eyes still wide.

Ashley nodded as if Max had shared something she already knew. "It was real," she said.

Max laughed an uncomfortable, humorless laugh.

"I accept there are mysteries in the world. Was it real? In my mind it was, and what's more real than that, you know?" He murmured, wishing away the panicky quiver in his stomach. "Why are you guys interested in The Crawford House?"

Ashley pressed her lips into a thin line and then glanced at Sid.

"We think The Crawford House is haunted too," Ashley said.

"Did you see something out there?" Max asked.

Ashley shook her head. "Just heard some weird stuff."

Max recognized the lie. Whatever they thought about The Crawford House it went beyond strange noises, but he sensed their unwillingness to open up.

"We've got to go," Ashley said, grabbing Sid by the shirt and tugging him up. "We'll see you around, Mr. Wolf."

They walked to Sid's bike, Ashley climbing on the knobs of the back tire, and rode away.

*a*fter the ice cream shop, Max's entire body seemed tense, as if the muscle memory of that long ago night in The Crawford house had as much to say as the mental one.

He needed a long ride to clear his head, and pulled into a gas station on his way out of town to fuel up.

"What's this country coming to?" The man who stood in front of Max, waiting to pay for gas, demanded. He folded his newspaper with a huff and slapped it on the counter.

The cashier, a petite girl no older than twenty-one widened her eyes.

"Sorry, Miss," the man said, half turning to Max and gesturing at the paper. "A little girl missing from the woods just down from her street. It's a crying shame what people are up to. You hear this good," the man continued, turning back to the cashier and directing his words at her. "Stay away from strangers. STAY AWAY! Don't ride with 'em. Don't even walk up to their car if they're asking directions. My sister's son disappeared walking to a park not two blocks from his house. Two blocks!"

The girl glanced at Max, and the cautious expression vanished from her face. She flashed him a brilliant smile.

"Oh, I'm careful," the girl stated, ringing up the man's newspaper and Styrofoam cup of coffee. "After those girls went missing a few years back, our school did a whole assembly on safety and self-defense." She poked two pink fingernails in a jab at the men. "Go for the eyes," she said.

"Good, good. That's the ticket," the man agreed.

"A dollar-fifteen please," she told him.

He set the money on the counter, and as she made change, Max focused on the man.

"Where'd you say that was?"

"Over in Lake City. I grew up there. Back in my day, you could stay out all night playing without a care in the world. Course my ma strapped us if we ever did that, but it wasn't over no boogeyman. It was because we skipped out on our chores. These days you got weirdos pluckin' kids out of their own neighborhoods. Men murderin' women and burning them in the woods. That's what that lunatic up north was doing. Had some old kiln on his property according to the paper."

"Yeah, I remember hearing about that guy. What was his name again?"

"Spencer Crow," the girl piped up. "I heard he was very handsome." Her eyes lingered on Max as she said the word.

"I'll take ten in gas on pump four," he told her.

She rang him up, brushing her fingers over his palm when she handed his change back.

"That's your bike?" she asked, looking out the window at his motorcycle.

"Yeah, she's mine."

"I love motorcycles," she offered, leaning forward on the counter. Her long dark hair brushed her suddenly more visible cleavage.

The man gave Max a significant look and smiled.

"You should get one," Max told her. "Not enough women ride bikes."

He hurried to catch up with the man as he left the gas station.

"I think that young lady was hoping for a date," the man told him.

"A date is the last thing I need," Max laughed, though he could almost hear his mother disagreeing with him. "Listen, I'm a teacher at Winterberry Middle School, and the girl who just disappeared was in my class. There have been other kids who have gone missing too."

"There have?" the man looked surprised. "I haven't read anything about it, and I get this paper every single day. I read the whole thing too. Even the obituaries. My wife says it's morbid, but at least once a month, we know someone listed in there. How are we to pay our respects if we don't even know when someone has passed?"

"Very true," Max agreed. "Do you know if any other kids have disappeared from your sister's town?"

The man shook his head. "Not that we've heard of, and we've been pounding the pavement over there, hanging up fliers and trying to question people ourselves. She's got a detective on the case now, but they gave her the cold shoulder when she first reported the boy missing."

He opened his car door but made no move to get inside.

"See, part of the problem is my sister is poorer than a church mouse. She lives in this shabby apartment building full of down-on-their luck families, some of 'em with five, six kids running the streets all hours of the day and night. But Chris wasn't that way. He wandered, sure, what kid doesn't, but he was home for supper every night at six sharp when his mama got home from work. She knew the minute he didn't show up, something bad had gone on."

"Do you think she'd be willing to talk to me?" Max asked.

"Oh sure, yes, sir, she would. She's desperate to get people talking about her son."

The man wrote his sister's phone number on the back of his gas station receipt.

"I'll tell her to expect a call."

～

"HELLO?" Max heard the woman's searching voice on the line, and knew he'd reached the mother of the missing boy. Her voice teemed with hope and fear, the fear slightly outrunning the hope.

"Hi, Ms. Rowe?"

"Yes, this is her." Her voice rose another octave.

"My name is Max Wolfenstein. I ran into your brother yesterday, and he told me your son is missing."

The woman paused on the line, and Max wondered if she'd hung up.

"Yes, he mentioned you."

"I'm a teacher here in Roscommon, and we've had several disappearances as well."

"You have? Of children?"

"Yes. I'm not sure if there's any connection, but it strikes me as odd. Can you tell me about the day your son disappeared?"

The woman sniffled, and Max stared at his map of northern Michigan, studying the X marks for the hundredth time in search of some similarity his mind was overlooking.

"Chris didn't come home for dinner. He never missed dinner. It was March 17th, a Thursday. He's a good boy. He got into trouble now and then. All boys do, I think, but he always made it to dinner."

"Did he attend school that day?"

"Yes, school let out at two-fifteen, and he rode the bus home. He had plans to meet two other boys from the neighborhood at the basketball court. He never arrived. Somewhere between our apartment and the park, he disappeared."

"People saw him ride the bus?"

"Yes. The bus driver said he got off the bus at our stop. She didn't watch him walk into the building, but Nancy Perdy did. She lives in the apartment above us and spotted Chris coming up the sidewalk. He waved to her. She said he looked normal, smiling, kind of in a rush, probably to go play with his friends."

"Did anyone witness him leaving the building?"

"No," she sighed, "but the police searched the building and we did too, me and my brother and a few neighbors. His basketball was gone."

"And no one in the neighborhood found the ball?"

"No."

MAX TURNED ONTO HOWARD STREET, the street where Chris Rowe lived in an apartment with his mother. According to his mom, his father had died when Chris was only a baby, and she'd never remarried.

As he drove down the street, he immediately noticed the state of disrepair. The apartment buildings were not only out of date, they were grubby and unkempt. A crumbling abandoned building stood next to the apartment. Max wondered if anyone had searched that.

The park that Chris had been walking to that day looked equally haggard. Knee-high weeds were the only vegetation in sight. A rusted swing set offered a single swing dangling by two chains. A paved parking lot of spider web cracks and two netless hoops served as the basketball court.

It was a far cry from the picturesque parks Max had played in as a boy.

Several boys played a basketball game. They looked around

twelve or thirteen, the same age as Chris, maybe even his friends.

Max parked his motorcycle and watched the kids, gazing at more derelict houses, buildings with faded paint and parking lots. He waited until the boys took a break and then walked over.

"Hey guys," he said.

They looked at him, but didn't speak. One of them glanced at his motorcycle and nodded approvingly.

"Sweet ride," he said.

"Yeah, thanks. Listen, do any of you guys know Chris Rowe?"

Two of the boys frowned. They glanced at each other. The third nodded.

"Yeah."

"Were you here playing ball the day he went missing?"

"I was out of town," one boy answered. He was the tallest of the three with hair buzzed close to his head and beady brown eyes.

The second boy, likely awaiting a growth spurt, shook his head.

The third nodded. He stood in between the other two, lanky with shaggy brown hair and so many freckles they nearly obscured the features of his face. Max had to study him to make out his nose and mouth in the sea of freckles.

"I came here to meet him, but he never showed up."

"Did you see anything that day? Cars you didn't ordinarily see in the neighborhood? That kind of thing?"

Freckles shrugged and glanced at his buddies. "Nah, not really."

"Not really?"

He shrugged again. "I don't know, I saw a black van. It seemed normal enough, but later on, after Chris disappeared, kids started calling it the boogeyman van."

"Why?"

The boy who'd been out of town piped up. "Because the driver offered Ethan Becker some candy. Ethan's Jewish, like real Jewish, you know? He only eats Jewish stuff."

"It's called kosher, dufus," the third boy told him, bouncing the basketball at his face.

The boy swatted it away.

"Yeah, that. Anyway, the guy gave him the creeps, and that's the day Chris went missing."

"Would Chris have taken the candy?" Max asked, disturbed by the story of a man in a van offering candy.

"Oh yeah, for sure. He ate candy like a fat kid even though he was skinnier than most girls. He'd have definitely taken it," Freckles admitted.

"Does anyone know if the police spoke with Ethan about the man in the black van?"

"The police didn't talk to nobody," the first kid said. "We live in the same building as Chris, and the police never came to our place."

Freckles nodded.

Max frowned.

"How about Ms. Rowe? Anyone tell her the story?"

Freckles nodded.

"I did. About a week after he went missing. I told her and Chris's uncle when they were out putting up flyers. Mrs. Rowe and my ma drove me to the police station. The cops left us sittin' for two hours before they finally wrote down what I said. But I swear the guy wrote it on the back of a menu for that barbecue joint over on ninth street." He snatched the basketball from his friend and lobbed it at one of the basketball rims. It missed by a good five feet.

"Air ball," the first boy called.

"Where can I find Ethan Becker?" Max asked.

"He works at his dad's shoe store after school. Go about three blocks that way. It's called Becker's."

The store was empty when Max arrived.

He spotted a boy, close to the same age as the other boys, standing on the sidewalk, a spray bottle and a rag in his hand, washing the windows.

The kid turned when Max pulled the motorcycle up to the curb.

"Ethan Becker?"

The boy frowned and leaned close to the window as if searching for someone inside the store. He took a step toward the door.

Max held up his hands.

"I'm a teacher. I just wanted to ask you a few questions."

The boy's eyes darted inside the store again, but he turned to face Max, clutching the spray bottle tight in his right hand. Max suspected if he moved on the kid too fast, he'd get a face full of window cleaner.

"My name's Max," Max offered. "I'm helping Ms. Rowe find out what happened to Chris."

It was only a small lie, but he suspected mentioning Ms. Rowe's name would ease the kid's suspicions. "I met some kids at the basketball court who said you saw a black van the day Chris Rowe disappeared." Max figured he'd better get right down to it. The kid looked uneasy, and he doubted the parent in the store would leave him talking to a strange man for long.

Ethan looked in the direction of the basketball court. "I already told Ms. Rowe everything I know."

"Can you tell me too? Just what you remember?"

Ethan fidgeted, shifting from one foot to another and glancing up at the sky as if trying to jog his memory.

"I was walking to the store, and a guy in a black van pulled up. I'd never seen the van, and it didn't have any windows except in the front. A guy rolled down his window and held up a Twix bar. He said he was trying to find a gas station. If I'd get in and show him the way, he'd give me the candy bar."

Max recoiled. The story was even more disturbing hearing it firsthand.

"He wanted you to get in the van?"

Ethan nodded. "I don't eat store candy. Plus the guy creeped me out."

"What did he look like?"

Ethan shrugged. "Normal, I guess. Dark eyes, kind of dimmed glasses, you know like guys wore in the sixties and seventies."

"Clean?"

Ethan nodded. "Yeah, no beard or nothing."

"Why did he creep you out?"

Ethan blinked at his feet. "He umm…. he seemed like he was pretending. He had this real high voice. Ever seen *Animal House*?" Ethan looked up at him, then glanced toward the store window.

"The movie?" Max asked, not following.

"Yeah, yeah. Dean Wormer's that real uppity guy who runs the school. The guy in the van sounded like Dean Wormer, but he dressed like a hippie."

Max nodded, though he wondered if the man in the black van had been playing at sounding sophisticated to lure the young man into his van.

The door opened and a man not much taller than Ethan stepped out. He wore a crisp white shirt tucked into black trousers.

"Can I help you, sir?" the man stepped in front of Ethan blocking him from view.

"No, thank you," Max said, taking a step back. "I'm a teacher. Max Wolfenstein." He held out his hand, and the man shook it, though wearily.

"He's helping Ms. Rowe find Chris," Ethan blurted.

The man nodded and nudged Ethan toward the door.

"I need you to take out the trash, Son. You can finish the windows later."

He pushed his son through the door, and offered Max a curt nod before following him inside.

19

"Milk, medicine droppers, Polaroid camera, and steak knives," Sid said, picking through his backpack.

"And my baseball bat," Ashley added, clanking her metal bat against the curb. "And keep your eyes on the sky. You see any birds and we're out of there."

They'd neared the edge of the forest when a voice startled them both.

"What are you guys doing?" Shane asked, kicking up his skateboard and balancing it on the tip.

Sid shot her an anxious look and shook his head.

Ashley shrugged. "Walkin."

"Into those woods?" Shane nodded at the woods where Melanie Dunlop had disappeared several days before.

"No, into the mall. Obviously." She rolled her eyes, and Sid grinned.

"Can I come?" Shane asked. He tossed his head back, his blond hair returning to a sheath across his forehead.

"No," Sid whispered under his breath, but Ashley's head had already tilted up and down.

"Sure, why not?" She ignored Sid and traipsed into the woods, stomping branches beneath her sneakers.

"Are you guys looking for Melanie?" Shane asked as they walked beneath the awning of trees.

"No," Sid griped, eyes cast toward the sky in search of vultures.

"You okay, man?" Shane asked.

Sid didn't answer and dropped his jaw when Shane got a running start and ran right up the side of a tree, grabbing a branch above him and swinging his legs up. His upper body arced back, and he dangled, his golden hair waving below his head.

A blue jay squawked and fled from the tree, its bright blue body vanishing into the higher branches.

"Why did you let him come? He'll make fun of us with The Thrashers," Sid whispered to Ashley.

Sid's belly felt like a pit of writhing snakes. He didn't understand why, but suspected it had something to do with the way Ashley laughed when Shane had flipped into the tree.

"Three is better than two, Sid. We need all the help we can get if we run into the monster."

Sid grunted and picked up a stick, poking at the dirt and avoiding looking at Shane as he gracefully swung down from the tree.

"Swear you won't tell anyone what we're about to show you?" Ashley asked, turning to face Shane.

He stopped, pulling a face and squinting at the forest floor.

"You didn't find her, did you? Melanie?" Shane whispered.

Ashley screwed up her face.

"No, gross! What do you think, we're leading you to her body?" Ashley cringed.

Shane released a whoosh of breath and ran his hands through his hair, a mannerism that made Sid want to hack off every piece of his golden hair with a pair of rusted gardening shears.

"Haven't you read "The Body" by Stephen King? It's in his book *Different Seasons*. Crazier things have happened," Shane replied.

"*You've* read it?" Sid asked, as if he expected Shane to be illiterate, though he knew full well he wasn't. He'd heard Shane read aloud in English class. He never even stumbled over the big words like procrastinate or bewildered. Sid, on the other hand, who was an exceptional reader in his own head, turned into a stuttering ignoramus when forced to read out loud during class.

"I won't show you until you promise to keep them a secret."

"I swear," Shane said, resting a hand on his chest.

Ashley led him to the clearing where they'd built the raccoon den.

Shane walked up to their little raccoon tree house and peeked into the opening.

"Wow," he said. "I've never seen baby raccoons before."

"Want to feed one?" Ashley asked.

She pulled the backpack from Sid's back and took out the milk and medicine droppers.

Shane lifted a raccoon out and cupped it in both hands as he sat on the ground.

"Hey, little dude," he told it. "Where did you find them?" he asked Ashley.

"In a tree. We think their mom got hit by a car."

"Bummer," he said.

"Want the other dropper?" Ashley asked Sid.

He shot Shane a grouchy look and shook his head. "You go ahead," he murmured.

Ashley lifted Alvin from the den, rubbing his soft head beneath her chin.

"Hey, Alvin. How's your day been?"

"Alvin?" Shane asked.

"Alvin," Ash repeated, lifting the raccoon. "And you're holding Simon. Theodore is the little pork chop still in there. He'd guzzle all the milk if you let him."

After they fed the raccoons, they walked back toward the road.

Sid had never taken the camera from his bag. He sensed Ashley didn't want to reveal what else they'd been looking for in the woods. Keeping the secret suited him just fine.

"We could go to the arcade," Shane suggested as they left the woods.

The summer day lazed around them. Sun splashed across the metallic hoods of cars parked in driveways.

Sid saw sprinkler's sending arcs of water across green lawns.

In Mrs. Lincoln's yard, her windmill flamingos didn't move a feather. The leaves didn't rustle in the trees. The heat had the thick stifling sensation that reminded Sid, unpleasantly, of being tucked into the dumbwaiter several days before.

"I can't," Ashley said. "I've got to mow Mr. Bauman's yard, and then run to the market for Mrs. Jasper."

"Dang. Are those like your jobs or something?" Shane asked.

"I'm saving for the Huffy Pro Thunder. I only need twenty-two dollars and it's mine. I have eight right now, fourteen bucks to go."

Shane whistled.

"I've seen that bike in Sampson's. It's totally bitchin."

"What about you?" Shane asked Sid.

Sid looked up sharply, a flush rushing from his neck to his forehead before he could demand his body to play it cool.

Shane watched him as if he were dead serious, not asking so that when Sid said yes, he could laugh in his face.

Sid wanted to go to the arcade. He had dreamed two nights before that he'd defeated *Donkey Kong* and won back Lady, but when he tried to imagine riding his bike alongside Shane on his skateboard, he stumbled instead into a vision of Shane luring him into the park where Travis and the other Thrashers would hide in the john, waiting to grab him and stick his head in the toilet for a bogwash.

"Nah, I don't think so," he said at last. "My mom said something about burgers at the Pin Wheel today."

It was a lie. His mom never wanted burgers at the Pin Wheel. The last Friday of the month they went as a family because their father insisted the boys deserved a greasy burger and fries once in a blue moon. Gloria Putnam disagreed, but went along with it after too many arguments with her husband to count. However, they'd gone to Pin Wheel two weeks before. Their next trip wouldn't be until July.

Ashley knew as much, but Sid didn't let her catch his eye.

"Okay, see you guys later," Shane said, pulling his skateboard from the bushes.

Sid and Ashley had walked to the woods, so they continued home on foot.

"You'd like him if you gave him a chance," Ashley said after several minutes of silence.

"Like a needle in the eye," Sid grumbled.

"Come on," Ashley argued. "What's your deal, Sid. He's been nice."

"He's boring, Ash. Okay. He's one of those perfect everything dudes. Perfect hair, best at skateboarding, too cool for the cool kids, too cool for the dorks. He's like a shadow of a person."

Ashley started to disagree, but Sid cut her off.

"And he's probably pulling the prank of the year. He'll spend the summer befriending us and then lure us to some secret Thrasher hideout so they can beat the tar out of us before school starts back up in the fall."

Sid heard the explanation, weak and bordering on paranoid. He didn't believe a word of it. The truth was, he didn't want a third. Period. He liked Ashley and Sid as they were.

Ashley didn't say more about it. She rattled on about the Huffy Pro Thunder until they reached his street.

"My mom's making spaghetti tonight. Want to come over later?"

"I thought you were going to the Pinwheel," she mocked.

Sid's mouth fell open, but he clamped it shut. "I just didn't want to go with him, okay?" He heard the whine in his voice and wished he could cut out his stupid voice box and just be one of those cool, silent guys you sometimes saw in noir films. They wore black trench coats and smoked cigarettes, and gorgeous women fell all over them even though they never spoke a word.

Ashley shook her head and Sid noticed a wistful look in her eye. "I'm cooking dinner for my mom tonight."

"What? Can you even work the oven?"

Ashley glared at him. "Actually, smart-ass, I can. But I'm going to make tuna fish sandwiches, so I won't need to."

"Umm, I don't think that's called cooking."

"Whatever. I'll see you tomorrow, Sid." She offered him a light punch in the bicep and turned left, cutting between a row of houses leading toward her house.

"Okay," he yelled after her. "Call me early. Okay? Maybe we can take the camera out and look for, ya know…"

But she didn't respond and as he watched her run off, and his throat constricted around his words.

20

"Mr. Wolf?"

A girl's voice, as clear as if she'd spoken into his ear, flowed to Max out of the darkness.

He sat up in bed.

"Who's there?" he asked, his mind suspended between waking and dreaming.

He squinted into his dark bedroom. He made out the silhouettes of his dresser and the chair next to his closet.

Had a student snuck into his house?

He fumbled for his bedside table, flipping on his lamp, and extinguishing the shadows.

No girl stood in his bedroom.

His eyes flitted over the dresser scattered with his wallet, keys, and a few quarters. Beside his dresser, the previous day's clothes were draped over a chair.

He stood and shuffled to the door, looking down the dark hallway to the equally dark stairs. No sounds emerged, not even a breath broke the silence.

He slipped back into his room and closed and locked the

door. As he walked toward his bed, something scratched at his window.

He jumped back, imagining a girl's sharp fingernails clawing at the glass.

The scratching came again, and his heart galloped in his chest. He lunged to his lamp and flipped the light off, feeling exposed in the yellow beam.

In the cover of darkness, he peeled back the curtain, preparing for the face he expected to find pressed against his window.

His cat, Frankenstein, named after the scientist, not the monster, stood on his roof, paws pressed against the window pane. His yellow eyes glowed in the dark night.

"Jesus, Frankenstein," he muttered, putting a hand on his chest and feeling the rapid thud beneath his palm

Max opened the window, and the cat leapt inside, his black and white hair standing in a rigid arc from nape to tail.

The cat had been all that was left after his break-up with Cindy Montgomery two years before. She'd given him the kitten for the single Christmas they'd spent together. He remembered her confused and disappointed expression when she'd opened her own gift: a waterproof Timex watch. He'd realized later, after Jake elbowed him after Christmas dinner, that Cindy had expected a ring.

Frankenstein had outlived several of Max's, short but not so sweet, relationships since.

"Something spook you?" he asked, kneeling to pet that cat.

Frankenstein leaned into his touch, but remained alert, his tail a streak of agitated fur.

As Max stroked the cat and the hazy fear of being awakened dissipated, he realized he recognized the voice who'd spoken to him from the darkness.

It had been the voice of Melanie Dunlop.

Max walked into the hallway, turning on lights as we went.

He peeked into the spare bedroom, the bathroom, and finally, traipsed down the stairs into the living room.

A book lay on the living room floor. He grabbed it, not bothering to glance at the title and returned it the shelf. The house was empty.

"I dreamed it," he sighed, retiring to his room and crawling back into bed.

Frankenstein curled into a ball and rested his head on his tail.

"Melanie Dunlop," he whispered and then shook his head, thinking back to his conversation with Ashley and Sid from the day before. The ghost story had clearly planted a creep seed in his head, and he'd dreamed her voice in his room as a consequence.

Creep seeds were a term invented by one of his college professors during psychology 101 and referred to unnerving events of the day that later wove themselves into dreams.

Max's experience at The Crawford House had definitely left a lasting impression, one he'd never made sense of. Though in the years since the incident occurred, he'd decided he'd made it up. Fear mingled with a powerful boy's imagination produced the images Max saw that night. Nothing more.

He leaned over and flicked off the lamp, listening to Frankenstein's purrs as he drifted back to sleep.

Sunlight filtered through the slants in his blinds when Max woke. He rolled over, mouth falling open, when he spotted the time: ten forty-three a.m. He couldn't remember the last time he'd slept later than seven o'clock in the morning.

His feet tingled from the heavy ball of fluff curled on his ankles.

"Ok, Frankie, move it or lose it," he murmured, wiggling his legs until the cat stretched, shot him an irritated look, and hopped down from the bed.

He followed the cat down the stairs and into the kitchen, stopping abruptly at the mess on the floor.

"What the..." he bent down to take a closer look. A trail of colorful cereal lay scattered along the linoleum.

He picked up a piece of the cereal and sniffed it.

"Fruit Loops," he murmured, smelling the faint aroma of lemons.

Max stood and set the single yellow loop on his counter, eyeing it wearily.

He didn't own a box of Fruit Loops. He stopped eating sugary cereal in high school when the football coach had told him he'd never make the team if he didn't build some muscle, which meant protein. Max had started eating eggs for breakfast the next day. He never did play football.

By the time his body achieved the desirable physique of an athlete, Max had shifted his focus to the basketball team and considered the football players to be lunkheads who likely lost half a cup of braincells every game.

Frankenstein sniffed the cereal and then batted a loop with his paw, sending it skidding across the floor and under the kitchen table.

Max walked to the door and turned the handle. It wiggled, but otherwise stayed in place, the lock engaged.

He thought of the voice from the night before, the girl's voice, Melanie Dunlop's voice. Maybe she had run away and for whatever reason had broken into his house and dropped a handful of Fruit Loops on his kitchen floor.

"Like Hansel and Gretel," he said out loud before shaking his head in disbelief. "Better take pictures of this, Frankenstein. Detective Welch will definitely want to see the latest clues I've discovered."

His sarcasm was lost on the cat who continued to chase the fruit loop beneath the table.

Max grabbed his broom, swept the cereal into the dustpan,

and threw it out the back door. He could have deposited it in the trash can. It was right there, but when he started to lift the lid something in him squeezed, and without thought, he opened the door and tossed it into the yard. The colored hoops disappeared into the grass.

He brewed his coffee and gazed around the kitchen. The microwave sat on the counter. A jar of quarters sat on his kitchen table. If a burglar had broken in, one who left Fruit Loops in his wake no less, wouldn't he have taken those items?

He wandered out of the kitchen and into the living room, noting the television and VCR. Again, nothing appeared amiss, except a single book laying face down in the center of the carpeted room, just as one had the night before.

But he'd picked it up and returned it to the shelf. Hadn't he?

He knelt and grabbed the book, flipping it over.

Heart of Darkness he read out loud, by Joseph Conrad.

He'd taught the book the previous fall to the seventh grade students, a class that Melanie Dunlop had been in.

He set it on the coffee table and then picked it back up, returning it to his bookshelf, making sure it was held snugly within the other books. He pushed against the side of the bookcase. It didn't budge. He hadn't expected it to. The bookcase was an antique made from solid oak and heavy.

When he sat down at his table with the newspaper, he was disappointed to see no mention of missing kids.

Melanie Dunlop's disappearance had shifted to page two.

ax drove slow through town, watching the early morning travelers walking to jobs. Mrs. Kenmore, who owned Minnie's Flower Shop, heaved a large potted flower out her door. When she saw Max, she grinned and tilted her head in a wave. He lifted a hand to wave back.

The town felt emptier than usual with the school buses absent from stoplights and no groups of kids piling at street corners as they waited for the crossing guard to wave them by.

He generally met the summer with mingled exhilaration and sadness. He missed the kids over summer break, missed the routine of his day-to-day life and the students' boisterous energy.

Throughout the summer, he'd return to the school a few days a week as he started preparation for the upcoming year, but during the first days of his break he often felt an odd purposelessness, a questioning of not only his big life choices, but also the little ones, like what will I do today?

Instead of that niggling self-doubt, Max found himself fixated on the voice of Melanie Dunlop and thoughts of the other kids: Vern Ripley, Simon Frank, and Warren Leach. Three still missing and one dead.

He slowed and directed his motorcycle to the curb, climbing off and leaving his helmet on the seat of his bike.

Baby Love, a boutique store specializing in all things baby, looked empty on the early Saturday morning, but thankfully the little open sign glowed red.

He'd received an early morning call that Matthew Herman Wolfenstein had arrived into the world at four a.m. Max's parents were already at the hospital. Max had promised his mother he'd pick up a gift and meet them there.

As he approached the store, he gazed through the window at the display. A crib draped in satiny blankets spotted with little yellow ducks sat on a matching duck rug. A glider chair held a pile of plush blue and pink ducks.

One child had left the world the week before, and now another had come into it. Hundreds, no thousands more had been born and died in the interim.

As Max gazed through the window, a reflection appeared in the glass beside his own. He looked toward it, expecting another patron hurrying into the store for their own early morning gift. Instead, Melanie Dunlop gazed at him in the glass. Her eyes looked dark and hollow; her lips parted as if she was about to speak.

Worst of all was the red gash across Melanie's throat.

Shocked, he spun to face her, but the sidewalk stretched on before him, empty.

"Mom, can I talk to you about something?"

Maria Wolfenstein stood back to survey her handiwork. She'd spent the morning cooking and baking for Jake and

Eleanor and had stocked their refrigerator and freezer with food.

"Casserole on the second shelf?" she asked him absently. "Yes," she agreed before he could answer. "Knowing your brother, he'll only see what's at eye level and poor Eleanor will spend the next week eating sauerkraut."

She switched the dishes out and then smiled, triumphant.

"What would you like to talk about, Maximillian?" she asked, turning to face him.

He started to speak, but she held up a finger. "Did you get the mobile set up?"

"Yes."

"Okay, then. We deserve a little break. How about a cup of coffee and cake?"

"Sure, Mom."

After Maria had sliced them each a hunk of Black Forest cake and poured coffees, she followed Max onto the sunlit porch. They settled into wrought iron deck furniture.

"You used to say Grandma Stein spoke to ghosts," Max started.

Maria sipped her coffee and regarded him. "Oh yes. My mother had the sight to be sure," Maria agreed, cutting a forkful of cake and holding it up to her nose. "You can smell the cherries. Have a bite, Maximillian. Don't insult me with your meager appetite."

Max laughed and took a bite. "I may be many things, Mother, but a stingy eater isn't one of them. It's delicious as always."

He took a second bite and followed it up with a sip of coffee. "Did you ever see things? Ghosts?"

"Yes, indeed. We live in a haunted world. Every being leaves something behind. That's what my mother used to say. When I was a girl in Hamburg, we lived during the most dreadful time in the history of Germany. The horrors..." she trailed off, gazing at her cake in woeful astonishment. "I still cannot think of them, not truly. Most of us did not believe in Hitler's cruelty. My very best friend's mother was in the National Socialist Women's League, a major supporter of the Nazi Party. The city was haunted, the whole country, really. Death everywhere you turned. My mother nearly went mad with it."

Max leaned back in his chair, watching a boy whiz by on a bicycle.

"The ghost I encountered, the one I knew was a ghost, was a little girl. I say little, but back then she was my age. Gitta was her name, and she had lived in the flat beneath ours. Her family was Jewish. They owned a little store that had closed after the boycott. The Nazis had taken her family two years before. I still remember their screams, still to this day. The crying and pleading. Her father offered to pay the Nazi soldiers."

Maria's face pinched with the memory.

"I remember the sounds of Gitta and her mother's footsteps pounding up the stairs and down the hall. The mother beat on our door and begged us to let them in. My father stood at our door, his face like stone. My mother held me and rocked me, tears pouring down her cheeks, and I didn't understand. I couldn't. My mind had not yet grown enough to comprehend the evil that exists in this world. My parents did not support the Third Reich, but we were powerless against them."

Maria paused, the color gone from her face as she gazed into the yard across the street, though Max knew it was not the neighbor's newly planted flowers she observed.

"A couple years went by and sometimes I wondered what happened to Gitta, but if I brought it up, my mother would shush me and say not to think about her because I would let her in. Well, that only made me think about her more, and one night after I'd said my prayers, I climbed into bed and had only just closed my eyes when she whispered my name. *Maria*, she said from beneath the bed."

A chill crept down Max's spine, and in his mind he heard his name, Mr. Wolf, spoken in his bedroom.

"I thought, my goodness Gitta has escaped," Maria continued. "And I popped out of bed and looked for her, but she was not there. No one was there. A few nights later, she spoke my name again from the crevice beneath my bed, and again, I did not find her. I grew determined to catch her. I lay in my bed with my mother's hand mirror tilted toward that dark crack. And this time when she spoke my name, I saw her in the mirror. Her face looked like driftwood, gray and gnarled, and her eyes were dark and shining. She looked sunken."

Maria rotated the gold band on her ring finger as if it were a talisman and might protect her from the memory.

"Gitta opened her mouth and a flood of ash poured out. I screamed and dropped the mirror, cracking the glass. My mother and father rushed in. They'd been asleep in bed. They looked almost as terrified as me. I couldn't even speak to tell them about Gitta and the ashes."

Max's skin crawled and he shifted in his chair.

"My mother slept with me that night. In the morning, I told her all about the girl. We cleaned my room that day. Moved the bed to the opposite wall, swept the dust and dirt free. My mother burned candles and said a prayer. I never saw Gitta again."

Max finished his coffee, his arms prickling with goosebumps. As he'd done with his own terrifying childhood tale, he wanted to dismiss her experience as the wild imaginings of a child in wartime.

Instead, he said, "I think I'm being haunted."

She finished her cake, sliding the fork over the porcelain to get the last of the frosting.

"Have you invited someone in? A spirit?"

"The hell if I know." He threw up his hands.

"Words, young man," she scolded him.

"Sorry, Mom. The heck if I know." He winked at her. "It's the girl who went missing, Melanie Dunlop. I heard her voice the other night in my room, and then I saw her reflection in a store window."

Maria frowned and reached a loving hand to Max's, caressing his fingers. "You are my sensitive child, Max. My heart. I love Jakey like my own two legs, but Jake is a thinker, and you are a feeler. It's always the feelers they come to, the ghosts. The thinkers simply think them away."

"It means she's dead, right? If I'm seeing her ghost, she's dead?"

"I've never met a live one," Maria murmured. "What a shame, a young girl, hardly more than a baby." Maria pressed her hands into her cheeks, her eyes filling with tears. "So much suffering in this world."

"Could it be a hallucination?" he wondered out loud. "Something I'm imagining because I've been thinking about her so much?"

Maria tilted her head to the side. "The mind is tricky. That's true enough, but what does your heart tell you?" She leaned over and placed a hand on his chest.

He closed his eyes. "That she's dead."

22

---

*A*shley and Sid fed the raccoons and returned to the street.

"Here," Sid pulled a dollar out of his pocket.

She didn't take it, planting her hands on her hips.

"What's that for?" she asked.

Sid's parents rarely gave him pocket money, and when they did, he spent it on candy within an hour.

"My dad gave it to me for helping him haul some old furniture down from the attic."

"Don't you want to get candy?"

Sid shook his head and waved his t-shirt away from his body as if suddenly hot.

"I'd rather you get your bike a little sooner."

Ashley smiled and took the money shoving it in the back pocket of her shorts.

"Thanks, Sid," she said.

"So where to?" he asked. "We could see if Benny McKenzie has his pool open."

Ashley shook her head. There was only one place Ashley had

wanted to go since the idea had popped into her head two days earlier.

"The Crawford House," Ashley said.

Sid paled, slowing his walk.

"Let's go tomorrow, Ash. It's too hot today. The bugs will be terrible."

"Not any worse than they were back there." She hiked a thumb at the woods behind her. "Look, you don't have to go inside. Deal? I just want to poke around there and see if we notice anything."

Sid sighed, and Ashley noticed how he dragged his feet as they walked out of their neighborhood, skirting the southern end of town.

The woods that ran behind the train tracks buzzed with gnats.

Sid swatted them away. "Ugh, I swallowed one," he complained.

"Breathe through your nose."

Ahead of them, Ashley spotted birds circling above the trees. She counted twelve vultures floating in the still sky.

"Sid," she croaked, grabbing his arm.

"What?" he asked.

She pointed to the birds, and when he saw them, he turned as if to run the other way.

At the end of the street, Ashley saw Shane Savage walking toward the woods, oblivious to the birds circling above.

Ashley didn't think. She sprinted down the street.

Shane hadn't noticed her. She darted forward and grabbed his hand, wrenching him back as he stepped onto the grassy embankment edging the trees.

"What are you doing?" he asked, surprised.

"Don't go in there," she told him, trying to catch her breath.

Sid lumbered toward them, less than a half a block away, but red-faced and visibly winded.

Ashley looked into the sky where the birds continued to hold vigil over whatever lurked beneath them.

"It's in there," she said.

"What? What do you mean?"

She pointed a shaky finger toward the birds.

Shane frowned. "Okay? So, there's like a dead opossum in there or something."

He started to pull away, to walk back toward the tree line, but she snatched the back of his shirt in her hand and pulled so hard she almost ripped the fabric.

"It's not a dead opossum, Shane. There's..." she looked for Sid. She wanted him there to back her up. If they both told their stories, it wouldn't seem so nuts. He'd stopped, hands planted on his thighs, as he wheezed for breath.

"He doesn't look so good," Shane murmured.

"He's fine. Come on." She dragged Shane toward Sid.

"No, I-"

"Just give us five minutes, okay. Five minutes, and if you still want to go in there, whatever. It's your funeral."

Shane gave her a funny look, but she didn't offer more.

When they reached Sid, he'd managed to stand back up straight, but his mouth still hung wide as if trying to suck as much air in as humanly possible.

"Screw running," he panted.

"I don't see track in your future, Sid Putnam," Shane told him.

Sid flipped him the finger and then wandered to the curb, sitting down and stretching his legs out in front of him.

"We've got to tell him about the monster, Sid," Ashley said.

"What monster?" Shane asked, looking back and forth between them.

"You... you go first," Sid puffed.

Ashley glanced at Shane, noticing his long dark eyelashes and then frowned, exasperated with her own stupid thoughts.

Shane revealed little as he listened first to Ashley's story of the boy who attacked her in the night followed by Sid's.

"We think it might be Warren," she said at the end.

Shane picked up a stone in the gutter and flicked it across the road. It hit the opposite curb before bouncing into the grass.

"You think Warren killed Simon?" He shook his head in disbelief.

"Warren went into the woods not far from where Simon's body was found," Ashley explained. "Maybe he knows they found the body, so he's hiding out."

"The boy you described in the woods doesn't sound like Warren. Warren is big. He can't exactly creep around unnoticed," Shane countered.

"He might be disguising himself," Ashley insisted. "I didn't get a good look at him. It was dark and-"

Shane shook his head again.

"Warren's mom came over a few nights ago. I heard her talking with my mom. Warren said something odd a few weeks ago to his mom. He told her he thought an animal had been stalking him in the woods when he'd walked home that night. He kept hearing it and thinking something had been watching him. He'd been scared."

Ashley frowned. "But we heard Travis talking, and he said Warren went missing on purpose."

"Travis is a jack-ass," Shane said.

"Here-here," Sid cheered in agreement.

"So, if it's not Warren, who is it?"

Shane shrugged. "Beats me, but I'd say if there really is something after kids in the woods, it got Warren too."

"But Warren's big," Sid said, unable to hide the tremor of fear in his voice.

"Which makes him an easier target, right?" Shane asked. "He's not exactly quiet, and he's damn easy to see if he's walking in the woods."

Sid looked visibly ill. "We can't go to The Crawford House without weapons, Ash," he said.

"What's at The Crawford House?" Shane asked, looking back and forth between them.

"We think it's hiding there, living there maybe."

~

MAX PARKED his motorcycle in Jake's driveway and waved at his brother sitting on the front porch.

"Mom asked me to bring you a block of cheese. Don't ask me why, just take it."

Jake laughed and took the white cheese, setting it on the glass topped table beside him.

"After all the food Mom crammed in the refrigerator, I can't imagine where she expects us to put it," Jake grumbled.

"Feed it to the neighbor's dog," Max suggested, sitting next to his brother. "Listen, while I'm here, I wanted to ask you a few questions about one of the missing kids, Vern Ripley."

"Moonlighting as a sleuth?" Jake asked. "Oh, I forgot, you're on easy street until September. If you've got all this time, maybe you could come pick up the midnight to three a.m. shift at our house. Apparently, that's Matthew's most hated time of day. He cries nonstop whether he's nursing, just got changed, or you run laps around the house and bounce him like a basketball."

"Well, no wonder he's crying if you're bouncing him like a basketball," Max told him dryly.

"Ha-ha," Jake retorted rubbing his bloodshot eyes. "Good grief, I want to go back to work. Is that terrible? Eleanor's like the walking dead, and I'm not far behind her. If Mom weren't coming over to help, I think we would have given the baby up for adoption."

Max laughed and patted Jake on the back.

"You heard what Mom said. The first few weeks are the worst. In a month, you'll be on easy street."

Jake offered him a bleary-eyed look of astonishment. "I hope you have twins someday, Max."

"Me too, pretty ones with big boobs."

Jake sputtered a laugh and slapped his thigh. When he leaned his head back on his chair, he closed his eyes.

"I could sleep for ten solid hours right now."

"You do that. But answer my question first. What's the deal with the Ripley family? Kids at school implied the kid's stepdad is a brute. I talked to Goldie, and she seemed pretty defensive about him."

Jake opened his eyes and gave Max a weary glance.

"Darwin Ripley. He's a little rough around the edges, but brute seems like a strong word. He's a mechanic over at Joe's Auto Body. He's insured his truck with us for the last five years, and usually comes in with Goldie, though I haven't seen her in months."

"Because her kid is missing."

"Yeah, you said that. And it is strange that Darwin never mentioned anything, but we don't exactly sit around and have tea when he comes in. Goldie's real sweet, a little hardened. I don't think she's had the easiest life. She bakes us cookies every Christmas. I can't tell you much more than that, Max."

"Ever see the kid, Vern?"

Jake shook his head, rubbing his neck.

"Ouch! oh, man, got a kink right there." He shoved a thumb into the base of his skull and rubbed. "I've aged ten years in three days. No. The boy never came in with them. Sometimes Goldie brought their daughter in, a tiny little thing like her mama, not a day over five, I'd guess."

"Did you ever notice bruises? Anything like that on the mom or daughter?"

Jake huffed and cast Max a frustrated glance.

"You better not ask anybody else that question. I don't know Darwin well, but if he got wind of the implications, he might stop by your house with a steel pipe."

"I'm not asking anyone but you and maybe Dad. I'm just trying to rule out the possibility that he had a hand in his stepson's disappearance."

"You're trying to rule it out? Now you sound like a cop." Jake sat up and looked squarely at his brother. "Max, I'd leave this to the real cops. You're getting in over your head."

"Yeah, well, kids are missing and nobody's doing shit about it. How would you feel, Jake? Now that you're a dad. If your kid went missing? Wouldn't you hope people were looking? Asking questions?"

Jake's face fell.

"Yeah." He nodded. "I guess I would."

When Max pushed through his front door, the first thing he noticed was the book laying on the carpet in his living room.

He paused, the door left ajar, and gazed at the book.

Finally, he walked in, picked it up, not needing to glance at the cover to know it was *Heart of Darkness*, before he tucked it snugly back into the shelf.

Then he went to his garage and retrieved his power drill and eight screws. He screwed the bookcase into the wall.

23

They returned to Ashley's house.

Shane opened cardboard boxes in the garage, pulling out a flathead screwdriver and a pair of gardening shears.

Ashley went inside to retrieve her metal baseball bat. "Sid grab that tennis racket," she said when she returned to the garage.

He picked it up and frowned. "Half the netting is missing," he complained.

"It's fine," she said. "You just need something you can swing if we get attacked."

The day grew muggier as they hurried back to the woods. Sid dragged the tennis racket on the ground, and it thumped and scraped over the pavement until Ashley finally snapped at him to lift the damn thing up. He slouched as if he were a flower wilting beneath a boiling sun, and Ashley shot him impatient, hurry up glances that he ignored.

She knew he was tired, but she also knew most of his slothful behavior could be attributed to Shane. Sid didn't like him and wanted to make sure Ashley knew it.

155

The ceiling of branches and dense leaves broke the heat and all three sighed as they moved through the sun streaked forest. They stopped often, listening for the sounds of movement, breath, or something foreign against the backdrop of birdsong.

When they reached the house, Shane didn't pause, but instead barreled up the steps, shoving through the front door with a splintered crash.

Sid grabbed Ashley's hand. "You said we weren't going inside," he griped.

Ashley stared at the dark opening of the house and her mind swerved to Mr. Wolf and the story he'd shared days earlier.

Shane poked his head out. "You guys coming?" he called.

Ashley pulled her hand from Sid's. "It's okay. We're safer in a group, but if you really don't want to go in, you can wait out here."

His eyes bulged, but she didn't wait for him to argue.

She walked up the stairs and stepped into The Crawford House.

Shane had already started into the lower floor.

Ashley and Sid followed.

Shane walked ahead of them into the room filled with old coffins.

"Look," Ashley whispered, pointing at a pile of discarded clothes in the corner of the room.

Shane picked something up and Sid gasped, backing into a wall of cobwebs.

"Get em off, get em off," he muttered, swiping at the back of his neck where he felt their sticky softness tickling his neck.

"Shh…" Ashley demanded. "Hold still." She pulled the cobwebs from Sid's hair.

Shane held up a small plastic bracelet, ripped jaggedly from whoever had worn it.

"The Northern Michigan Asylum for the Insane," he read out loud followed by an address in Traverse City.

"So, it's just some nutter," Sid babbled, gesturing toward the door. "Let's get out of here. The guy might be crazy."

"These are kids' clothes," Shane said.

He lifted the pants from the pile of clothes. He was right. They looked to be around their size maybe a little shorter than the same pants Shane wore.

"That doesn't mean anything," Sid argued. "Maybe the guy stole some clothes, realized they didn't fit, and then left them here."

Shane lifted up a coffin lid and leapt back, sending the lid crashing back down. Both Ashley and Sid jumped, Sid letting out a little squeal of terror.

"What is it?" Ashley asked.

Shane glanced at them, shuddered, and then pushed the coffin open, holding his arm out long as if he didn't want to get too close.

Ashley walked closer, but Sid backed toward the wall holding up his tennis racket.

In the center of the mildewed silk lining lay an ugly rag doll.

She leaned close and realized the doll was not merely cloth, but appeared to have human hair and bones. She saw two yellowing bones jutting from the blue fabric wrapped over the doll's lumpy body. Its face was a crude ball and its eyes were two blue buttons.

"Those are bones," Shane murmured. "And teeth."

Ashley stared awestruck at the two teeth poking from the red gash in the doll's face.

"What?" Sid squeaked, standing on tiptoe, but not walking closer. "Like a dead person's bones?"

"It's a doll," Ashley told him waving him over.

He walked toward them slowly, not lowering the racket.

He recoiled when he saw the doll and quickly spun toward the door, but they were alone.

"It's his," Sid whispered.

"It's the creepiest thing I've ever seen in my life," Shane muttered.

Only Ashley didn't speak. She swallowed the lump in her throat and reached a shaky hand toward the doll.

"Don't touch it," Sid hissed, grabbing her shoulder, but Ashley shrugged him off.

She picked the doll up and turned it around, studying it.

"This looks like Vern Ripley's hair," she started. "I don't know him very well, but..."

"Whoa, yeah. His hair does look like that," Shane said, peering closer at the doll.

The doll's hair was a distinctive shade of red-brown.

"The shirt too," Sid said, though his voice was barely a whisper.

"Huh?" Ashley asked.

"I saw Vern in it once. I remember because I thought my brother would like it. Zach likes to fish."

The blue fabric was covered in little orange fish with black eyes and sharp white teeth.

She lifted the doll up and inspected it.

"I don't think you should touch it, Ash," Sid whispered.

Above them, the door banged open.

"What was that?" Sid squeaked.

Shane stared at the ceiling. "Just the wind, I think."

Ashley tucked the doll into her backpack.

"What are you doing?" Sid asked, shaking his head.

"I'm taking it. I want to get a closer look at it, but I think we should get out of here."

Voices sounded overhead. "Spray that window," a familiar voice commanded. Travis Barron's voice.

"Crap," Shane muttered.

"We're trapped," Sid croaked.

They crept to the foot of the stairs and listened. Travis and whatever bumbling imbecile he'd brought with him worked their way through the rooms. They heard the sound of aerosol cans as the boy's spray painted the walls above them.

"What total ass bags," Ashley muttered.

She wasn't a fan of The Crawford House, but it seemed awfully disrespectful to walk through and spray paint the walls and furniture that had once belonged to a family.

They heard the clomp of footsteps on the stairs.

"They're going to the second floor," Shane said. "Let's make a run for it."

They sprinted up the stairs, Sid bringing up the rear.

Above them, they heard Travis let out a high-pitched scream. "There's something in here," he shrieked.

Shane looked back, laughter erupting from his lips. They burst through the front door, running for the woods.

Ashley glanced back in time to see Travis running from the house, his face a white mask of fear. When he spotted Ash, Shane, and Sid, he stopped, his goon friend smacking into his back. Travis turned and shoved the friend away.

Ashley didn't wait to see what he'd do. She ran for the shelter of the trees. They zigzagged through the forest, sprinting until Sid panted that he needed a break.

When they stopped, they all grew completely silent, save Sid's overloud inhales and exhales, as they listened for the crunch of branches.

"I don't think he came after us," Shane said, a smile spreading over his lips. "But seriously, that was priceless. Did you hear him scream?"

"He... he," Sid paused, drawing in a gulping breath. "He sounded like a little girl."

"And his friend ran right into him," Ashley added, her own laughter coming in unison with Shane's and Sid's.

Soon they were laughing so hard all three had collapsed to the forest floor. Sid was stamping his feet on the ground as he simultaneously laughed and struggled for breath.

When the fit ended, Ashley sat up, her jaw and belly aching from her guffaws.

Travis's angry face popped into her mind, and her laughter ebbed away.

He'd be gunning for them now, no two ways about it.

"Man, I wish I could have tape recorded that," Shane said, pulling himself up. "What a perfect prank on the last day of eighth grade. To play Travis pissing himself in The Crawford House."

"Yeah," Sid agreed.

The two boys high-fived. Ashley took off her backpacked and opened the zipper. She peered at the doll inside.

"What are you going to do with it?" Shane asked, stepping closer to look as well.

Sid did not move closer to the bag. His grin faded as if the realization of why they'd been in The Crawford House had just come back to him.

24

*M*ax parked his motorcycle on the curb in front of the ramshackle apartment building. Long strips of pale yellow paint peeled from the facade. The owner had likely considered it cheery, but in its state of demise, the yellow reminded him of curdled milk rolling down the side of the building.

Four tarnished black mailboxes hung by the door, one dangling sideways where it had fallen, or from the look of it, been ripped from the wall.

Across the street, Max noticed the Skeleton Crew Bar, a squat windowless brick structure. He could imagine the dark, smoky interior, country music blaring from the jukebox on most nights, a room of regulars slamming beers and dragging each other into the street for fistfights.

The neighborhood left something to be desired, that was for sure.

He tried to envision a kid growing up in one of those apartments. Where did he play? In the brown weeds that grew along the gravel parking lot?

Beyond the bar and apartment building, a series of warehouses and industrial businesses stood. He noticed a storage lot, a salvage yard, and further down a liquor store that boasted beer and lotto.

He found the front door to the apartment building unlocked and likely broken since the knob didn't turn at all when he pulled on the door. He started up the stairway, narrow, dark, and smelling of vomit.

At the top of the stairs, he found two doors, but only one was labeled.

According to his notes, Nicholas Watts lived in Apartment B.

Max knocked on the scratched door, and noticed a splintered indent in the lower right corner, as if someone had kicked it.

From across the hall he heard rhythmic thumping, and moments later, the undeniable sounds of moans and grunts as someone neared their climax.

He knocked a second time, leaned close to the door, and listened.

He heard a man's voice low.

"Don't fucking touch it," the man growled, and Max took an automatic step back, his blood chilling in an instant.

The door didn't open, and Max forced himself close a second time, pressing his ear to the flimsy plywood.

From inside, he heard a whimper and the soft whoosh of "Please," spoken by a woman. The word was cut off so quickly, Max knew the man had either clamped a hand over her mouth or tightened his hold on her throat.

"Fuck all," Max whispered.

He slipped down the steps, light on his feet, and hurried to his saddlebags, all too aware that whoever was occupying the second floor apartment was likely watching him through the window above. He rifled through his bag and made like he was pulling out documents while quickly sliding his tonfa into his pants.

His tonfa were two narrow, but strong, wooden sticks with small handles jutting from the sides.

He didn't have other weapons, and he usually didn't carry the tonfa, but he'd been practicing with them at the martial arts studio the night before and had forgotten them in his saddlebag.

The handles of the sticks poked him painfully in the stomach when he moved, but he tried to appear official as he organized the papers and walked determinedly back into the building.

When he reached the second floor, the moans across the hall had subsided.

He pounded on the door.

"I'm here about your missing son," he called.

To his surprise, the door jerked open and a thin woman with red-rimmed eyes gazed out at him. A red welt showed on her cheek in the distinct shape of an open hand.

"Mrs. Watts?"

The woman blinked at him, her hand lifting toward her face, and then quickly dropping back to her side. Her hair had been pulled into a bun, but looked as if someone had grabbed the side of her head and yanked fiercely, wrenching half of her hair loose.

"Can you come out and speak with me for a minute?" he asked.

"No!"

It wasn't the woman who answered, but a man who stepped from behind the door. He stood as tall as Max's own six-feet-three inches, but outweighed him by a hundred pounds. Thick arms and a muscular chest hovered over a round belly. In his younger days, the man could have been a bodybuilder, but he'd gone soft and Max smelled why. The man reeked of beer.

On the table behind them, Max spotted twenty or more beer

cans scattered across the cheap plastic surface. More empties littered the counter.

"It's okay, Denny," the woman said, reaching out a trembling hand and patting one of the man's meaty forearms. "This man is here about Nicholas."

"That little shit for brains?" Denny snapped.

The woman jumped and her eyes darted to Denny's large hands.

"Are you Nicholas's father?" Max asked, feeling his blood pressure rise at the man's insensitive comment.

Max didn't want to talk about Nicholas. He wanted to pull out his sticks and beat the man bloody. Denny outweighed the woman by two hundred pounds. He was the worst kind of bully.

"Wish I wasn't." Denny made a grotesque sound as he cleared his throat and walked to the counter, hocking a ball of spit and snot into the sink with a metallic thud. "Run off is what he did and took my five bucks with him."

"Will you come in?" The woman cast hopeful, almost desperate eyes on Max, and he knew he'd never get her outside. Denny would slam the door in his face before he let her leave the apartment.

"Sure, yeah." He walked stiffly, the sticks jabbing his belly.

"Can I get ya something?" she asked, pushing several beer cans aside. "We have beer or orange juice? Or tap water?"

Max shook his head.

"No, nothing for me, Mrs. Watts, thanks. I hoped to ask you a few questions about the day Nicholas went missing."

Denny lumbered to a kitchen chair, yanked it out, and plopped down. His eyes narrowed on his wife, and she hurried to the refrigerator, grabbing him a can of beer, wiping the condensation on her skirt before popping the top and handing it to her husband.

He guzzled half of it one gulp, burped loudly, and slapped the can on the table.

"You can call me Joan," she said.

She lifted a self-conscious hand to her head and winced, confirming Max's theory that Denny had pulled her hair. She didn't bother fixing it, likely too tender to touch.

"It happened in March. Denny gave Nicholas some money and asked him to run down to the corner store for beer."

Max frowned. "He's twelve, right?"

She laughed, embarrassed, and shot a quick glance at her husband who glared at Max.

"Denny's friend owns the store, so..." she shrugged. "But he didn't come home. After about a half hour, I walked down there and Brody, the store owner, said he never saw him."

"Little fucker took my money and ran," Denny snarled, finishing the beer and crumpling the can in his hand.

He kept his eyes trained on Max's face as if daring him to challenge his statement.

Denny threw the can behind him in the vague direction of the sink, but it bounced off the counter and landed on the floor.

He didn't even have to look at his wife this time, Joan had already seized another beer from the refrigerator and set it in front of him.

"Five dollars isn't much to run away with," Max said.

"He didn't run away," Joan whispered so low Max barely heard her.

Denny leaned forward on his elbows. "What d'you say?" he demanded.

Color rose in her face, making the bruise burn scarlet. "I just... I don't think he ran away, Denny. I think... umm..." But she didn't finish.

Denny's hands turned into fists, and his eyes bore into her.

"There have been other kids who have gone missing," Max

said, directing his words at Denny. "There's a chance he was abducted."

Denny snorted. "Who'd want him?"

Joan's face fell, and her bottom lip quivered. Her eyes welled, and she turned sideways so her husband wouldn't see her tears. She cried silently, her bony shoulders hitching beneath her threadbare blue dress.

Max wanted to hug her, to pat her back and tell her it would be okay, but as he pictured the woman's life spread out before her, he knew even if her child came home it would never be okay.

"I have a photo on my motorcycle. It's a sketch of a possible abductor." Care to come down and take a peek? You might recognize him.

It was a lie. He didn't have any such photo in his bag and he didn't have a plan for what he'd do with Joan if he got her out of the apartment, but he couldn't just walk away.

Joan sniffled and wiped her face on a dish towel.

Denny shook his head, no.

"Just for a second, Denny. I'll come right back," she pleaded.

Joan followed Max to the door.

He stepped into the hallway and started to turn back, but in a flash, Denny was up and hurling himself across the room. He grabbed Joan by her hair and dragged her back into the apartment, wrenching the door closed.

Max swore as his foot, which he'd stuffed into the opening not a moment too soon, was pinched between the frame and the door.

Denny grunted and opened the door further. Max knew if he managed to slam the door a second time, his toes would be broken if not severed.

Max slipped one of the tonfa from his pants and shoved it into the opening, pulling his foot free. The door crashed against the stick, but didn't close. Max pulled out the second tonfa and kicked the door as hard as he could.

As the door crashed in, it hit Denny with a sickening crunch of bone.

Denny howled.

Max plunged into the apartment, observing everything as if through a fish-eye lens.

Denny clutched his nose, which spurted blood down his gray t-shirt, which featured a rifle and the silhouette of a buck. Joan backed into the corner, blood-shot eyes wide, and her arms crossed protectively over her chest.

"Come on," Max said, holding out his hand.

"Over my dead body," Denny exploded, flinging a handful of blood to the floor with a splatter.

Joan stepped away from the counter, and Denny's fist shot out, catching her in the back of the head and sending her sprawling to the kitchen floor. Max watched her hands slide through Denny's blood.

Denny's other fist darted toward Max and Max jumped back, hitting a kitchen chair that skidded into the wall. He lifted both tonfa up, the short end of the sticks pointing toward Denny, the length of the tonfa pressed against Max's forearms.

Denny stared at him, and his mouth broke into a smile as if he'd bested his opponent before the fight had even begun. Denny lunged forward and swung. Max ducked and jabbed the tonfa beneath Denny's rib cage.

The man shrieked and brought his knee up. It narrowly missed Max's nose, but found his eye. The pain struck Max dumb. His eye felt as if it had exploded in his head, but he didn't pause, instead gritting his teeth and throwing himself sideways before Denny could bring two meaty hands down onto his back. Max went down on one knee, another explosion of pain in his kneecap. Denny ran at him and Max jabbed both sticks hard into Denny's crotch. One caught on the man's jeans but the other drove home, connecting with the soft yielding space between the man's legs.

Denny's eyes shot wide, and he released a blood-curdling sound that caused Joan to cry out in fear. Max jumped up and brought a stick down hard on the back of Denny's neck.

The man fell forward still clutching his balls.

"Come on. Now!" Max barked, grabbing Joan's blood-slick hand and hauling her from the floor. She was crying and trembling, her feet skidding as Max dragged her toward the door.

"No, I can't. He'll kill me if I leave." She reached out and grabbed the doorframe, clutching it.

The door across the hall had opened and a man and woman, both smoking cigarettes, watched them. They looked only mildly interested, and Max wondered if he they'd called the police. He doubted it.

"He'll kill you if you stay," Max shouted.

When she didn't budge, Max leaned close to her face. "What if Nicholas comes home Joan? You want Denny to raise him because that's what's going to happen if you walk back in there. You're as good as dead."

She still shook her head, but when he tugged her forward, she allowed herself to be led.

She followed him down the stairs, crying and murmuring.

"Put this on," he told her, thrusting his helmet into her hands and swinging his leg over his motorcycle.

She lifted it, but paused, her eyes locked on the apartment building, her mouth hanging open. Denny struggled down the stairs, one hand wedged between his legs, and the other clutching a wooden baseball bat.

"Holy shit," he muttered, wondering suddenly how in the hell he'd gone from searching for a missing kid to fleeing a bloody fight scene in less than twenty minutes.

He revved the engine and jerked Joan toward him, practically dragging her onto the bike behind him. The helmet clattered to the sidewalk.

"Hold on!" he screamed as he roared away from the curb.

For a horrifying instant, her hands didn't clutch his back. He was sure she'd either fallen off or simply climbed off to aid her enraged and bloodied husband. And then he felt her tenuous grip clutch his waist, and he sighed, putting his head down to drive.

25

*H*e should have taken Joan to the police station, but in his shock, he drove to his place of refuge: his parents' house.

In the nearly hour-long drive, he wondered what the woman behind him was thinking.

He didn't stop to ask her. He couldn't stop because his legs had begun to shake. He tried to tell himself it was the vibrating of his bike, but he knew better.

His parents' house stood like a lighthouse in a gale. If he could just get them there, everything would be okay.

When he pulled into their driveway, he spotted his mother in the side yard, digging in her garden. His father sat on the porch reading a newspaper. They both looked up at the sound of Max's motorcycle.

Joan climbed off and Max saw gooseflesh covering her arms. Despite the warm day, motorcycle rides were chilly. He hadn't even thought of her meager attire when they'd fled her apartment.

Her hair, messy earlier, lay in tangles on her thin shoulders. The welt beneath her eye had gone from red to blueish gray, and tiny red spiderwebs had begun to seep into her right eye. When she blinked, she cringed as if even that small gesture hurt. Dried blood coated her hands and forearms where she'd slid through Denny's blood.

"Damn, I'm sorry," he told her, gesturing at her arms and legs. "I didn't think about how you were dressed."

She gazed at him dazed, as if not comprehending.

"You're cold," he explained.

She looked down and let out a weak laugh.

"That's the least of it," she murmured, limply pressing a hand to her cheek.

"This is my parents' house," he explained. "Probably seems odd I'd bring you here, but it's safe and we can talk about what to do next."

Joan glanced toward Max's father, who now stood and watched them inquiringly.

Max's mother came around the house. Her gardening clothes were streaked in dirt.

His mother stopped before them, her smile fading when she saw Joan's face before drifting to the woman's bloodied hands.

"Oh dear, what's happened?" she asked, searching Max's face.

"Mom, this is Joan Watts. We've had a bit of trouble and…"

"What sort of trouble?" Max's father asked, stepping from the porch and walking toward them.

"Hi," Joan whispered, offering Max's mother a bony hand.

His mother took it in both her own, ignoring the blood. Her hands were large and soft, and they seemed to swallow Joan's.

"My goodness, you're as cold as a Popsicle. Come inside, honey. Let's make you a cup of tea and get you cleaned up."

Maria led Joan away, and Max sighed, relieved.

Herman stopped in front of Max, glancing toward the woman as she passed. He said nothing, waiting for Max to explain.

Max rubbed his jaw and took a deep breath, still trying to make sense of all that had happened.

"She's the mother of one of the missing kids," Max told his dad. "I went to her apartment in Mesick to ask her some questions. Her husband was in the process of giving her a severe beating. I interrupted them."

Herman's eyes had gone wide behind his spectacles. He folded his newspaper and tucked it into the back pocket of his trousers.

"What happened to her husband?"

"I kicked the shit out of him."

Herman briefly closed his eyes, his mouth pursing into a tiny little bud. It wasn't anger that flashed across Herman's face, but fear.

"And now what will you do with the wife? Hmmm. I'd imagine her husband is looking for her at this moment. Growing angrier with every second that has passed since he watched her climb onto the back of a strange man's motorcycle."

Max frowned. He hadn't thought about that part. He was good looking, young, drove a bike. He intimidated regular men, but jealous psychopaths? He'd never pissed one of those off before.

"What was I supposed to do, Dad? Leave her there to get beaten to a pulp? Did you see her? She can't weigh more than a hundred and ten pounds. Her husband is two-fifty. If I hadn't shown up, she'd probably be dead right now."

Herman sighed and touched the dark splotches on Max's shirt.

"His blood, not mine," Max explained.

"Good. You're a good boy, Max. This was not a good idea, but... well, we're not always given many choices, are we? Come on. Let's call Frank."

"Frank Bellman?"

Herman nodded. "He's not with the force anymore, but he'll know what to do."

When they walked inside, Max spotted Joan in the living room. Maria had wrapped an afghan around her shoulders and she held a mug of tea in both hands.

"What a day," Joan sighed.

She'd showered and changed into a pair of Max's pants that his mother had saved in that strange way that mothers would hoard their children's clothes, as if they wouldn't be out of style by the time their grandchildren came along to claim them. He hadn't fit into them since he was fifteen. She'd also put on one of Maria's heavy crocheted sweaters. Her auburn hair lay in a thick wet sheath down her back.

"Has he always done that?" Max pointed at her face.

She picked at her apple cake and looked away, tilting her head in an almost imperceptible nod.

"I shouldn't talk about him. He'll be angry."

Max's mouth dropped open. She intended to go back to him. "I'm a stranger to you," he said, thinking of a therapist he'd dated briefly.

She had told Max it wasn't her personality or her academic training that made people open up to her. It was her detachment. They didn't know her. They didn't have to fear they were isolating their community by revealing their secrets. "Nothing you say to me will get back to your husband," he promised.

She nodded, glanced at him, and pushed her dessert around the plate.

"Appfoocooking," Joan said, slicing a forkful of the cake. "That's what your mom called this."

"Apfelkuchen," he corrected her. "It's German, but it's probably easier just to say apple cake."

"Apple cake," she sighed. "It's very good, but..."

"But you're not hungry?"

Joan nodded.

While Herman had called Frank, Max had eaten two roast beef sandwiches, inhaling them while standing at the open refrigerator. His appetite only mildly satiated, Max followed the sandwiches with a slice of cake and a glass of milk. Now he had the drowsy fullness of overconsumption.

Joan set her cake aside and lifted her mug of tea.

"It started before we got married," she said, gazing into her cup as if afraid to see Max's expression as she told her story. "I was already pregnant then. Seventeen years old and stupid in love with Denny Watts."

She blushed with the memory.

"He was the quarterback." She laughed. "I wasn't a cheer-leader. I never played sports because my family never had the money for the uniforms and shoes." And well," she opened her arms. "I've always been scrawny. I couldn't believe he liked me. Maybe I would have waited…" She set her cup down and pulled at the curled corners of the doily beneath her plate. "Anyway, I didn't wait. And I got pregnant just like my mom said I would. I was four months along the first time he slapped me. I had gone to his house to watch a movie, and he wanted to… make love. I was so tired during the first trimester. I threw up a lot. I told him I wasn't in the mood, and he backhanded me. He cried after, apologized, and swore he'd never do it again."

Joan spoke in an off-handed way, as if she were telling someone else's story, not her own.

"But he did," Max said.

"Yeah, a lot."

"Why did you stay with him?"

Joan frowned, the tiny crease between her brows giving the first hint of her true age. Otherwise she looked young, far too young to have a twelve-year-old child, and too young to have spent more than a decade getting beaten by an angry husband.

"That's always the question, isn't it? And people ask it with all this judgement. Why do *you* stay? I have answers. I have a thousand reasons. Our son, money, because for many years I loved him, for the good times, out of fear. I'm not sure if anyone who hasn't been there can understand. I've met other women who live with angry men and they understand. I've left him a couple times."

"And he makes you come back?"

She laughed and touched a thin gold necklace resting in the hollow beneath her throat.

He saw three gold hearts intertwined.

"Just the opposite. He becomes the man I fell in love with again. He quits drinking, buys me flowers, sends me notes at work. He asks me out on dates. He buys presents for Nicholas. Last time he bought us a car."

Her face contorted bitterly.

"He wrapped it around a tree six months ago, a few nights after Nicholas went missing. He'd been at the bar all night. He told the policeman he was searching for our missing child, but..." she shook her head. "He'd been at the bar. There was a woman in the car too. She had a concussion. Denny wasn't hurt, but our car was totaled. Now I take the bus again."

Joan scooped up a tiny forkful of cake and put it in her mouth.

"This is very sweet," she said. "It's delicious."

"Maria Wolfenstein believes sugar and tea can cure anything that ails us."

"My mom didn't cook," Joan said, still gazing at the strudel. "She worked two jobs. One in the factory and the other at the laundromat. My father stayed home with us kids, but... well he didn't cook either. Like Denny, he preferred to drink."

Max watched her, the vacant look in her eyes as she shared some of the most intimate aspects of her life, a life so foreign to his own, he struggled to imagine it.

"What happened the day Nicholas disappeared, Joan?"

She looked up and the distance in her eyes faded. He saw

pain course in. Her shoulders turned inward, and she slumped forward slightly.

"Nicholas is the only thing I've done right. He's the only thing I... live for, maybe even the only thing I love anymore."

A tear slid from her eye, down her cheek, and disappeared into the knit sweater.

"It hadn't been a good day. When Denny asked Nicholas to go to the store, he'd already finished a twelve pack. He'd come home from work mad. Another guy at the plastics factory had gotten a promotion Denny wanted. He didn't eat dinner. Said it tasted like dog food and threw it in the trash. Mine and Nicholas's food too, plates and all." She started working the doily again, her fingers pressing and pushing against the fabric.

"I should have taken Nicholas and left. I wanted to. A few times I'd started to say let's go to a movie to give your dad a few hours alone, but I knew Denny would have gone into a rage."

Max imagined the man drunk, and getting drunker as his wife searched for any escape for her and her child.

"When he sent Nicholas for the beer, I was relieved. I thought he'd drink until he passed out and everything would be fine. But then Nicholas didn't come back. It was cold that day. Nicholas had left in his snow boots and winter coat, but he hadn't taken his gloves. After I went to the store and found out he'd never been there, Denny went nuts. He drove to the arcade and screamed in George Kassum's face. George is one of Nicholas's school friends. George looked terrified. No one had seen Nicholas. Denny drove all over town like a maniac, squealing in and out of parking lots, driving a hundred miles an hour on the back roads." Joan paused and closed her eyes. She put her fingers up to her lips.

"Did you call the police?"

Joan shook her head.

"Not until the next day. I tried and Denny ripped the phone out of the wall. I had to go downstairs and borrow Mr. Shafer's phone. He's a vet on disability who lives beneath us. A nice man. He used to give Nicholas bubble gum. The police came out, but honestly, they took one look at our place and wrote me off. We're poor. My husband's a drunk. They know him at the station. Denny's been brought in more than once. They figured Nicholas ran away. They wouldn't blame him if he did. Neither would I, I guess."

She tucked her fidgety hands into her lap.

"Do you think he ran away, Joan?" Max asked.

She shook her head.

"What do you think happened?"

She looked up at him, her eyes filled with tears. "I think someone took him," she whispered.

26

Sid sat cross-legged on Ash's bed, pulling at the fringes on a pillow. He gazed at Ashley's backpack slung over the back of the chair at her desk.

The desk was not a usable workspace. It was covered with paperback books, homework, cassette tapes, clothes not yet put away, and a scattering of pictures Ashley insisted she was organizing into a scrapbook despite the book itself never having made an appearance.

The doll lay inside the backpack, and Sid couldn't shake the feeling it sat in the claustrophobic little pouch, listening to them.

"Why can't we just call 9-1-1 from a payphone and report an anonymous tip? I mean people do that, right? They can't tell it's us from our voices."

Ashley shook her head. "Sid, you said yourself, your parents would tune you out if you mentioned weird stuff at The Crawford House. They won't listen. If we don't do something soon, that monster will get another kid."

Sid frowned and pulled one of the tassels free.

"Hey," she snapped, yanking the pillow away. "My Grandma Patty made that for me."

He looked at the tassel in his hand, shocked. He hadn't even realized he was pulling on it. "Oh shoot, sorry, Ash. I swear I didn't mean to."

"It's fine," she said, flinging the pillow across the room where it landed on a papasan chair. "By the time they do anything, it might be too late. We can go during day and set a trap."

Sid groaned and leaned back on her bed. His head hit the wall with a thump. "This sounds like a terrible idea from a scary movie. We go out there to set a trap, and two days from now our pictures are on the back of milk cartons."

"It only attacks at night," she reminded him.

"You don't know that. Warren went missing during the day."

"I have a theory about that. I think he messed around in the woods after school. He and Travis were arguing that day. Maybe he didn't want to go home, so he walked around in the woods. He lives like five miles from school. If he walked home, that would have taken him ages."

Sid crossed his hands on his stomach and stared at the glow in the dark stars attached to Ashley's ceiling. He didn't want to agree. The summer vacation he'd imagined when school let out had been swallowed by Ashley's growing obsession with the monster in the woods. If left up to Sid, he'd pretend he'd never encountered it. And maybe they hadn't. It had been so dark that night.

"What if it's not real, Ash? What if it's like Travis playing an epic joke on us?"

"Then who killed Simon? And who took Vern, Warren, and Melanie?"

Sid sat up and swung his legs over the side of the bed. Ashley's dresser was covered in pictures of her mother and Grandma Patty. Sid had liked Patty too. She had called him Bear because he was Ashley's best friend, and since she'd nicknamed

Ashley Pan when she was a baby, she'd said it was only fitting Sid be Bear like in the *Jungle Book*.

He liked the nickname Bear; it sounded strong, fierce. It made his size something powerful instead of embarrassing. Unfortunately, he made a better comparison to a teddy bear than the real thing.

"I'll go with Shane then. Or by myself," she said.

"With Shane?" Sid scowled, wishing Shane Savage would disappear. "Fine, I'll go. But how are we going to trap it?"

Ashley picked up a snow globe and shook it.

Sid watched the tiny white flakes drift over a Christmas village.

"I'm not sure, yet. I told Shane we'd meet him at the willow over at Denmore Park. We'll make a plan there."

"ARE YOU SERIOUS, MAX?" Jake demanded. "She's not an abandoned puppy. She's a grown woman with an abusive husband who's probably roaming the streets with a shotgun as we speak."

"He doesn't have a car," Max said, knowing his comment would only infuriate Jake.

Jake's eyes bulged, and he sucked in his cheeks and bit down, his signature *trying not to say something he'd regret* expression.

"You've gotta stop, Max. You're not the hero, okay? You're an English teacher at a middle school. You're playing with fire and you know who's going to get burned? Mom and Dad. Why would you bring her to their house? Why didn't you just go to the police?"

Jake was right, but Max's own anger had arrived at the party, and it wouldn't be quelled.

"Jake, don't put your bullshit on me. I get it. You're stressed having to play domestic dad and all, but the man was ready to cave in her goddamned skull. Would you prefer I left her there to get her brains splattered on the kitchen table?"

"No, Max," Jake sighed, his anger giving way to disappointment. "I would have preferred you take her to the police and left our parents out of it."

He said nothing more, but he turned and gazed into the living room, where their parents sat cooing at the baby.

"Hi, Eleanor," Max grumbled when he noticed her watching from the kitchen.

She gave him a sympathetic smile and a half wave.

Max had taken Joan to a women's shelter in town after first stopping at the police station so she could file a report against her husband. The officer who took photos of her face seemed busy and distracted, snapping the shots quickly and only half listening as Max and Joan described what had transpired earlier that day.

He'd returned to his parents' house to find Jake, Eleanor, and the new baby. Jake had not been pleased to see him.

Maria stepped into the hall. "Stop arguing this instant," she scolded her adult sons. "Look at the beautiful baby boy in there. Do you want Matthew to hear his daddy and uncle fighting?"

"Mom," Jake muttered.

"Mom, nothing," she interrupted. "I'm grateful your brother brought Joan to us. He saw a woman in need, and he helped her. And he trusted us to help her too. I hope you will be so lucky to have such a compassionate son, Jake. Now both of you go play with that baby."

Max tried to engage with his new nephew, but his frustration at Jake's comments got the best of him. After an hour, he excused himself with a fake appointment and slipped from his parents' house.

Halfway across town, he spotted Ashley Shepherd ducking beneath a large weeping willow in Denmore Park.

He pulled his bike over and hopped off, following the path she'd taken.

He found Ashley, Sid, and Shane Savage sitting at a picnic table tucked within the willow branches, as if they'd pulled the table into the tree canopy for cover.

Something lay on the table between them, a doll of some sort, though it looked like something Miss. Cutler would have the kids make in home economics with its crude stitching and weird misshapen arms and legs.

Shane glanced up and spotted Max.

He grabbed his backpack and dropped it on top of the doll, his eyes sending a silent warning to his friends as he nodded toward where Max stood.

Sid looked up and blanched.

Ashley, ever the stealthy one, turned slowly and gazed at Max. Her expression revealed nothing. "Hi, Mr. Wolf," she said.

He watched her slide the bag from the table, and when she removed the bag, the doll disappeared with it.

"What are you guys doing out here?"

Ashley shrugged. "Hiding from Travis Barron."

Max nodded.

He knew enough about Travis Barron to find the story believable, though he doubted its truth in that moment.

"DO YOU THINK HE SAW IT?" Ashley asked after Mr. Wolf left.

"Even if he did, he doesn't know what it is," Shane offered.

"Neither do we," Sid said, crossing his arms over his chest and looking irritated.

"True," Shane agreed, though his confirmation didn't mollify Sid, who looked grumpily toward the branches Mr. Wolf had slipped through moments before.

"Maybe it's a voodoo doll," Sid interrupted excitedly. "Like in

Trilogy of Terror. What if someone made a voodoo doll of Vern to kill him!"

Ashley cocked her head to the side. "Possible, but even so, figuring out the doll isn't the priority."

"What's *Trilogy of Terror*?" Shane asked.

"I think the only way we can trap it," Ashley continued, ignoring Shane's question, "is with bait."

Sid wrinkled his forehead.

"Like earthworms?" Sid asked. "I don't see how-"

Ashley cut him off. "Not fish bait! Monster bait. With kids. With me."

Both boys stared at her with mingled confusion and horror.

"No, no way," Sid said. He uncrossed his arms. "You're mental, Ash."

"There's no other way," Ashley insisted.

"Okay, let's say we try it. How would we use you as bait?" Shane asked.

Sid glared at Shane, but Shane ignored him.

"We find the birds," Ashley explained. "That's the key. Once we find the birds, I go into the woods, make a lot of noise, and ride like hell to The Crawford House. We rig it so I can run through the front door and jump out a window in the back of the house. As soon as I'm in, you guys secure the openings so he can't get out. We call the police and say one of us fell and got hurt at The Crawford House. The police come and they find him inside."

"That's a terrible idea," Sid said.

"It could work," Shane mused.

"And it could also not work. The monster could catch you and rip your throat out like Simon Frank's."

Ashley frowned, but refused to imagine Simon dead in the woods.

"He won't catch me. I'm getting my bike in two days."

"You saved enough money?" Shane asked, face brightening. "That's so awesome."

Sid cast him an incredulous look. "Are you both insane? This is the worst idea I've ever heard!"

"You've got forty-eight hours to come up with a better one," Ashley challenged him. "In the meantime, we've got to board up the other windows and doors at The Crawford house. Sid, you'll have to steal more nails from your dad."

27

"Max?" Max looked up from the bench where he sat watching two other guys stick fighting on the padded blue mats.

Joan stood just inside the glass door, smiling hesitantly.

"Hi," he said, standing and striding over to her. "How are you?"

He hadn't seen Joan since he'd left her at the women's shelter three days before. He'd spoken to her once on the phone to ensure she'd settled in, and she reassured him they were treating her well.

"I hope you don't mind my showing up like this. The shelter comes into town on Fridays, and I saw your motorcycle." She pointed toward the window where his bike was parked near the curb.

"No, it's great. I'm happy you stopped in."

"Is this where you learned to use your stick things?"

"Tonfa," he told her. "That's the name of the stick things. This is my dōjō. I've been practicing martial arts here since I was a kid. My parents wanted to minimize how frequently I was getting beat up."

"You got beat up?" she asked, genuine concern in her eyes.

"Not anymore," he promised.

Joan looked beyond him to the men on the mat. One circled the stick around his head and brought it to rest against the other man's neck. They laughed and bowed to one another.

"Seems like very peaceful fighting," she said.

"It's less about fighting than mastering self-control. Though the sticks can come in handy when fighting is necessary."

"I remember," she murmured, and her hand lifted to the yellowing bruise on her cheek.

She looked different from the first day he'd met her. She had replaced her thinning blue dress with form fitting jeans and a purple t-shirt that read Go Bobcats in large yellow letters. She glanced down at her shirt and smiled.

"Martha, the director at Ellie's House gave me some clothes."

"You look nice," he told her, and he meant it.

She did look nice. She'd brushed out her long auburn hair, and it fell in a wave down her back. Her blue eyes looked brighter, the red mostly gone now.

"I'm finished here for the day. Can I take you to lunch?" he asked.

Across the street, several women left the Village Market, grocery bags clutched in their hands. They walked toward a blue conversion van.

Joan saw them and she took a step toward the door.

"I can drop you off at Ellie's House," he assured her.

She watched the woman and seemed to consider his offer for another minute. "Okay, yeah. Let me tell Martha."

As Max gathered his gym bag, he watched Joan jog across the street, her hair blowing out behind her. A strand caught on the branch of a flowering magnolia tree and she laughed, batting at the branch as another woman joined her. The older woman smiled and helped Joan disentangle her hair. She plucked a pink blossom and pushed it behind one of Joan's ears.

He was struck again by how young she looked. Had he met her on the street, he would have pegged her for a college girl, bright-eyed and tackling a degree in elementary education or social work. She had the fresh-faced sparkle of a woman standing on the precipice of a transformation.

Max watched Joan talking. She pointed toward the martial art's studio, and the woman gazed at the building, a tiny furrow wrinkling her brow.

He slung his bag over his shoulder and pushed through the door, waving at the women as he walked across the street.

"Hi, I'm Max Wolfenstein. I thought I'd take Joan to lunch."

"You're the man who helped her?" the woman asked, her eyes kind but weary. She had long silver hair pulled over one shoulder and wore an outfit not unlike Joan's, jeans and a t-shirt advertising Kramer's Auto Supply.

"Yes. And thank *you* for helping her."

Martha nodded, glancing back at the women who'd piled into the van.

"Joan, I generally advise against social engagements so soon in the process."

"Oh, it's not like that," Joan said quickly. "Max is investigating the missing children."

"Missing children?" Martha asked, eyes widening.

"Yes, several from here in town, and I'm discovering others. Including Joan's son, Nicholas."

"That's terrifying," Martha said, resting a comforting hand on Joan's arm.

Joan nodded and patted the woman's hand.

"I'll bring her home in an hour, two at the most," Max promised.

"Please do," the woman told him. "And I'm Martha Page. Nice to meet you, Max."

"You too, Martha."

He and Joan walked down the sidewalk.

"Pizza?" he asked her after they'd covered half a block.

"Sure."

"Uncle Leo's makes a killer Hawaiian. They also have great subs if you're in the mood for a sandwich."

"Nicholas used to say pineapple on pizza should be illegal," she laughed.

Max smiled.

"I've always been a rebel." He winked at her. "Have you talked to Denny?" He hated to ask, but couldn't stop the question running through his mind.

She tucked her hair behind her ear and frowned at the sidewalk.

"No, Martha coordinated the delivery of a restraining order through the police in Mesick. I... I'm afraid to know what he's thinking right now."

"He has no idea where you're at?"

She shook her head. "I don't think so."

"That's good," he murmured, pulling open the door to Uncle Leo's and gesturing for her to go first.

The hostess sat them in a half-moon booth near the salad bar.

After they ordered, Joan wrapped her hands around her plastic cup of lemonade. "Have you found out anything more, Max? About the kids?"

He sipped his tea and nodded. "I think so. A twelve-year-old boy went missing from Lake City three months ago. Another kid in the area was approached by a man in a black van."

"What does it mean if a man took him? Does that mean he's... he's...?" But she couldn't get the words out. She buried her face in her hands. "Nicholas has been my reason for living. Without him." She shook her head. "What's the point? What's the point of living if my son is gone?"

Max drew in a breath, struggling for the wise words he should have been able to conjure. Instead, he slipped a hand across the table and clasped hers. Her hands were small, the bones felt tiny and fragile beneath her cool skin.

She didn't look at him.

"You keep going, Joan. You're the only advocate he has, the only person who will keep the pressure on the police, who will pass out fliers, and who will fight for him."

Joan's eyes looked troubled.

"They wouldn't listen to me, Max. They never took me seriously. I should have been screaming from the rooftops. Instead I went right back to life as it had been, working, serving Denny his beer and getting slapped for my efforts."

"You can't go back to yesterday because you were a different person then," he said. "It's from *Alice in Wonderland*, one of those quotes that's stuck with me since I was a boy. You're not the same woman, Joan."

She blinked at him, her expression so hopeful and scared it made his heart ache.

"I'm afraid that it's too late, that I've failed him," she whispered.

Max shook his head. "No," he surprised both of them with the passion in his voice. "You didn't fail him, Joan. You know what you did? The bravest thing of all. You got out. You left, so when Nicholas returns, he'll have a new life too."

"A new life," she said, looking toward the window where a group of women walked by, arms linked, laughing.

"My maiden name is Joan Kimberly Phillips. My mother wanted to name me Kimberly, but my father insisted on Joan, his mother's name. My grandmother had a temper, and she never touched us kindly, only to whip my brother and I as children. I used to imagine how my life might have turned out differently if I'd been named Kim."

Max smiled. He'd had similar thoughts as a boy, especially when his teachers had insisted on calling him Maximilian rather than Max. He'd once begged his mother to change his

189

J.R. ERICKSON

name to Mike. She'd faced him across the table and told him Maximilian meant great, and emperors and leaders had shared his name. After that he'd puffed up a bit each time someone at school called him Maximilian.

"Kimberly's a beautiful name," he said.

"Kimberly Phillips," Joan said, reaching out her hand.

He shook it and grinned. "Wonderful to meet you, Kim," he told her.

*I*t took almost three hours to nail boards over every window and door at The Crawford House. They left only two openings, the front door and a window in the back of the house. Ashley would reach the window by running down the main hallway and through the kitchen.

They nailed boards to both the front door and back window as well, but left one side free. When Ashley got the monster into the house, Shane would nail the window shut after Ashley jumped through into a pile of pre-arranged blankets. Sid would nail the door shut on the opposite side of the house.

Together, they'd ride to the payphone at the end of Turner Street, the closest phone to the house. They estimated they could be there in four minutes.

"Are you guys going to the Summer Shindig tomorrow?" Shane asked as they traipsed back through the woods. They were hot and sweaty and dirty, but both Ashley and Shane wore smiles of satisfaction. Sid looked dour, tiny creases between his eyebrows that seemed to deepen with each passing hour.

"Heck yeah," Ashley said. "Mrs. Hagerty, the principal's wife, makes popcorn balls every year. They're so good. I'd go just for those."

"Mr. Pinot's meatballs are pretty good too," Sid added. "My dad always tries to replicate them after the Shindig, but his end up tasting like hamburgers covered in spaghetti sauce."

"I've never gone," Shane admitted. "My dad says it's a waste of taxpayers' money and gets all pissy about it every year, but he's out of town so my mom's going to drop me off."

"Why don't you ride your bike?" Ashley asked.

Shane shrugged. "My mom's freaked about Warren. She doesn't want me riding in the dark."

Ashley nodded. "If she knew what was really out there, she wouldn't let you leave the house."

⁂

Max spotted Joan, now Kim, across the grassy expanse where the town had set-up the Summer Shindig. In years past, he'd volunteered, usually grilling burgers or helping build the bonfire, but he'd opted out this year.

When the volunteer sign-ups had circulated months earlier, Max had left his name off the sheet, imagining instead a long motorcycle ride out west. Maybe he'd spend an entire month traveling, even driving down to Mexico. Instead, when he'd learned of the missing kids, the trip left his brain as if it had never been there at all. He'd only remembered it that afternoon when he recalled his reason for not volunteering.

"Kim," he called.

She looked up from the table where she carefully filled Dixie cups with strawberry lemonade.

Martha, director of Ellie's House, stood beside her. When she saw Max, she offered him a wave and nodded at Joan, who slipped from behind the table and walked over to Max.

He wanted to hug her, but instead took both her hands in his and squeezed. "You look beautiful," he told her.

She blushed and reached self-consciously to the hem of her green t-shirt, which read Safe Haven Vet Clinic. When she glanced at the shirt, her eyes lit up, and she pointed at the words.

"I got a job today!" she announced, grinning.

"At Safe Haven? That's great. I took Frankie there to sacrifice his manhood. He still hasn't forgiven me."

She laughed. "Is Frankie your dog?"

"My cat's full name is Frankenstein Wolfenstein, and now that I say it out loud, I realize I'm one of those dreadful cat parents who ruined his life by giving him a name destined to be the focus of bullies everywhere."

"Frankenstein Wolfenstein," she repeated, still laughing. "It has a nice ring to it."

"Especially if you're an emperor during the renaissance period. These days, I'm not sure it makes the cut. But enough about Frankenstein Wolfenstein. How do you like the Summer Shindig?" he asked.

He gestured at the park emblazoned with twinkle lights, though the sun had not yet set. Picnic tables held potted daisies. Kids played tag while parents stood around drinking lemonade and chatting.

"I love it. We never had anything like this in Mesick. It's as if I've stepped into another world."

"New life, new world," he told her.

"Yeah." She touched her face where the bruise had nearly disappeared.

"Can I grab you a drink? I have it on good authority that the table over there," he pointed to a table manned by his friend Randy from the martial arts studio, "has spiked cider."

"Okay, sure," she said, running nervous fingers through her long auburn hair.

"Here," he said, grabbing two lawn chairs. "Hold our seats."

She sat down, crossing and then uncrossing her legs.

"Randy Bo-Bandy, I need some of the good stuff."

"Max!" Randy high-fived him across the table. "Do tell," he said, winking and nodding his head at Kim.

Max smiled and shook his head. "That's Kim Phillips. She's new in town. And we're just friends."

Randy arched an eyebrow and shook his head disbelievingly.

"Sure you are." Randy handed him two cups of cider with large black x-marks on the side. "The parents insisted I mark the cups this year. Apparently last year a few pre-teens were acting rather giggly after their cider."

Max took a sip. "Where are your wife and kiddos?"

Randy gestured with his ladle toward the bonfire where his wife, Greta, helped their twin boys put marshmallows on sticks. "They're middle schoolers next year, Max. Better watch out."

Max laughed and walked away. "Thanks, Randy," he called over his shoulder.

When he returned to Kim, he saw her brush at her face where a sparkle of fresh tears faded from her eyes.

"Are you all right?" he asked, looking beyond her to where a group of kids held sparklers.

One of their fathers walked amongst them with a lighter, lighting the tips. The sparklers erupted, shooting sparks into the dusky evening sky. They chased each other around the fire, their sparklers held out like magic wands.

"My son should be there," she said. "He should be playing with sparklers and eating too many roasted marshmallows. His biggest worry should be whether he'll make the soccer team next year."

"I'm sorry, Kim. I'm sorry I haven't found out more."

"Max," she turned to face him. Her eyes reflected the flames in the growing bonfire. "You've changed my life. I don't expect you to find Nicholas. I don't even know if we can find him.

Please," she put her hand on his forearm. "Please know how grateful I am for everything you've done."

A tall slender woman with short golden hair that framed her face walked into the park. She wore a figure-hugging black dress and black sandals. It was an outfit completely unsuitable for a park bonfire and cookout, but it made heads turned. Within minutes she had a group of men around her, laughing too loudly at her jokes.

Kim glanced at the woman and back to Max. "Is it just me or does that woman keep staring at you?"

Max didn't have to turn around to know who Kim was referring to. He sighed and looked skyward. "Sheila Hopkins. I dated her for about six months last year."

"She's very pretty," Kim said, tugging her t-shirt lower. She wore jean shorts and faded tennis shoes.

Kim looked beautiful. She was an entirely different kind of beautiful than Sheila, with her made-up face and tanned, aerobicized body.

"She is pretty," Max agreed. "Not so much on the inside, though."

Kim frowned and tilted her head to the side. "She must be very funny," she added, as the man beside her let out a bellow of laughter and slapped his leg.

Max tried not to roll his eyes. He'd witnessed Sheila's effect on men. Funny was not how he would describe her. Disarming, maybe. She said things to shock people, to knock them off kilter.

"Why did you break up? Is that too personal?" Kim asked, taking a drink of her cider. She balanced the cup on her knee.

"It's no great story. After dating a few months, I realized we weren't compatible. Sheila's the type of woman who needs undivided attention. She can't share. If I stayed after school to grade papers or went for a solo motorcycle ride, I'd get the silent treatment for days. I had the feeling she wanted a man she could put on a shelf and take down when it suited her. The rest of the time he needed to sit on the shelf and admire her from across the room."

Kim smiled.

"Sounds like a sad life for the man on the shelf."

"Exactly," Max agreed. "And my mom didn't like her. A bad review from Maria Wolfenstein is the kiss of death in our family."

Kim chuckled. "Why didn't your mom like her?"

Max glanced back at the group, and Sheila caught his eye, trying to hold it, but he swiveled back around to Kim.

"She sensed that she was... fake. I never probed much into it. By the time my mom told me her feelings, I'd already started to distance myself. She said Sheila needed a good tragedy, some heartache to add depth to her character. It's a strange thing to say, but it made sense to me. I wanted to meet the person beneath the pretty exterior.

"In a way, the mystery is what drew me to her. I kept waiting for the big reveal. Everyone has a secret, right? But nope, no skeletons ever leapt out of the closet, unless you count the jealousy and pettiness."

Kim rubbed her arms. "Your mom must love me then; tragedy is my life's motto."

"Was. Tragedy was Joan's life motto. Kim's is triumph."

"Triumph," Kim said. "That sounds like a powerful word. I feel like I should do something more to complete the transition from Joan to Kim."

Max bent down and picked up her purse. "Do you mind?" he asked.

She shook her head and watched, perplexed as he rifled through her bag.

He pulled out a paper grocery discount card with Joan Watts printed on the front.

"Walk with me," he said, taking her hand and leading her to the bonfire.

He felt the softness of her skin, the warm wetness of her palm against his.

They stopped at the fire and he handed her the card.

"I hereby release Joan Watts from her life of tragedy. With the destruction of this card, Kim Phillips is born."

Kim grinned and crumpled the card up before throwing it high. It disappeared into the flames.

29

*M*ax watched Kim's profile, the curve of her pale cheek, the narrow slope of her nose, the small mound of pink lips that stretched into a smile. The flames brought out the red in her hair, and as the fire echoed in her blue eyes, he saw a flash of glee, as if she truly had liberated herself from tragic Joan's life.

"How do you feel, Kim?"

She turned and gazed at him, her eyes searching his. "Hungry," she replied, laughing.

Max gestured to a table of food. "As you should be on the day of your birth. Plus, Annie Kohl brought her famous stuffed mushrooms. They're unmatched."

They filled their plates and walked to a picnic table. Max watched Ashley and Sid arrive at the Shindig, their heads dipped close together as they talked. He tried to catch their eyes and wave, but they pushed on toward the bonfire, oblivious to him.

"Do you know them?" Kim asked, following his gaze.

Max nodded. "Both were in my seventh grade English class this year. They're as thick as thieves, those two."

"Nicholas has two friends like that. Fred and Marty. They called me every day for two weeks after he went missing. Fred's dad drives a semi-truck and he passed out fliers in more than thirty states."

"That's good," Max said. "It just takes one person who knows something."

"Yeah. I pray every night that tomorrow's the day someone picks up the flier and recognizes Nicholas. That I'll wake up to Martha knocking on my door with the news someone found him. He fell and hit his head and got amnesia, but someone saw the flier and took him to the police."

She tried to smile, but it slipped off her face. "I've resorted to fairytales." She shook her head. "Worse, soap operas. That's something that happens in soap operas, not real life."

"Don't question anything that gives you hope," he told her. "Keep believing for Nicholas's sake and your own."

He heard his advice and considered his own tendency to question extraordinary events. The book for instance, the Fruit Loops, the reflection in the boutique's window. He was a fine one to give advice about believing.

Kim dropped her eyes to her plate and picked up a mushroom, slipping it into her mouth. "Yum," she said, eating another.

"What did I tell ya?" he asked.

Kim's eyes flitted back to the bonfire, where a kid drew a stick topped with a flaming marshmallow from the fire. He laughed and hopped up and down as his dad tried to steady the stick so he could blow it out.

Her chewing slowed, and Max watched the joy from eating the mushroom drain from her face.

He tried to imagine her feelings, but knew he'd never understand. Every pleasant experience was strangled by the unknown. Every thought was followed by where is my son.

They could erase everything that defined Joan Watts, but it

wouldn't change that a part of her, the most critical part perhaps, had been stolen. She lived and breathed, but with only half a heart.

"Max. Hi, how are you?"

He stiffened at the sound of Sheila's voice behind him.

When he turned, she stood, scanning Kim distastefully.

"Oh, hey, Sheila. How's it going?"

"Grand. I was promoted to Head of Marketing last month, so life is good."

"Congratulations," Max told her, withholding his comment that she couldn't have chosen a more suitable career.

"Still teaching middle school?" she asked, wrinkling her nose as if she'd smelled something rotten. She shifted her attention to Kim. "I told him a thousand times he should teach at a big university. I mean middle school? What a waste of those gorgeous brains."

She reached forward and wiped a manicured finger across Max's cheek.

He recoiled, and she laughed.

"You had a bit of mushroom there," she said and then looked pointedly at Kim.

"My son's in middle school," Kim said. "I'd give my right arm for him to have a teacher as wonderful as Max."

Sheila wrinkled her brow. "Well, that's fine and good for your son, but that's not looking out for Max's best interest is it?"

"Looking out for my best interests is no one's jobs but my own. Well Maria Wolfenstein gets a say now and then." He winked at Kim.

Sheila feigned a smile and adjusted a single diamond earring in that coy way she'd done many times during their courtship. Swivel earrings, examine nylons, drop her head so her hair fell over her face.

He'd seen it all and, unfortunately, had taken the bait more times than not in those first weeks. Now he recognized the clever ruse and wanted no part in it.

"Sheila, this is my friend, Kim," he said, reaching out and resting a hand on Kim's lower back, a gesture far more intimate than he'd intended. Her warmth seeped through the t-shirt and into his fingertips.

"A pleasure," Sheila said, though she offered Kim a dismissive glance. "I thought I'd see you here." Sheila directed her gaze back to Max. "I hoped we could talk."

He stood quickly, his paper plate catching on his shirt and plummeting to the grass.

Kim leaned down to pick it up, but he touched her shoulder.

"I've got it," he told her. "Yeah, listen, Sheila now's not great. I have to umm...-"

"Loan me that book," Kim jumped in, standing. "You said we could swing by your house to grab it, and I really need it tonight so..."

Sheila glared at Kim, but when she shifted her attention to Max, she smiled coolly. "Some other time. You have my number, Max."

She turned and walked away, her heels disappearing into the grass. Max wondered how she stayed upright.

"We don't have to go," Max said. "I should have just said no, but-"

"We can go," Kim offered. "Watching all the kids makes me sad."

"It's early, though. I hate to take you back to Ellie's House. I have a couple bottles of red wine at home if you're interested? I hope that doesn't sound presumptuous."

Kim smiled and nodded. "That sounds like something Kim Phillips would enjoy."

~

J.R. ERICKSON

"Hey, Ash!"

Ashley looked up from where she sat with Sid, who was on his second helping of potato salad.

Brenda Dean waved at them. "You guys in for capture the flag?"

Sid looked at Ashley and gave a short shake of his head.

Ashley bit her lip and looked toward the woods. "There are twinkle lights all over the place, Sid," she said.

Sid snorted. "And you think twinkle lights will stop it?"

"There're kids too, in groups. Unless it's trying to get caught, it's not in there," she insisted. "Yeah," she called back to Brenda.

"Awesome!" Brenda gave her a thumbs up. "You're with us. Sid, you'll be on Norm's team."

"Noooo," Sid whined, flicking his eyes to Norm, a tall freckled boy who was so competitive he'd pushed a special ed girl the year before after she'd bested him in a drawing contest. "Norm is a total show-off. I don't want to be on Norm's team."

"Oh, come on, Sid. You wanted to do something fun, right? Here's your chance."

Sid dragged his feet as they walked across the grassy field separating the park from the woods.

The Shindig committee, a group of parents and kids, had strung white twinkle lights along the branches that edged the woods. However, deeper in, the forest lay thick and dark.

Ashley spotted Shane Savage on Norm's team and gave him a half wave.

He nodded at her and smiled.

"Okay, everybody on my team wears camo bandanas. Don't take them off either," Norm announced, walking through the kids and thrusting bandanas into their hands.

"We've got yellow bandanas," Brenda said, grinning. "So we can actually see each other."

Norm shot her an annoyed look, but her team laughed.

Ashley tied the bandanna around her bicep.

"Our flag is hunter orange because Brenda didn't think she could handle the camouflaged one." Norm gave them all a look as if Brenda were a total wimp.

"And ours is light blue," Brenda added, holding up the light blue flag.

"The territories are divided along the trail sign." Norm pointed at a small wooden sign that explained the several trails that wound through the woods. "Everything to the right is our territory and everything to the left is Brenda's. If you get tagged, you're frozen until one of your own team frees you. And don't even think about moving your flag once it's hidden," he added, glaring at Brenda's team.

Ashley rolled her eyes. Norm was a notoriously poor sport who bent the rules to win. If anyone was going to move their flag, it would be Norm.

"May the best man win," he added, offering Brenda his hand.

"Or woman," Brenda snapped. When she extended Norm her hand, he jerked his back and smoothed it through his short brown hair.

"Better luck next time," he said.

Sid offered Ashley a pained expression before following Norm, Shane, and the rest of their team into the woods to the right of the sign.

"Five minutes and the game starts," Norm added before slipping into the trees.

Brenda wanted to hide their flag on a knobby oak tree at the end of their territory. Ashley climbed the tree and tied it around a branch.

After the team broke apart, Ashley slipped into the trees, stealthily moving out of her team's territory and into Norm's. She hadn't expected to get into the game, but the look on Norm's face had her wanting to see his expression when she captured his flag.

She hunched down and ducked under a dense pine tree, running smack into Shane Savage.

He grunted, but managed not to fall over.

"Oops, sorry," she apologized, rubbing her chin where she'd struck his shoulder.

"I think you hurt yourself more than me," he said, squatting back down. "So, am I frozen or are you frozen?" he whispered, laughing.

"Let's call it a wash," she said. "Are you trying to find the flag or just hiding from Norm?"

He laughed and shook his head. "Don't you know Norm is invisible with his camouflaged bandana on?"

"I like capture the flag, but Norm takes it to a whole new level."

"Norm takes everything to a whole new level. Did you see him in dodgeball the last week of school? He whaled Sally Hansen in the face with the ball so hard her glasses broke."

"What a dick," Ashley murmured, her desire to get the flag stronger as she imagined poor Sally crying over her broken glasses.

"Catch you on the flip side," she said, starting forward.

Shane's hand shot out and grabbed her wrist.

She froze as Norm, squatting low and shuffling through the forest like a soldier, crept by.

Shane smirked, and Ashley clamped her teeth together to keep from laughing.

Norm had painted two streaks of black paint across his cheeks.

Ashley thought of tagging Norm, but knew if he saw her and Shane, he'd throw a tantrum and likely insist the game be started over.

Norm disappeared into the darkness.

Shane laughed silently, and the tremble of his shoulders was too much. She spurted a laugh, her breath catching, and dropped to her knees on the bed of leaves.

"Shhh... " Shane told her, putting a hand on her shoulder as his body bucked from the quelled laughter.

Their laughter subsided and Ashley took a deep breath "Seriously, that guy is a freak," she giggled.

"And that's if you're being nice," Shane added.

A scream pierced the quiet, and Ashley jumped up, heart racing.

30

*S*hane stared at her, smile gone, his blue eyes wide and confused.

"What was that?" he asked, though they both knew it had been a girl's scream.

The girl screamed again.

They pushed through the trees, running toward the sound.

Other kids had come out of their hiding spots. In the darkness, Ashley watched dark figures running haphazardly. She couldn't make out faces. Voices called and branches snapped.

The forest, silent moments before, filled with sound.

"Who screamed?" someone yelled.

"Was it a joke?" Brenda's voice drifted through trees.

Another scream pierced the night, this one different from the first.

Sid's scream

"Oh God, oh God, oh God," Sid was mumbling, and Ash ran toward the sound.

A flashlight beam waved across the forest floor.

Sid stood staring at a leafy ground, his flashlight shaking. The light flitted across blood-splashed leaves. At the edge of the trampled grass lay the body of Krista Maynard, an eighth grader. Blood gushed from a wound in her throat.

Ashley knelt, pulling her bandana from her arm and stuffing it against the girl's neck. Warm blood seeped through the bandana.

"Sid, give me your bandana. Shane, yours too," Ashley commanded. "Somebody run for help. Shane, get Mr. Freeman."

Mr. Freeman taught social studies at the middle school. He was also a volunteer firefighter and a paramedic.

Shane thrust his bandana into Ashley's free hand and sprinted away.

Sid had not moved. The flashlight continued to weave and bob.

"Sid, give me your damn bandana," Ashley boomed as Krista's blood saturated Shane's.

Other kids stepped from the trees.

"Is that Krista?"

"Oh my Gosh, what happened? Did she run into a tree?"

Ashley heard their murmurs, but trained her eyes on Krista's face. The girl's eyelids fluttered. Blood had soaked into her blond hair making the light strands that fanned out behind her look dark.

The seconds dragged and suddenly Mr. Freeman was there along with Sid's mother who was a nurse.

Someone pushed Ashley aside, and she stood on shaky, stiff legs.

When she emerged from the trees, parents and kids stared at her, horror-struck. She looked down. Her light blue t-shirt was streaked in blood.

MAX POURED the wine and corked it, pausing when he heard murmured voices.

Kim sat on his back porch, hardly a place for a casual conversation at almost eleven pm.

Kim laughed.

He took their glasses and pushed open the screen door with his hip.

Kim sat alone in an Adirondack chair. Her pale legs were crossed, and her hands rested on her knees.

"Who were you talking to?" he asked, surveying the dark yard beyond.

"Oh, just-" she smiled and turned her head as if to ask the person their name.

She craned around in her chair looking toward the side of his house. A tall hedge of juniper trees separated his yard from his neighbors. Kim stood and walked down the steps, peeking around the house, and returning a moment later with a puzzled expression.

"She was right here," she said. "I can't imagine where she ran off to."

Max looked into the shadows of the yard, the skin on the back of his neck prickling.

She.

"What did she look like?"

Kim bit her lip. "A bitty thing with bleached blond hair. She couldn't have been over eleven or twelve."

Max handed Kim her wine and walked down the stairs. The grass was cool against his bare feet.

He looked toward his neighbor's house and then gazed at the dark tree line fringing the backyard. Nothing stirred.

"What did she say?" he asked.

Kim sipped her wine thoughtfully. "She said, 'It's a full moon tonight.' I agreed with her and laughed because I got a chill. And then you came out..." Kim trailed off, looking at him, concern tinging her voice. "What is it, Max? Are you feeling ill?"

Max shook his head and returned to the porch. "She said it's a full moon?"

On the cusp of his words he heard sirens in the distance.

Both he and Kim looked toward the sound, but it faded away and the quiet night took over once more.

"Eerie," she murmured, shivering.

He nodded and wished eerie was where it ended.

"Shall we go inside?" he asked, gazing toward the trees crowding his backyard, hiding the wildness that hid within them.

He'd never feared the woods. Few kids who grew up in Northern Michigan did, but the woods in the day differed from the woods at night. Like Dr. Jekyll and Mr. Hyde, in daylight the woods were sun streaked and filled with the comforting sounds of birds and chipmunks. At night, darker things reigned. They crept out from holes and caves, their eyes glowing and their teeth gleaming. Few children walked into a dark forest without such thoughts.

"Yeah," Kim agreed, rubbing her hands over her arms as if she'd gotten a chill. "Do you ever get the sense you're being watched?" she asked, following his gaze to the trees.

He nodded, and broke his stare, pushing open the back door and releasing a flood of light onto the dim porch.

Kim followed him through the kitchen and into the living room. They sat on opposite ends of his gray suede couch. The conversation that had been so easy on their drive home from the Shindig seemed stilted. They sipped their wine in silence.

"I feel like a meteoroid."

"A meteoroid?" Max asked.

She nodded.

"Nicholas loves outer space. We made a paper mâché solar system for his room. Denny probably destroyed it. I hate to think what else he's done." She took another drink and pressed the glass against her forehead. "I feel like I'm drifting in space. No path, no gravity, just adrift."

"My mother would say, rest in the uncertainty of this moment," he told her. "She used to tell my brother and me that all the time growing up. Whenever we were anticipating something or recovering from a break-up. I didn't get it as a kid, but it's come in handy as an adult. I had no idea how much uncertainty there was in life. I still don't. Not at the level you do, anyway."

Kim stood and walked to his bookshelf, examining his photos. The shelf held pictures of his graduation from Michigan State University. He stood wedged between his beaming parents, holding his diploma. He saw photos of himself posing next to his new motorcycle, photos of a family cruise they'd all taken several years before.

His face fell as he watched Kim studying his pictures. His life looked like happily ever after. One smiling, shiny day after another.

He hadn't seen any family pictures in her apartment. The frames had probably all been smashed by her violent husband.

"Uncertainty," she said after several minutes of silence. "Right now, in this untethered space, I think that's why I stayed with Denny. I don't think I had a word for it before this moment, but the uncertainty is what I feared most of all. At least with Denny, his fists were familiar. I don't even know how to be in this life. Am I still a mother? When someone asks if I have children, what do I say?"

Max winced at her question, imagining his own mother if she ever lost her sons. Her heart and her legs, she had called them just days before. And more than once in his lifetime, she'd told Max he and Jake were her life's purpose.

"You say yes," he told Kim. "And then you tell them all about Nicholas. Why don't you start with me?"

Kim's head drooped, and she continued to face the bookshelf.

"I gave birth to Nicholas on Valentine's Day. My Valentine's baby, I called him. Denny brought me one of those big heart-shaped boxes filled with chocolates. He ate all of them except the cream-filled kind." Kim laughed and touched a finger to a framed photo of Max and Jake as children dressed in matching powder blue suits. "I didn't care. I'd never been so in love."

She turned to Max with red-rimmed eyes.

"Not with Denny, but with Nicholas, my son. He lay on my chest and blinked up at me with those milky blue eyes. He weighed less than five pounds, but he gained weight fast. I remember his doctor told me not to introduce cereal into his bottle because he'd get fat."

She laughed.

"Fat! Nicholas ran from the moment he woke up in the morning until he fell into bed at night. Fat was the last thing he would be.

"He loved outer space before he could walk. We lived in a little trailer in those days, and I'd sit with him on the porch and look at the stars. Tinkles, he called them. He started to talk about aliens in elementary school. All of his art projects showed googly-eyed aliens and giant silver discs flying through space."

Max watched her shoulders relax as she spoke. She lifted her head and walked purposefully to the window, peeling back the curtain and peering into the night sky.

"He learned about the moon and how its cycles affected the tides. He used to mark the new moon and the full moon on our calendar at home. He liked to fish and play basketball. He request-ed lasagna for his birthday dinner every year and angel food cake with whipped cream and sprinkles. He hated carrots. He used to pick the carrots out of soup if I tried to sneak them in there."

Her eyes shone in the moonlight slanting through the

window. She walked to the lamp and flicked it off. Only the eerie white glow lit the room. Kim's skin looked translucent, almost glowing in the darkness.

"He loved to read. Every other Friday we walked to the library, and he checked out books by Ray Bradbury."

"*Fahrenheit 451?*" Max asked.

Kim nodded. "But *The Martian Chronicles* was his favorite."

Max smiled, remembering reading the same books as a boy.

What had happened to the space loving child? If they were in a happily-ever-after novel, the boy would have been abducted by space aliens. The aliens would worship him, and later he'd convince them to return to Earth to rescue his mother from her abusive marriage. Nicholas and Kim would live happily ever after on a planet with six moons and pink waterfalls.

"He read for hours," she went on. "In the summer he read ten books a month."

Max didn't know what had compelled him to stand and go to her, but he'd barely registered the thought when his hands slipped around her waist. She tilted her face, and he kissed her, sinking his hands deep into her wavy hair.

She tasted of wine and something deep and sweet, memories he thought, memories of her son.

When he drew away from her, his breath hitched.

"I'm sorry," he said. "I shouldn't have-"

But she cut him off by pressing her finger to his lips. She took his hand and pulled him toward the stairs.

ASHLEY'S MOTHER rushed to her and squatted down, grabbing her shoulders, gazing at her with panicked eyes, and then pulling her close.

"Sid's dad called me. Oh Ashley," she moaned, and buried her face in her daughter's hair, mumbling her name several more times before leading her daughter to her gray Chevy coupe.

Ashley waved to Sid, who sat in the back of his parents' minivan. He looked at her, dazed, before lifting a limp hand in a farewell wave.

The car stank of cigarettes, a bad habit her mother indulged in only while driving, but never when Ashley was in the car.

Despite the stink, the car was clean, the ashtray empty. Ashley spotted her mother's white smock draped over the backseat next to a paper plate with two chocolate cupcakes.

When they pulled onto the road, Ashley's mother glanced at her, grimacing. It was the blood. Ashley had seen a similar reaction out of every person who'd laid eyes on her since she departed the woods an hour earlier.

She reached a hand to Ashley's knee and squeezed.

"Want to talk about it, honey?"

Ashley swallowed; her mouth dry. She coughed and swished her tongue around, searching for a drop of saliva. She found nothing and closed her eyes, leaning her head against the seat.

She didn't want to talk.

She'd spent the previous hour talking, explaining the events in the forest to Mr. Freeman and then to one policeman and a few minutes later to another and then to a group of kids who'd surrounded her when the cops had made the mistake of leaving her alone for half a second.

Sid had undergone something similar, though she'd seen him crying, his hands shaking as he tried to describe finding Krista after he heard her scream.

No, she hadn't seen what had attacked Krista. No, the girl hadn't spoken. No, she didn't see an animal. No, she didn't see any suspicious persons. Yes, she knew Krista, but only barely. The bandanas were hers, Shane's, and Sid's. Her mother had taught her to staunch a wound. No, she hadn't moved Krista.

Her mother didn't press, but when they pulled into the driveway, Rebecca did not immediately jump from the car.

"This is my fault, Ash. I should have been there with the other parents. I might not have been able to prevent what happened, but I could have comforted you. Sid's mother was there, his father too."

"It's not your fault, Mom," Ashley croaked. "I need a drink of water."

She jumped from the car and ran into the house, aware she'd forgotten to lock the front door when she'd left that evening. She was equally aware something could have crept in while they were away, something that could've been concealed by the shadows.

Ashley grabbed a glass and filled it to the brim.

She gulped the water as her mother entered the kitchen and flipped on the light.

Dark eyes gazed at Ashley through the window over the sink, and she jumped, dropping the glass. It shattered, causing her mother to cry out.

It was only her reflection.

But the relief was short lived.

Her stomach rolled, the water somehow not agreeing with the stone her stomach had been clenched into since seeing Krista's bloody throat.

She lurched into the bathroom, yanked up the lid on the toilet and vomited.

*M*ax pulled open the door to a stony-faced Jake.

"Hey, what's up?" Max asked, half closing the door as he stepped onto the porch.

"I've been trying to call you since seven am. Why didn't you pick up?"

Max frowned and looked toward the phone in his living room. "Must have been sleeping hard."

"Well, did you hear what happened at the Summer Shindig?"

Max's heart sank. "I was at the Summer Shindig. What are you talking about?"

"Eleanor's sister, Jan, called this morning. Krista Maynard was attacked last night. Something ripped her throat half open. They rushed her to the hospital in Grayling. She's lucky to be alive."

Max's mouth dropped open.

Jake shifted his weight and narrowed his eyes into Max's house.

Max turned and saw Kim, wearing only his t-shirt, freeze on her way to the kitchen.

"Oh," she looked up, startled, pulled the shirt lower, and backtracked toward the stairs.

"You've got to be kidding me," Jake grumbled.

Max didn't bother with an explanation. The truth was obvious enough.

"Who attacked her? What did she say?"

"Ripped her throat out," Jake repeated enunciating each word as if Max had regressed to the ignorant little brother with a penchant for asking why... why... why until Jake was forced to stuff a pillow over his head and run from the room. "I'm pretty sure she wasn't in a state to talk."

"Did any of the other kids see anyone?" Max demanded.

"Anyone? Max, we're talking about an animal here. A rabid cougar or something. Krista's dad and some other men went into the woods with shotguns this morning. Whatever it is, its hours are numbered."

Behind Max, something crashed. He jumped, and Jake took a step back.

Max stepped into the living room, Jake on his heels. All the books on his bookshelf lay on the floor. The bookcase itself had not moved, and the pictures of him and his family didn't tremble. Max also knew he'd screwed the bloody thing tight to the wall. Not even an earthquake could have rocked it free.

"What the-?" Jake asked.

Kim appeared in the doorway, her face white.

"What was that?" she asked, though her eyes, too, had landed on the books. In the center of the pile of books lay *Heart of Darkness*.

Max opened his mouth to offer an explanation, but he blurted something else altogether.

"I don't think it's an animal," he said.

Jake turned to him, briefly distracted from the books.

"Max, don't go there, brother. I'm telling you. Whatever

insane ideas are percolating thanks to your not-so-healthy obsession with spook movies and weird books, they will cost you your job. Get me?" He looked at his watch and muttered under his breath.

"I've got to go. Matthew barely slept last night, which means Eleanor barely slept, which means I'm on diaper and feeding duty. I only came over because you didn't answer your phone and I started worrying the cougar got you too. Glad your situation isn't that dire," he added derisively.

He slipped out the door.

"Give Eleanor my love," Max called, tempted to flick his brother off. It was immature and unkind considering his brother had come over to check on him, but his final comment had been cruel. Max had noticed the color flushing Kim's face.

Max closed the door harder than necessary. "I'm sorry," he said, stepping toward her, but she'd turned and walked into the kitchen.

"Another child has been attacked?" she asked.

"They believe it's an animal."

"But you don't?"

He shook his head.

"Why not?"

"I'm sorry about what Jake said or didn't say. I'm sorry he was rude."

"Why don't you think it's an animal?" she asked again.

He brushed his hands through his dark hair, catching his fingers in a tangle and trying to work it free.

"Here, let me," she told him.

She pushed her slender fingers into his hair, gently pulling the strands apart.

"I don't have a reasonable explanation. It's a sense. I've had it since I discovered the first child had gone missing. It hasn't left."

She stepped back and studied him.

"I'm going to get dressed, and then I'd like to talk."

Max made a few calls to get the gist of the previous night's events from his friend, Randy.

"Greta's nervous as hell," Randy told him. "She's convinced she and the boys should spend the summer at her mom's place down in Lansing. As if they're going to be safer with a bunch of gangbangers."

"I don't think Lansing is known for its gangbangers," Randy," Max told him.

"Well, gangbangers or not, my boys are safer in our woods with a Winchester and a pocket of shells."

"We're going, Randy!" Greta shrieked in the background.

Randy lowered his voice. "Jesus, Mary, and Joseph, it's like we found out there's a flesh-eating plague spreading through town. Greta's friends from a block away are coming over to coordinate travel plans. Good riddance," he said. "But I'm not getting run out of town by a juiced up alley cat."

"Did Krista say a big cat attacked her?" Max asked.

"No, no. That's just the newest theory. I myself figured some nasty kid out there hit her with a stick, or worse, pulled a switchblade on her. But apparently, one of the paramedics spread the rumor it was clearly a bite. As if anyone in this town is an expert on wild animal bites."

Max managed to wrangle the rest of the story from Randy, though he didn't know much more than Jake. The kids had been playing capture the flag when Krista had started screaming. The paramedics had carried her from the woods and loaded her in an ambulance. Police had questioned all the children, but no one saw a thing. Max hung up the phone, a vision of Simon Frank thudding against the back of his eyelids.

He found Kim on the back porch.

She'd put on her clothes from the night before and stood drinking coffee and leaning heavily against the rail. The intoxication of the night before, the magic, had disappeared with Jake's news. It was almost as if his brother had seen it lying there between them, stuffed it in his Jeep, and driven it away with him.

"What happened, Max, with the books?" Kim asked.

He gazed at her, taken off guard by the question. He'd expected her to continue questioning him about the animal. Oddly, he'd forgotten about the books.

"Have you ever been haunted?" he asked, stunned as the words left his lips.

He'd never considered himself a hard man of science, not in the least. He'd loved Shakespeare as a boy, by God. Those works were filled with spectral figures and hauntings, but at the end of the day, it was fiction. He'd never had to ponder the legitimacy of Shakespeare's characters because they'd never appeared in his home and demanded his attention.

Proof that the paranormal existed, that all the quacks offering to read your palm or chat with your dead grandfather might actually have a toe dipped in the realm of spirits, had only rarely crossed his mind. The closest he'd come to such a contemplation had been his single night in The Crawford House, and he'd managed, rather quickly, to explain that away as a figment of a child's terrified mind.

Kim studied him, but she didn't answer.

"I believe one of the missing children, Melanie Dunlop, is..." He paused and weighed the words: *haunting, visiting, terrorizing me.* "I think she's contacting me."

"Contacting? Melanie is the girl who went missing last week?"

Max nodded and waited for Kim's disbelieving laugh.

Instead, she turned back to the yard. Her profile was delicate, the soft slope of her cheekbone down to her chin. He'd kissed her face the night before, so fragile he'd grown furious for an instant, furious her husband had ever hurt her. She had felt small in his arms. Holding her had been like cupping a butterfly in hands.

"The girl I spoke to last night, out here?" she asked.

"I think so."

Max walked inside and retrieved a yearbook from the pile of books on his living room floor. He paused, gazed at his copy of *Heart of Darkness*, and then grabbed that too.

He flipped to the page in the yearbook where Melanie smiled out from a black and white photograph. Each child had their own little square. Though immortalized in the glossy pages, some of them, Simon Frank and likely Melanie too, would never share their grade school pictures with their own children. *Look, honey, mommy used to bleach her hair.*

He held the book up for Kim, and she looked at the image, the groove between her eyebrows deepening.

She blinked up at him. "Her hair was lighter, the girl last night, but that looks like her."

"She dyed her hair a lot," Max explained.

"Maybe she just ran away," Kim suggested hopefully. "Maybe she's hiding out in the woods and trying to get your attention."

Max closed the book and set it on the patio table. "It's possible," he agreed, but if Melanie had run away, why did Max hear her voice in the night? Why did his books keep crashing to the floor?

Because she's obviously a ghost, he thought sarcastically, as if a ghost could ever be an obvious explanation.

"What do you think, Kim? When you really try to dig into that question. Was the girl you spoke to alive?"

Kim set her coffee on the rail and shook her head. "What else could she be?" her voice rose on the last few words. She clutched the rail as if the world might tilt at any moment and spill her into the sky.

Max found he couldn't speak the words out loud. "This book

has been appearing on my living room floor since the day after she vanished."

Kim took *Heart of Darkness* and studied it.

"What's it about?"

"A man who travels up the Congo River into an indigenous area of Africa to meet an ivory trader. He becomes fascinated by an ivory trader who appears to have been accepted by the natives. It's a book I teach nearly every year, a way to begin the conversation about ideas of acceptable cruelty relative to perceived cruelty."

Kim appeared confused. "I've never read classic books. I got my diploma by going to night school, though I always thought it would be interesting to understand why so many people loved the classics. Nicholas said reading Shakespeare was like watching paint dry."

Max laughed. "That's pretty typical. I love the classics, but when I was thirteen, I hated reading anything other than H. P. Lovecraft and Stephen King," he confessed.

"What would this book have to do with Melanie?"

"We read it in class first semester. But other than that, I don't know."

Kim flipped through the pages. "We penetrated deeper and deeper into the heart of darkness," she read out loud. "What is the heart of darkness?" she murmured.

"The heart of the Congo, but more likely the heart of men," Max explained.

Kim's blue eyes flitted over the pages. She closed the book and set it next to her coffee mug.

"The heart of men," she whispered, and she clenched her eyes shut as if a spasm of pain had torn through her.

Her cries were silent at first, but then grew louder as she shrank down to the porch.

"I'm sorry, Kim," he told her, squatting down beside her and putting his arms around her quaking body. She was thinking of

Nicholas, of course she was, and if Melanie Dunlop was dead, her Nicholas might be dead too.

Kim shook her head, wiping the tears from her red cheeks. "I'm not strong enough, Max. I can't…" she started to cry again.

Max held her, feeling again as if Kim were a fragile butterfly.

"*I*'m on house arrest today," Sid mumbled into the phone. "My mom's been having a hairy canary over what happened at the Shindig. She even went out and bought us oven pizzas and ice cream for lunch. She's bribing us to stay inside. She keeps looking at me funny, like maybe one of my ears got bit off and she's just now noticing it."

Sid talked high and fast, trying to make a joke out of his mother's worry.

Ashley sighed, gazing toward the door her mother had walked through at eight that morning. Rebecca didn't have a choice. No one else would pay their bills, but Ashley had barely slept the night before. Each time she started to drift down into the darkness of sleep, Krista's pale face above her bloody neck would float into focus and she'd jolt wide awake.

"My mom asked me to stay inside too. I told her, I would, but the house is so quiet. How are you, Sid, really?"

She listened to the pause, the television in the background. It sounded like a cartoon, Wile E. Coyote chasing after Road Runner.

"Creeped out," he admitted. "I had nightmares last night. I

thought it'd come for me, you know? The boy in the woods. I thought he must have seen me last night. I was so close to Krista, so he'd come for me next."

Ashley sighed and picked up the paperback copy of *Hell House*. It was the last thing she wanted to read.

"Me too," she muttered, not adding that Rebecca had crawled into bed next to her.

They'd both been terrified, mother and daughter, but for very different reasons.

"Are you still going to get your bike tomorrow?" Sid asked.

"Yeah, absolutely," Ash replied, feeling her shoulders relax at the mere mention of the bike. "I'm helping Mrs. Penny clean out her basement for a garage sale in the morning. She offered me ten bucks. That's all I need."

"Cool," Sid said. "I'd come over and all, but even if my mom dropped me off on your doorstep, she'd worry all day. I better stay close to home."

"Yeah, I get it," Ashley agreed, not averse to staying tucked safely in the living room for most of the day.

"Ash," Sid started. "About Thursday. I'm not sure if we should-"

"We have to," Ashley insisted. "Now more than ever."

Sid didn't respond. Ashley wondered what she'd say if he pulled out. Could she and Shane do it alone?

"Okay," Sid sighed. "I'll call you later."

BY THE TIME the phone rang at seven o'clock, Ashley had grown so bored she'd cleaned her bedroom.

She'd organized her books, put the scattering of papers from the previous year's schoolwork in her desk, and even vacuumed the carpet.

She ran to the living room and grabbed the receiver on the second ring.

"Shepherd Residence," she said on the chance it was her mother calling to check in on her. Rebecca Shepherd hated it when Ash answered the phone with a simple 'Hello?'

"Another body's been found," Sid whispered.

"Wait, what?" Ashley turned off the television and pressed the phone closer to her ear.

"A body," Sid repeated. "In the woods by Warren's house. It's a kid. It's in bad shape. I heard my dad on the phone."

"Holy crap," Ashley blurted. "It's got to be Warren, right?"

Her heart thudded, and she gazed through the picture window feeling removed as she watched Mrs. Lincoln walking Kermit, who tugged and pulled away, sometimes snapping at the leash behind him.

"What?" Sid yelled.

Ashley heard his mother in the background, but she couldn't make out her words.

"I'm talking to Ashley," Sid shouted. "I already washed my hands. Okay, fine. Ash, I've got to go. Time for dinner. My mom's trying to pretend everything's normal."

"Meet me after?"

"There's no way they'll let me out."

"Sneak out, dummy. Meet me in front of Trinity Church."

Trinity Church was located at the end of the block on the street where Warren lived, or had lived, she really didn't know.

Sid sighed, but agreed. "Okay, but we can't stay out long. My parents will probably check on me ten times tonight."

Ashley flipped the channels, but there wasn't any news on until eight p.m., another half hour to wait. She walked down her driveway and glanced up and down the street. She wasn't sure what she expected, but the quiet surprised her.

No police cars with sirens flashing drove down the road. No

sirens wailed in the distance. People weren't gathered on street corners talking in fearful whispers.

"Because they don't know," Ashley thought out loud.

Sid's uncle was a cop, which meant Sid's dad knew before anyone else. Sid often gave Ashley the scoop hours before it hit the news. Technically, Sid wasn't supposed to know either. Despite his parent's best efforts to keep him in the dark, he excelled at eavesdropping. He and Ashley had fashioned a range of contraptions for just that purpose, though the best continued to be the old glass against the wall trick.

Ashley half considered waiting for the news, but curiosity got the better of her. She grabbed her old bike from the garage and pedaled down the street, hanging a left on Parkdale Avenue in the quickest route to the woods flanking Queen Street.

It took ten minutes of furiously riding, but soon she saw the pulsing of red and blue lights through the backyards one street away from Queen Street. Now she spotted the commotion she'd expected to see outside her front door.

Five police cars were parked along the soccer field that butted up to the woods. Yellow tape had been strewn along the curb and drawn back to the woods, blocking the entire field and the woods beyond. People who lived on the street stood in the road, watching the police, talking and pointing.

An ambulance was parked on the grass, and as Ashley watched, two men carrying a stretcher departed from the trees. She stood high on her pedals, squinting. A white sheet lay over the stretcher, a lumpy form beneath it.

Along the street, several people gasped, and Ashley saw one woman fall to her knees. The man beside her tried to pick her up, but she shoved him away, letting out a wail that turned the heads of everyone on the block.

It was Warren's mom. Ashley had never seen the woman, and yet deep in her guts, she knew. Ashley slowly sat on the seat of her bike. The men loaded the stretcher in the back of the ambulance and pulled away from the curb. Their lights continued flashing, but the siren didn't sound. Ashley knew what that meant. It wasn't an emergency. They weren't rushing someone to the hospital. Whoever they'd pulled from the woods was dead.

Ashley spotted Sid's dad at the edge of the trees. Though she couldn't make out his face, she saw the hunch in his shoulders.

Warren's dad eventually coaxed his wife from the ground and half carried her to a pickup truck parked haphazardly on the curb. As they drove past, Ashley and Warren's mother's eyes met. The woman's mouth stretched wide and, for an instant, Ashley heard the screams filling the truck, but then they passed, and the sound faded.

*M*ax stared at the reading list for the coming year, but struggled to concentrate.

The day before, Warren Leach's body had been discovered in the woods. Like Simon, he appeared to have been killed by an animal.

Forgetting his lesson plan, he wrote their names: Vern, Simon, Warren, and Melanie. Beneath that he wrote the names of the other kids who'd gone missing: Chris and Nicholas.

"And who else?" he asked the still room.

Poster boards of the kids' final projects still hung on the wall. Melanie Dunlop had chosen a book called *The Cat Ate My Gymsuit*. Her pink poster was covered in drawings of angry black cats.

The intercom on the wall released a burst of static.

He waited, expecting to hear Assistant Principal Lundt's voice come through.

When she didn't, he walked to the intercom. Before Max could press the call button, a gravelly, child's voice came through the speaker.

"Help…," the voice croaked. "Help her."

Max froze, hand halfway to the button, his abdomen cramping as if he'd eaten bad Chinese food and his body might spit it out all at once.

He stared at the intercom, transfixed by the voice of Melanie Dunlop.

"Message for you," Mrs. Lundt announced, popping her head into Max's classroom.

Max gasped, and stumbled back into the desk behind him. He almost fell right over it.

Mrs. Lundt rushed in, grabbing his arm and helping to right him.

"Heavens to betsy," she exclaimed. "I didn't mean to startle you, Mr. Wolf. We called on the speaker, but you must have stepped out."

Max took the sheet of paper, unable to still his trembling hand.

She patted his back.

"It's devastating," she said. "Little Simon Frank and now Warren too. We're all rather skittish."

Max glanced at the intercom and then forced his eyes down to the note Mrs. Lundt had given him.

Please call Kim - urgent, he read.

"Thanks, Mrs. Lundt," he told her.

"Okay, then. If you need me…" She gestured at the speaker, and Max shuddered.

What had she said? Help? Help me. It had sounded like help her, which didn't make a whole lot of sense.

He barked a hysterical laugh at the thought of making sense of haunted messages through a school intercom.

Two days before, Jake had implied he was losing it. Max wondered if he was right.

He offered the speaker a final, weary glance and then returned to his desk.

"Reading list for seventh grade and I'm done," he promised the empty room.

The reading list for seventh turned into the reading list for eighth, and by the time he left the school, the sun had shifted into the western part of the sky. It would still be light out for hours, but the afternoon stillness had settled over the town.

As he drove to pick up Kim, he remembered her note. "Shoot," he mumbled.

He had intended to call her before he sat down to finish the reading lists, but he had completely forgotten.

As Max turned onto Sycamore Road, he saw flashing red and blue lights. A police car, parked at an angle, blocked motorists. A line of cars sat along the road.

As his eyes adjusted to the scene, Max realized more cars filled the parking lot at Safe Haven, the vet clinic where Kim worked. Six cop cars and an ambulance crowded the lot. People stood outside.

On the dark concrete, a white sheet concealed something bulky.

He climbed from his bike, forgetting the kickstand and allowing it to crash to the pavement. He barely noticed, moving from a walk to a run as he sprinted past the parked cars and onlookers.

His shoe caught on the curb and he sprawled forward on his hands and knees. He felt the asphalt scrape the skin through his jeans. Beside him a muted voice, screaming, met his ears. He turned and there, in the back of a police car, was Denny Watts. Denny's mouth was twisted in a furious scowl. He howled and leaned back in the seat, kicking the plastic barrier separating him from the front of the police car.

"Stop now, or I'm going to use force," an officer told him, pulling open the back door of the car.

Denny lunged sideways, landing half out of the car, his face less than three feet from Max's own as he stood frozen.

His gaze swiveled away from the bellowing man back to the white sheet, and he saw it was not entirely white. One part of the sheet was bright red, as if soaked in...

"Blood," Max rasped.

No one was providing aid to the person beneath it.

Max searched for Kim's face in the small crowd huddled by the door. He saw the veterinarian, Dr. Patterson. Two other women stood near him, both wearing cheery green Safe Haven t-shirts.

One of the women was crying, black rivulets of mascara streaking down her cheeks. The other woman looked as pale as a sack of flour. Her made up eyes and lips were clown colors against her stricken face.

Max managed to stand, but the world had gone silent. He saw Denny's mouth stretched wide. He saw the officer's mouths opening and closing. They were talking, yelling, barking orders. As he pushed through a stream of yellow caution tape, an officer grabbed him by the shoulder. The man's lips moved but still no sound.

"Kim," Max croaked, but he couldn't hear his own voice.

He shoved the cop out of the way and ran, reaching the sheet and snatching the corner.

The officer caught up to him and grabbed him from behind. As he jerked him back, the sheet pulled away.

Kim lay crumpled on the pavement in the fetal position. Though her hands were near her head, they had not been able to block the bullet that took off the right side of her skull. A mass of gray and red leaked through her auburn hair.

Max fell to his knees.

The officer held him for another moment and then released him.

The scene unfolded in slow motion. The humid breeze ruffled her hair. Dark blood oozed into the cracks of the pavement. The neckline of her green shirt was black with blood.

"Max, Max," a voice somehow broke through the silence, and Max looked up to see Detective Welch, the man he'd argued with weeks before. He held out his hand.

Max shifted back to Kim. A paramedic had begun to replace the sheet over her.

The sheet blotted out her green Safe Haven shirt, her pale neck where he knew the three hearts intertwined lay against her unmoving chest. The sheet drew up over her neck and then over her chin, the eye that was still left in her face, and finally her head.

The detective took ahold of Max's hands, and he pulled him to his feet.

Max tried to make his mouth work, but managed only to open and close it a few times.

The detective walked him to an unmarked car. He opened the passenger door.

"You're in shock, Max. I'll send one of the paramedics over."

Max sat heavily on the seat, legs splayed on the pavement.

The world of sound had returned, and it filled his head like a swarm of bees: sirens, people shouting, the low throbbing of someone's sobs.

Beneath it all, he heard Denny's voice muffled by the car, but not silenced.

"She asked for it," he screamed.

Max put his hands over his ears and closed his eyes.

He didn't know when Detective Welch returned to the car, but suddenly he was there, lifting Max's legs into the car as if he were paralyzed, and he was.

The detective climbed behind the wheel and pulled away from the curb.

"I spoke with your father, Max. He knows we're coming."

∼

MAX HAD NEVER BEEN a big drinker. Something to do with the lack of control he'd experienced the handful of times in college when his buddies had talked him into getting inebriated. Not to mention the humiliation of worshiping the porcelain god at some frat house while guys traipsed in and peed in the bathtub or the sink and snickered from above.

As he sipped his bourbon, he tried to remember those days. They weren't fond memories, but anything was better than the white sheet with the patch of red soaking through. He swallowed the last of the drink and made eye contact with the bartender, holding up a finger to signal 'one more.' Though he doubted one more would do the trick. Five more maybe, and then he'd stumble the five blocks home and collapse on the couch.

Maria and Herman Wolfenstein had tried to make him stay. He could sleep in his old room, they insisted.

But no, he couldn't. He couldn't get sloppy drunk at his parents' house. He needed strangers for that.

On the news, a reporter spoke of the attack at the Summer Shindig.

A man two barstools to Max's left huffed.

"I told the police. The guy in the black van is behind those dead kids. He's an escaped mental patient from the Northern Michigan Asylum. You ask me, that's what we've got running around in the woods. Some looney toon who's better off in a straight-jacket."

Max stared into his glass, tilted halfway to his lips. The amber liquid swirled and released its noxious aroma.

A moment later, the man's words registered. He'd said, "the man in the black van."

Max turned and blinked at him.

The man wore a blue and yellow Hawaiian shirt over cut off jean shorts. He was entirely bald, and his head was smooth, as if he'd shaved it. He drank from a tall glass of beer.

Max stood, still steady on his feet, and walked to the stool next to the man.

"Do you mind?" Max asked, gesturing at the seat.

"No, I do not. I like company myself. My ex-wife never did. About shit a cat if I told her my parents were coming for a visit. But that's why she's the ex now, isn't it?"

Max offered the obligatory laugh and gestured at the TV. "I heard you say something about a black van."

The man nodded, opened his mouth, and then narrowed his eyes at Max. "You don't own a black van, do ya?"

Max shook his head. "Just a motorcycle and a Toyota I drive in the winter."

"A Toyota?" The man scoffed, eyes big and watery. "You trust those foreigners to build your car? Might need to be in the looney bin yourself."

The man took another drink and eyed Max's glass.

"Smells mighty potent, what you're drinking there. If my hair hadn't already fallen out, I'd be worried that stuff would do the trick. You grievin' or celebratin'?"

Max gazed at the glass. He couldn't answer. He didn't want to see the sheet again, and yet there it was, looming in his mind, floating like a ghost.

"Can you tell me about the black van Mr.-?

"Mr. Rice was my father. Call me Tom."

"Nice to meet you, Tom. I'm Max."

"Mad Max," Tom said, smiling. "You must be mad to be drinking that paint thinner."

"Tom, I don't mean to be rude, but I've had a terrible day. I don't want to talk, but I need to hear your story about the black van."

Tom arched an eyebrow.

"Grieving then." Tom nodded. "Last time I had a drink like that was the day my mother passed. My pops and I drank a bottle of scotch." Tim grimaced. "Can barely smell the stuff now.

Scotch and gardenias. Can't smell one without the other. Those were her favorite flowers, gardenias." Tom shuddered.

Max finished his drink and started to lift his finger to signal to the bartender, but Tom stopped him with a look.

"It only makes it worse, Mad Max." He nodded at the glass. "Take it from someone who knows."

The bartender paused in front of Max.

"I'll take a coffee, please," Max told him.

"Good man," Tom said. "Anyhoo, I saw that black van about six months back when Vern Ripley went missing."

Max braced his hands on the edge of the counter. "Here in town?"

Tom nodded. "Cruising the street real slow like. I live not three houses down from Vern and his family. I saw him walk out the door with his sled. I went out to get the mail and then looked off down the street the way he'd been walking. That kid and the van were gone."

"You think the person in the van abducted him."

"I sure do, and I told the police as much, but they looked at me like I was a few crackers short of a full box. Damn coppers. Never have had much luck convincing them of things they ain't seen with their own eyes."

"Why did you say it was an asylum patient in the van?"

"Oh, that's easy. He left a calling card on the side of the road. Or maybe it flew out when he opened a door, hard sayin'. It was a blank sheet of paper. Stationary you call it. Printed right on the top was The Northern Michigan Asylum for the Insane."

"*Hi*, Linda," Max said, reaching out and squeezing the woman's arm.

"Oh, Max," she murmured. "Oh, Max I'm so sorry. I know you and Joan or Kim had become close. She was such a dear. We absolutely adored her here, and the animals, my goodness they treated her like a regular Dr. Dolittle."

Max smiled, but his chest constricted at her words. He swallowed and gulped a shuddering breath.

Over the counter he saw Kim's Polaroid beneath block letters that read STAFF. Kim was sitting, legs splayed with a Burnese mountain dog laying across her legs. The dog had exposed his belly to Kim and gazed at her with soupy adoring eyes.

His throat grew thick, and he blinked away rising tears, looking toward the window, not daring to glance at her photograph a second time.

"Linda, I stopped by because Kim called me yesterday. I wondered if you knew why?"

Linda frowned and swiped her graying hair behind her ears. She turned to a paper calendar that took up half the counter.

"The day is a little blurry now," Linda admitted. She brushed a hand beneath her eye where Max saw a single tear sliding over her cheekbone. "Mr. Yessif brought in his lab, Punkie. Kitty Jenson stopped by with her new schnauzer pup for shots. Hmmm…"

She tapped an unpainted fingernail on the calendar. "You know what? Joan left for her break that day. She's never done that before. Usually she sits in the staff room with an old paperback and drinks coffee and reads. She stepped out, and she came back five or ten minutes late."

"Do you have any idea where she went?"

Linda shook her head.

"I'm sorry, Max. I don't. Does this have something to do with the man who killed her? Her ex-husband?"

Max shook his head.

"I don't think so. I'm just trying to figure something out, I guess."

Linda nodded as if she understood completely.

"I hope you do, Max."

Max left the vet and stood in the parking lot.

In the center of the lot, a dark stain stood out from the other pavement. It no longer looked like blood, but he knew it was. It was the blood that had seeped quickly through the cracks, and that no amount of washing could erase.

He gazed at the stores on either side of the vet clinic. Across the street, a strip mall contained the arcade, a pet store, and several other businesses. To his right was a pawnshop. He glanced away from the pawnshop and then looked back. A small dark surveillance camera hung from the eaves.

The man behind the counter perked up when Max walked through the door. "Looking for a gently used television? Had a beauty come in just this morning?" The man patted the tv sitting on the counter.

"No, thanks. I'm wondering if I could see your video camera footage. I saw the camera outside."

The man nodded. "Oh, sure, yeah. You with the police? I suspected they might be comin' round to retrieve my tapes. Not enough people use video cameras, if you ask me. I watch the tapes just for entertainment. You wouldn't think they'd be all that interesting, but I've seen some oddities on here, let me tell you. I've had half a mind to call the National Enquirer after a few of the things I've seen on the late-night footage."

The man stood and shuffled into the back room.

Max heard him talking to himself, counting back the days.

"Lucky, you came by," the man said offering Max the VHS tape. "I tape over them every couple of weeks. Though in all truth, I probably would have set this one aside. I didn't watch it myself. I don't have a stomach for such things."

Max took the tape, the plastic cool and flimsy in his fingers. He didn't want to think what the video contained.

HE IGNORED the tape for two hours. It sat on his kitchen table, black and ugly, and inviting him to see its secrets.

Finally, he shoved it into his VCR and rewound the tape to the beginning.

He pushed play. It started taping at midnight on the day Kim died. He fast-forwarded until seven a.m. when he saw cars pull into the parking lot at the vet clinic. He watched Kim climb out of Linda's car. The woman picked her up at Ellie's House every morning for work. They held cups of Styrofoam coffees in their hands. Kim laughed at something Linda said as they disappeared into the building.

He fast forwarded again, stopping each time a car pulled into the lot, but he didn't catch another glimpse of Kim until tenthirty.

She walked away from the building, her purse clutched in her right hand. He watched her hurry to the curb and out of sight of the camera.

"Damn," he muttered, hitting pause.

She appeared to be walking in a straight line, which would take her across Sycamore Road. Max imagined the stores that lay directly across the street from Safe Haven Vet Clinic.

He hit play and watched the screen. After nearly twenty minutes, he saw Kim jog across the parking lot back toward the clinic. The image was too grainy to make out her face, and yet he saw the bounce in her step. She had learned something and wanted to tell him. She must have made the urgent call to his school just after that encounter.

He let the tape play and ignored the twisting in his stomach. What if he had called her back? Would it have changed everything? Would she still be alive?

"What did you find out, Kim?" he asked the empty room.

He watched the minutes tick by on the screen. The lot emptied and filled again. People hauled their pets from backseats on leashes or in cages. He saw a man with a cat, whose claws were sunk firmly into his shoulder, climb from the backseat of a station wagon.

Kim stepped from the building, and Max held his breath as she gently drew the cat away from the man, running her hands along its bristly back as she carried it inside.

If he'd never gone to her apartment that day, she'd still be alive. If he'd never busted in the door, insisted she get on his bike, and acted like some knight in shining armor jackass, she'd still be alive.

He wanted to argue with himself and insist that no, she wouldn't. Denny would have killed her that day or maybe the next day, but he didn't think Denny would have.

Denny wasn't the type of man that killed the person he had in his control. He killed when he lost her.

He killed her when he realized she wouldn't be coming back.

"How did he find you?" he asked, watching the screen.

The clock on the screen blinked six-fifteen when the rusted pickup truck pulled into the parking lot.

It wasn't a truck Max had seen, and yet his heart plummeted into his stomach the moment it pulled into the lot.

Denny sat behind the wheel. Max couldn't see him. The sun cast a glare across the windshield, but he felt him there, rage bubbling up as he watched the clinic. He had parked lopsided, one wheel on the curb. The engine idling.

Had Kim sensed him too?

Denny stepped from the truck. His arms were large at his sides. They didn't hang limp, but appeared taut, as if he'd flexed every muscle in his large body as he strode across the parking lot. He marched with purpose, like a military tank, impenetrable, as it lumbered toward enemy territory.

Several minutes lapsed, and Max realized he'd been holding his breath. He let it out in a rush of agony just as Kim fled from the building. The spring in her step had vanished. She looked shrunken, her shoulders bowed forward, her hands in front of her as if she were blindly searching for something to grab or somewhere to hide.

Denny followed on her heels. His mouth opened wide, and Max knew he'd yelled her name, screamed it maybe. His tone must have alarmed her.

She'd stopped and turned. Denny's arm lifted from his body, something dark clutched in his outstretched hand.

Seconds, no, not even seconds, passed.

Max grabbed a pillow from the couch and squeezed, his knuckles turning white as the blast of the bullet knocked her backward off her feet.

Behind Denny, a man in a white coat burst from the vet clinic, Dr. Patterson, two seconds too late. He barreled into Denny who outweighed him by a hundred pounds, at least. Denny went down.

The dark thing in Denny's hand skidded across the pavement, and another person from the clinic, Linda, ran into the parking lot. She picked up the gun and held it, pointing it at Denny, who lay on the pavement with his hands in the air.

Dr. Patterson stood and ran to Kim. He knelt beside her, hands fumbling to her neck, and then her wrists.

There was no sound on the videotape, so Max couldn't hear the sirens, but the first patrol car arrived within minutes.

Lights flashing, it jumped the curb, coming to rest in the grassy median between the road and the parking lot.

An officer stepped out with his gun drawn.

Max watched his head rotate from side to side as he took in the horrific scene.

More police cars arrived, and onlookers started to edge into the parking lot.

Max couldn't draw his eyes away from Kim.

On the pavement beneath her, he saw the expanding darkness as her blood, her life, flowed into the cracked cement.

No one had attempted first aid.

She'd died instantly.

That was something, at least, he thought, though it brought him no comfort as he watched the men in uniform slowly flood the scene. Two officers draped a sheet over her body.

They dragged Denny, the fight back in him, to a squad car. He looked like a wild ape thrashing and kicking at them. It took four men to haul him to the patrol car and force him inside.

Max dropped the pillow and slid off the couch onto his knees.

He didn't know when he'd begun to cry, but he felt the rawness of his cheeks as the tears, warm and salty, poured into the creases of his mouth. Tears dripped onto the carpet. They soaked the collar of his shirt.

He fell forward onto his hands and knees and allowed a desperate groan to rip free of his body. The groan faded to a whimper, and the energy drained down, dissipating into the fibers of carpet as he pressed his forehead into the floor.

_____

 he strip mall across the street from Safe Haven
contained four businesses, and Max studied each
from his car: Roscommon Bank and Loan; a women's clothing
store called Katie's; Furry Friends Pet Food and Supply, which
had litters of kittens for sale in metal pens along the front
window once a month; and finally, Paulie Goldman's arcade,
aptly named Quarters, which everyone referred to simply as
Paulie's.

Max had lost more than a few allowances at Paulie's, whiling
away hours in the summer much to his parents' distaste. Max
and his friends often wandered out at dusk, bleary-eyed and
with the green glow of the arcade screens showing behind their
eyes.

Max's mother had insisted he looked a shade paler every
time he stumbled out of the dark interior. It seemed as if he and
his friends had paid more than just quarters when they slipped
into the arcade, their pockets full and jangling, only to emerge
hours later broke and withered.

Max didn't have a clue where Kim had gone that final day,
but he had to find out. The need burned in him as if he were an

addict and the only drug that would satisfy his unquenchable compulsion was that bit of information.

He started with the bank. When he pushed through the door, a blast of cold artificial air swirled up around him, scented with potpourri and a comingling of the perfumes and colognes that had already passed through the brightly lit bank that morning. The woman behind the counter looked vaguely familiar.

He read her nametag as he stepped up to the hard edge of the gleaming Formica counter.

"Hi, Mr. Wolfenstein. How are you?" she asked.

He smiled, still searching and then he remembered. She was the mother of Gary Phillips. Gary had moved on to high school the year before.

"Mrs. Phillips," he said, tilting his head. "I'm okay. I hate to bother you-"

She waved a dismissive hand, gold rings gleaming on her thick fingers. "Nonsense. I haven't had a patron in an hour. And I love to see a friendly face."

Max nodded, wondering if she'd find it so friendly after he started asking questions about the woman who'd been murdered.

"Were you here when the woman across the street was-"

He didn't have to finish. She'd already begun a dramatic bobbing of her head. She clasped her hands at her chest and then shifted to an equally dramatic shaking of her head from side to side.

"It was just terrible. Horrifying! I saw the whole thing right through the glass there. Mr. Davis put that spray frost on the bottom, so I didn't see everything, but enough. I doubt I'll sleep well for another month."

Max tried not to reveal his own horror at the images he'd seen on the video. The horror wanted to appear there on his stiff face, a gruesome scowl that might never leave once he allowed it to slip into place.

Don't make that face, his mother used to say when he pouted. 'Your face will freeze like that and you'll spend the rest of your life looking like a whipped puppy.'

He remained impassive, though he felt the corners of his mouth tugging down to match Mrs. Phillips own look of dismay.

"Did the woman, Kim, come in?"

Mrs. Phillips bit the side of her cheek and then picked up a pen, pressing it against her lips, a shade of girlish pink that seemed more suitable for teenagers than a grown woman.

"No, I don't think so. We had a busy morning. Typical weekday. Karen worked as well, but she was covering the window. I don't remember seeing Kim. She didn't have an account with us, I don't think." Mrs. Phillips lowered her voice and leaned forward. "She was a battered wife. Apparently, her husband killed her."

Max nodded. Usually he found the small-town judge, jury, and executioner gossip daunting and even shameful, but instead he nodded.

"The chair would be too good for him," he mumbled.

Mrs. Phillip's eyes popped wide, but Max had already turned away. "Thank you," he called over his shoulder, as he pushed back into the warm day. He didn't dare turn to look her in the eye.

He moved along to Furry Friends, though he doubted Kim could have gleaned any groundbreaking news from the owner's son, a pimple-faced twenty-something who spent his days perched on a metal stool getting lost in his latest fantasy comic.

Max visited the store frequently to buy food for Frankenstein. Each time, Max found the boy slouched over the counter, eyes bulging as he flipped furiously through the pages of a comic book. The kid rarely bothered with a hello or a goodbye. He merely took the money and thrust Max's cash back into his hands, as if even ten seconds away from the story was ten seconds too long.

It surprised Max not to find the boy behind the counter. Instead, his father stood there, a large jovial man who also bred and trained German shepherds.

Max had gone to school with the man's oldest daughter. She'd moved to California just after high school, and as far as Max knew, never looked back.

"If it isn't Max Wolfenstein." The man beamed. "How are you, Son?"

Max smiled, again forcing his mouth to tilt up at the edges and the emptiness inside to retreat down again.

"I'm good, Jeremy. How are you?"

"Oh good, good. Got a new group of pups wearing me out, but I can't complain."

"I haven't seen you in here in a while. Usually your son-"

Jeremy's face darkened.

"Not exactly an ambitious young man, that one. Apparently, my wife and I lost some of our heavy hand with the second one because we can barely get him to the store, let alone convince him to talk to the customers when they come in." He chuckled and wiped a hand through his thinning hair. "He's healthy. I try to be grateful for the little things, you know?"

Max nodded.

He thought of Kim, cold and hard on a morgue table somewhere, waiting for the sharp blade of a scalpel to expose her secrets to a stranger's eyes. What he wouldn't give to say the words she's healthy.

"Everything okay, Max?"

Max looked up to find Jeremy's brows knitted together.

"Yeah, sorry. I drifted there. Jeremy, were you here yesterday when the woman was killed across the street?"

Jeremy frowned and shook his head.

"To tell you the truth, that's why Ben's at home. He saw the whole thing. He's pretty shaken up."

"Yeah, I'm sure. Do you know if he talked to Kim?"

"Kim?" Jeremy blinked at him.

"The woman who died?"

"My God, Max, did you know her?"

Know her. The words rolled around in Max's mind, a heavy metal ball clunking against delicate things. He thought of her red-gold hair falling over her pale shoulder, her eyes big and bright as she sipped her coffee and watched the sunrise. Did you know someone who'd come in and out of your life in mere days? Could he make such a presumption?

Max nodded, unable to commit to more, unwilling perhaps.

"My condolences, Max. What an absolute shame. Dr. Patterson is one of my oldest friends. They just loved her over at Safe Haven. The man is just shaken to his core by the whole thing."

"It's a terrible tragedy," Max agreed.

Max had begun to back away. His legs hit something flimsy. A stack of cat food samples as tall as Max himself topped over backward. They thudded to the floor, the hard little pellets inside the boxes crunching against one another.

Max turned and dropped to his knees.

"Shit, I'm sorry, Jeremy." He fumbled with the boxes and tried to stack one on top of the other only to watch them fall a second time.

He felt Jeremy's hand on his shoulder.

"I've got this, Max. It's a hobby of mine. My wife thinks I should have been an architect." He chuckled. He offered his hand and helped Max stand up. "This gives me something to do today, anyhow."

"Thanks, Jeremy. I'm just trying to gather some information about Kim's last day. Did Ben mention if she stopped in at all?"

Jeremey shook his head. "I'm sure she didn't. He said he'd

never met her, but saw her walking the dogs a few times across the way. He thought she looked really nice."

"Yeah," Max sighed, heading for the door. "She was."

He hit another dead end at Katie's Clothing Store. The woman who owned it had worked the day before and had never seen Kim.

As he pushed into the arcade, the onslaught of beeps, clinking coins, and the strange gravely voices announcing Game Over assailed him.

The dim interior appeared hazy. The neon signs and yellow flashbulbs of the pinball machines cast him from the bright world of day into a sort of backroom reality, as if he were getting a peek behind the curtain into another dimension.

For a moment, he stood transfixed by a yellow Pac-Man eating his way across the screen of the machine directly in front of him. The player, a girl of eleven or twelve, leaned close to the screen, her ponytail swinging as she rocked the controls from side to side.

As his eyes adjusted and the first intensity wore away, he propelled his legs onward. He wound deeper into the arcade, all the way to the back where Paulie sat behind a glass case filled with a scattering of cheap toys the kids could exchange for the tickets they won on Skee-Ball or other games.

Paulie leaned back in a wooden chair, tipped on its hind legs in that dangerous way parents loved to scold their kids about. His feet were stacked on the counter's edge, his legs crossed at the ankles, and he read from a comic book with a dark figure in a mask running from a building with a bloom of red smoke billowing in the distance.

He didn't look up, and Max wondered if the overwhelming sights and sounds of the arcade had desensitized him. He would likely struggle with deafness as he aged, maybe even go blind.

It was a depressing thought, a very adult thought, and Max frowned only to find his reflection in the mirror above Paulie's head frowning back at him. He suddenly looked old. Not older, but old, as if the mirror were a funhouse mirror and the trick glass had aged him thirty years.

"Hey, Paulie," Max said.

To Max's surprise, the man's head shot up instantly. With unnatural grace, he pulled his feet in, tipped his chair down, and stood, flopping the comic book on the seat behind him.

"Well, if it isn't Max Wolfenstein! You and Jake come in to duke it out? You never did best him on *Death Race*."

Max laughed and his shoulders relaxed. A bit of his dreariness flitted away.

"Nice shirt," Max grinned.

Paulie wore a *Pac-Man Fever* t-shirt in an orange so bright it looked hot.

"Funkadelic, right? Eight hundred tickets and you can have your very own." He gestured at the wall where several t-shirts hung. "This is my bread and butter right here." Paulie tapped a finger on his shirt.

"T-shirts?"

Paulie guffawed.

"Hell no! Pac-Man. Kids wait in line all day for that machine. Boggles my brain, man. Meanwhile, my favorite, *Zaxxon* sits lonely and cold half the day. Kids." He shrugged.

"Paulie, were you here yesterday when the woman across the street was murdered?"

Paulie nodded. "Yeah. That was heavy. A kid ran back here screaming. By the time I got to the front, a dozen kids had their faces pressed to the glass up there. A few ran outside, and then the whole pack followed. Damn idgits."

Max nodded. He didn't want to hear more about the shooting. He'd seen the video. He knew how it had gone down.

"Kim was the name of the woman who got shot. Did you know her?"

"Kim," Paulie said triumphantly, as if he'd been searching for her name in his head. "I knew it was something like that. I kept thinking Kelly, but yeah, now I remember, Kim."

"You met her then?"

"Yesterday. Unreal, right? She came in looking for a kid named Jordan. I pointed her to *Donkey Kong*. He's the high scorer. Course he dropped out of school and just plays video games all day," Paulie whispered from the corner of his mouth.

"Is he here right now?"

Paulie nodded. "Sure is." Paulie pointed to a skinny kid, young but hard looking.

His messy hair hung over the collar of his cutoff black t-shirt. Thin pale arms reached toward the controls. Max saw ink drawings of barbed wire around the kid's scrawny biceps.

Jordan barely glanced his way when Max paused beside him.

"Jordan?" Max asked.

The kid said nothing, only continued flicking the controls, eyes laser focused on the digital ape jumping from block to block.

Max wanted to interrupt him, demand the kid talk, but he saw the hard set of his jaw and the way he'd tensed when Max walked closer. He knew kids, and this one was a runner. If he pushed him, Jordan would likely disappear out the door.

Max stepped back, putting space between them. He fished for his wallet and pulled out a five dollar bill, an essential gold-mine to a kid like Jordan.

"I've got five bucks and five minutes," Max said. "I'm going to go snag a game of *Death Race*. You want the money, come find me."

Max found the game he and Jake used to play for hours. In the years since, the other kids had bested their scores by hundreds of points. Max fed a dollar into the change machine and grabbed the quarters that popped out. He slipped one into the game, glancing behind him as Jordan approached.

"What do you want?" Jordan asked. He thrust his hand out.

Max took the five dollars from his pocket and laid it in Jordan's, knowing the kid could grab the money and take off.

"Paulie told me you were here yesterday and Kim came in to talk to you."

Jordan shrugged.

"Do you know who I'm talking about?"

Jordan nodded.

"Sure, the dead lady."

Max cringed at his words.

"What did she talk to you about?"

Jordan's eyes flicked toward a kid playing Atari.

"We can go outside if you want," Max suggested.

Jordan recoiled and stepped back. "I'm not going anywhere with you, man."

Max gave him an irritated look. "I'm a teacher. Kim was my friend. Believe me, I have no interest in you beyond finding out what happened to my friend."

Jordan's hand closed around the money, and he slipped it into his pocket. He stared at the door, seeming to come to a conclusion. "Fine, but I ain't going to your car or any shit like that."

Max walked to the door and pushed into the humid day.

Clouds offered a flimsy shield against the sun's intensity, but the brightness after the arcade stung Max's eyes. He cupped a palm on his forehead and looked down at the sidewalk.

Jordan stopped near the door, as if he wanted to stay within arm's reach. "She wanted to know about this dude in a van," Jordan said.

"Okay." Max spread his hands in a *that's all* gesture. "What dude and what van?"

Jordan pulled a pen from his back pocket and started to draw a crisscross of barbed wire lines around his left wrist.

"Kim was livin' with my mom at Ellie's House."

"The women's shelter?"

251

"Yeah. My ma told her I almost got nabbed by some freaks last winter. Kim wanted to know what had happened."

Max blinked toward the tangle of ink lines. "Can you tell me about it, please?"

"Yeah, whatever. I was just walking out by the train tracks. Doin' nothin', and this black van pulled up."

"Black," Max murmured. It was not a question.

"The door opened, and this guy threw a blanket over my head and dragged me inside."

Max's head slowly rolled up to Jordan's face. The kid was unnaturally pale, but as he told the story, two matching blots of pink appeared on his cheeks as if he were embarrassed.

It stunned Max that it was embarrassment rather than terror on the kid's face.

"I figured they were a couple of faggots trying to get me to do weird shit. My dad taught me how to fight. I started kicking and punching. I bit the guy who'd grabbed me, and then I pulled the blanket off.

"The driver started swerving all over the place, reaching back. But the guy who'd pulled me in hadn't latched the door. It was sliding open and closed as we went down the road. I punched the guy who took me as hard as I could right in the nose. That's how you put a man down. Right here." The kid tapped a finger on his nose, and Max ached at the tough way he spoke, as if he'd had to defend himself other times, many times.

"I hauled ass out the door of that van. We weren't going too fast, but I skinned my elbow pretty good and the side of my face. I didn't stop. I was up and running before they even knew I was out. Lucky for me we were driving by the woods near the pit. I ran like hell into those trees. I knew the woods. I didn't stop to see if they were coming. I ran a mile before I caught my breath."

Max sagged against the building. "Did you call the cops?"

Jordan sneered. "The pigs? Fuck no. The only thing the pigs

ever did for me was throw me in foster care. And they'd do it again."

"Jordan, did you see anything in the van? Anything that would help identify the people who took you?"

Jordan had returned to his barbed wire. He clicked the end of the pen and stuck it back in his pocket.

"Yeah. There was a little plastic card hanging from a metal string thing. The guy who'd grabbed me wore it around his neck. I ripped it off. It said Dr. Lance and under that the Northern Michigan Ass."

"Northern Michigan Ass?" Max asked skeptically. It was far-fetched enough the man was wearing a badge identifying him as a doctor, but Northern Michigan Ass.

Jordan shook his head. "A-S, not ass. It was an abbrevi-what'sit. You know where you shorten the word."

"Abbreviation."

"Yeah."

"Where do you live right now, Jordan?" Max asked, glancing at his watch.

"Here and there."

Max lifted an eyebrow. "Where's your dad?"

"Not here. Can't say I blame him."

"And your mom lives at Ellie's House?"

Jordan narrowed his eyes. "Don't even try to pull that 'save the kid' shit, man. I see how you're looking at me, and the only thing I ever get for that look is trouble. I'll see ya around."

Max walked to his motorcycle. Halfway there, he made the connection.

"Northern Michigan Asylum," he said aloud.

*M*ax opened his door to find a vaguely familiar woman standing on his stoop. It took a moment to place her.

"Martha," he said, remembering the director from Ellie's house.

"Hello, Mr. Wolfenstein. Do you mind if I come in for a few minutes?"

The woman's face looked haggard beneath a layer of powder a shade darker than her skin. She sat at Max's table and folded her hands in front of her.

From the other room, Max heard a light thud.

Martha glanced toward the doorway. "Is someone else here?"

He shook his head.

"I haven't slept well since Kim was taken," she confided. "I've lost other women at the house. It's the burden we accept when we work with survivors of domestic violence. A burden I know all too well."

She pulled up her sleeve to reveal puckered white and pink flesh.

"My ex-husband tried to burn me alive. He threw gasoline

254

on me and held his cigarette to my blouse." Martha stared at the scar, tracing her finger over the raised flesh. "One of the women at the house once asked if I'd ever considered plastic surgery to remove this scar. I told her no, never. This was mine, all mine, my emblem of survival, a reminder of what I had endured, and why I do what I do."

Max held his mug of coffee, staring at the woman's arm and remembering Kim's scars. A white pucker of flesh on her back that looked like a cigarette burn. A ring of half-moons near her left breast that had resembled teeth marks. He shuddered.

"I'm sorry," he murmured. "I wish I could have done more. I think I screwed everything up the day I went to Kim's apartment. I put her in the path of death."

Martha shook her head. "Survivor's guilt. She married death when she was eighteen years old. When a man commits to killing his wife, only fate can intervene. My fate," she shook her wrist at him, came in the form of a neighbor with a wet blanket and a golf club. "I believe in God, Mr. Wolfenstein. God saw fit to take our Kim, but before he did, he let her live one last time, love one last time."

Martha bent over and pulled a plastic grocery sack from her purse.

"She didn't have much. There's more in her apartment, but of course that's evidence for the state until Denny Watts is prosecuted. She received a letter after her death from a woman in Washington. You knew Kim. You were helping her with Nicholas. I want to give you her things in the hope you will continue her search. There's no one else now. You understand?"

He nodded, his coffee suddenly cold beneath his fingers. He looked at the mug and lifted it to his lips to be sure, and yes, the coffee had gone from piping hot to frigid in seconds.

He glanced toward the living room where the copy of *Heart of Darkness* lay on the floor.

"This letter came for her today. I read it, but I'm afraid I don't understand the implications. I thought you might." Martha handed him an envelope.

Max took the letter from the envelop and read it silently.

Dear Joan,

Thank you for reaching out. Yes, Percy is my brother, my only sibling, and I regret that I could not see him more in the two years he has been institutionalized. After he returned from South America, he was a different man. He started to write and call me about a terrible conspiracy. He claimed a doctor at the asylum was kidnapping children and performing experiments with them. As you can imagine, I was immediately concerned for my brother's mental health. I was unable to see him before he was institutionalized after appearing at the hospital with a gun.

I have visited him several times in the two years since. He is highly sedated due to paranoid delusions. The doctors believe he suffered a psychotic break during his time in the Amazon.

I believe there is no merit to his claims. He is merely a sick man.

Best of luck in finding your son,

Jody Hobbs

Max folded the letter and looked at the return address on the envelope.

"Washington State?" he wondered.

Martha nodded.

"There's a phone number for the woman in Kim's notebook. I do hope you can help, Max. And thank you."

Martha stood and patted Max's arm before leaving.

Max opened Kim's notebook. She'd filled the pages with dates, musings, and little notes about groceries. Twice he saw his own name. The date he first met Kim was listed next to the words Saved by Max.

He studied the words until they blurred.

"Saved by Max. No, doomed, not saved, but how could she have known that at the time?" he asked no one.

He picked up the phone and dialed the number listed next to Jody's name in Kim's book.

A woman answered.

"Hi, is this Jody Hobbs?"

"Speaking." She spoke in a high, clear voice.

"My name is Max Wolfenstein. I'm a good friend of Kim Phillips. I believe you were corresponding with her?"

"Yes, though corresponding implies a long communication and in fact I only spoke with her on the phone once and received a single letter. I wrote back to her as well, but haven't heard back."

"That's because she's deceased," Max told her, staring at the hairline cracks in the plaster beside his phone.

"Oh dear, I'm sorry to hear that."

"Jody, I'm curious to know why Kim reached out to you. Her son has been missing for several months. I'm assuming from your letter that Kim came across something pertaining to Nicholas."

"Yes, well, she described it as chasing white rabbits, unfortunately. She knew I was likely a dead end, but wanted to follow every lead that came her way. She found an article published two years ago by Abe Levett, a journalist for *Up North News*. He interviewed my brother about a trip he took to the Amazonian jungle. My brother unfortunately suffered a mental breakdown of sorts and started down a delusional path, which culminated in his appearance at the Northern Michigan Asylum for the Insane. He was in the possession of a pistol and threatening a doctor there. Percy is a very sick man."

"I see. Did Kim believe your brother was connected to Nicholas in some way?"

The woman sighed.

"As I mentioned, she knew it was likely a dead end. I'm afraid I can't be of more help, sir. My husband just pulled in to the driveway and I have to go."

Max thanked Jody for her time and disconnected the call.

He dialed zero for the operator.

"How can I connect you?"

"I'd like the number for the newspaper, *Up North News,* in Traverse City, please."

"Connecting you now," the woman said.

"*Up North News,*" a gruff voice barked into the phone.

"I'm trying to reach Abe Levett."

"Hold," the man snapped.

A younger man came on the line. "Abe Levett here."

"Abe, Hi. My name is Max Wolfenstein. I'm calling about an article you wrote for *Up North News* almost two years ago. You interviewed a man named Percy Hobbs."

Abe didn't speak for moment, and Max heard muffled talking as if he'd covered the phone with his hand as he spoke to someone.

"Max, I do remember Percy Hobbs, but I'd prefer to call you back from my home phone. I'm on my way out the door in five minutes. Can I call you back in twenty?"

"Yeah, sure." Max rattled off his number, wondering if the reporter was giving him the brushoff.

Twenty-five minutes later, the phone hadn't rang and Max paced back and forth in his kitchen.

Seeking a target for his anger, he cursed Abe Levett under his breath. He opened a cupboard and grabbed a cup, slamming the glass on the counter too hard. The shattering glass was drowned by the ringing of his telephone.

Max stared, dazed at the shards of glass flecking his gray and white checked counter.

The phone rang a second time, and he snatched it up, still stunned at the shattered glass.

"Yes?" Max said, half-expecting the voice of his mother or Jake to be on the other end.

"Abe Levett here. Is this Max?"

"Yes, it's me," Max sighed, lifting his phone and drawing out the cord as he walked to his table and slumped into a chair.

"Percy Hobbs called me about claims of a child abduction by a doctor at the Northern Michigan Asylum."

"And was it true?" Max asked, thinking of the stories by two separate unrelated witnesses of a black van with ties to the Northern Michigan Asylum.

"I could not substantiate those claims," Abe admitted. "But if you want my gut. I think there was a kernel of truth. Was the whole elaborate story true? That's hard to say."

"Can you tell me about them?"

"Hold on," Abe told him. He spoke to someone on his end of the line.

"Orla, can you grab my notes on Percy Hobbs from the December 1981 file?"

Max waited, listening to rustling in the background.

Orla, Abe had said, a unique name and one Max remembered. He'd read about her in the newspaper. She'd been one of the women abducted by the serial killer from the Leelanau area. Abe Levett had broken the case wide open. He'd also written a long series of articles about corruption at the Northern Michigan Asylum.

Abe cleared his throat, murmuring out loud to himself for a moment.

"Okay yeah, yeah. I remember. He was rather clandestine about the whole thing. He'd found something while traveling in the Amazon, something other worldly he'd claimed, and a doctor from the asylum had stolen it. The doctor was kidnapping children in order to use this thing. He wouldn't give me specifics, but he wanted attention brought to the doctor and the children. The doctor, as you can imagine, was furious and sued us for libel. My editor's a maverick, but he didn't want to take this one on.

"I tried to corroborate Percy's story, but he went into the

institution right after this all went down. I couldn't validate any of his claims. He did travel to the Amazon, and he lost two traveling partners. I could trace that information through flight records and a few interviews with the family of his colleagues who were lost in the rainforest."

"Has anyone contacted you about this recently, Abe. Did a woman named Kim Phillips call you?"

"No, I'm sorry. You're the first I've heard speak Percy's name in a year."

"Can I ask why you wrote his story? I feel as if most people would write off such outrageous claims as nuts."

"I've seen too much, Max. And I know people. Was his story true? He believed it with every ounce of his being. He believed it, and when I tried to interview the doctor, he came off all wrong. Slick as ice. He knew just what to say, but his eyes told me something else. The man lied. He lied as if it were his nature. And let me tell you another thing, that asylum has more skeleton's in its closet than a graveyard has bones in the ground."

"But how could you let it go, then? I mean, if you believed this doctor was abducting children," Max heard his voice rising.

"Whoa, slow down. I didn't have any proof. Not the name of one single missing child. I wrote that article thinking some parents might come out of the woodwork to tell me about their missing kids. None did. Not a single one."

*a*shley hopped up and down as she stood on the stoop of Sid's house, pounding on the front door.

Despite the events of the previous days, the thought of buying her new bike chased away the dark clouds that had been accumulating. She'd thought of nothing else since she'd woke at nine o'clock that morning.

Sid's mother, Gloria, pulled the door open, eyes wide.

"Goodness, Ashley, give that hand a rest," she said, narrowing her eyes at Ashley's raised hand.

Ashley dropped her arm. "Is Sid home?" she asked, barely able to contain her excitement.

Gloria cocked her head. "He's home, but he has dinner at his grandmother's house in exactly two hours. Which means I expect him to walk back through this door at four forty-five pm. And no going in the woods."

Ashley nodded up and down.

"Yes, ma'am. I promise."

"Sid!" Gloria called, retreating into the house. "Ashley is here."

Sid popped his head into the hallway and grinned. "Hey. I just finished my model airplane. Want to see?"

Ashley shook her head. She pulled the wad of cash from her back pocket.

Sid clapped his hands together. "Yes! You've got the rest?"

"Twenty-two dollars exactly," she said, waving the bills as if she'd just won the lottery.

"Mom, I'll be back in a little while," Sid called.

Gloria returned to the front hall, her face pinched with worry.

"I mean it when I say don't go in the woods, you two. If I so much as hear from a neighbor you chased a frisbee into the trees, you won't be leaving this house for a week, Sidney. Understand?" She stared at Sid and then shifted her attention to Ashley.

Both kids nodded their agreement, though Ashley was secretly grateful her own mother hadn't worded her warnings so strongly.

Sid stuffed his feet into his tennis shoes, not bothering to untie them first, and followed Ashley out the door. He grabbed his bike from the garage, and she climbed on behind him.

Ashley tilted her head back and let the warm breeze blow her long dark hair out behind her. Her body seemed weightless, light as a feather. It was a term she'd uttered plenty of times when they played light as a feather, stiff as a board, but not a sensation she'd ever truly experienced.

When they burst through the glass doors into Sampson's Bike Shop, the owner looked up and smiled.

"Is it time?" he asked.

Ashley pulled out her money and fanned it for a second time, her smile so wide her cheeks ached.

Mr. Sampson rolled the Huffy Pro Thunder off the little wooden platform it sat on.

"Every time you take her out," he insisted, swiveling his eyes between Ashley and the bike as if speaking to them both, "you perform the ABC, a quick three-point inspection that ensures safe travels. Bonus points if you've got one of these little helpers too." He pulled a worn playing card from his pocket.

Ashley saw a haggard man hiking up a mountain with a large walking stick.

"Saint Christopher," he explained. "The patron Saint of travelers. But if Chris can't make the journey, the ABCs should get you there."

Mr. Sampson squatted down next to the bike.

"A is for Air." He put his thumb and forefinger on the tire and squeezed. "Feel that?"

Ashley grabbed the tire.

"Nice and firm, as it should be," he told her.

Ashley nodded, struggling to pay attention as she gazed in wonderment at her new bike.

"B," he continued, standing up, "is brakes. Let's walk her outside for this one."

Mr. Sampson held open the door as Ashley wheeled the Huffy Pro Thunder onto the sidewalk.

Her legs were light and springy as she climbed onto the bike. She clutched the rubber grips on the handlebars, solid and strong beneath her fingers. The bike itself seemed to buzz with the anticipation of its first ride. She pushed off with one foot, standing as she pressed the pedal down, and the wheels started to turn.

"Now hit the brakes," Mr. Sampson said.

Ashley depressed the brakes, and the bike jerked to a stop.

"Responsive," Mr. Sampson beamed as she returned to where he and Sid stood. "That's how you want them. And last, but certainly not least, C, the chain."

Mr. Sampson bent down and tugged the chain. "Make sure she's secure every time."

"Got it, yes. Thanks, Mr. Sampson," she babbled, so

desperate to get on the bike and ride, she jiggled her foot up and down.

Mr. Sampson grinned and then held out his hand. "It's been a pleasure doing business with you, Miss Shepherd."

Ashley shook his hand and then looked at Sid. She didn't have to speak. He climbed on his bike and pulled next to her. They rode away from the sidewalk, down the center of the empty street.

"Don't forget to name her," Mr. Sampson called after them.

Ashley pumped the pedals, her legs pushing faster and faster as she sped down the street. She'd left Sid in her dust. The Huffy Pro Thunder sliced through the warm day as if it were made of steel, but a special kind, steel that was weightless and powerful.

She reached the end of the block within seconds and depressed the brake. She came to a stop, setting one foot down and marveling at the bike beneath her.

She leaned down and kissed the handlebars.

Sid caught up with her, his smile matching her own. "Wow, that bike flies!" he said.

"Starfire," Ashley said. "Her name is Starfire."

Starfire was one of Ashley's favorite superheroes from the DC comics. She could fly at supersonic speeds and absorb solar radiation, and best of all, she used star bolts to attack her enemies.

"Yeah," Sid nodded his approval. "Starfire," he said. "And she's purple like Starfire's costume."

For an hour, they sped through the neighborhoods in Roscommon. Ashley rode faster than she'd ever ridden in her life.

At times, the wheels took over, and Ashley lifted her legs out to the sides and watched the pedals spin.

When she left Sid at home, she rode back to her own house, pausing at the end of the driveway.

Despite promising her mother she'd stay out of the woods, Ashley wanted to try out her new bike on the trails.

She steered into the woods, checking the sky for birds, but spotted only a flock of dark clouds creeping across the sky. Rain would follow.

Grandma Patty called the rain tears from heaven. She told Ashley that's how they knew God was still paying attention.

Despite the coming rain, Ashley pushed on. She could ride for a half hour and then tuck the bike safely into the garage.

She flew over roots and jumps, the bike landing with a soft whoosh. "Starfire's got this," she shouted.

As she raced through the trails, birds took flight from the dense brush on either side. A squirrel fled across her path, chittering angrily as he raced up a tree.

A cardinal soared from a tree, and she watched his scarlet wings flap into the high branches.

As her bike rocketed forward, she sensed movement beside her. Twigs snapped and leaves crunched underfoot, sounds too loud to belong to a chipmunk or bird.

She glanced back and saw a flash of a person ducking behind a tree.

Her heart dropped into her stomach, and she almost slowed and stopped. As she started to compress the brake, another twig snapped behind her. Something darted from the bushes.

Ashley shrieked and jammed on the pedals, pumping her legs and trying to pick up speed. Her hair fanned out, and something touched it. She imagined the monster gaining on her, its mouth open to reveal jagged, blood-soaked fangs.

Panting, eyes blurring from sweat, she pedaled harder into the forest.

As she came around a curve in the trail, a familiar and unsettling laugh rang out.

Whipping her head sideways, she caught sight of Travis

Barron as he threw a thick branch into the front wheel of her bike.

The wheel caught and her bike jerked to a stop, sending her flying over the handlebars.

Ashley landed on her hands and knees, skidding through prickly brush. A splinter gouged in the soft webbing of her fingers, and she cried out.

Before she could stand, Travis kicked her in the ribs.

"Stupid bitch," he hissed. "Dumb spic bitch who thinks she's better than me. You and your four eyed, fat little friend."

He spat, and she felt the glob of wet slide down her cheek.

Furious, she started to stand, and he kicked her again in the back. She sprawled forward.

His friend, a freshman at the high school with a long ugly face and shaggy dark hair smiled as Travis picked up her bike and threw it into a tree.

"Keep her down," Travis ordered him.

The boy stepped on Ashley's back, pushing her into the gnarled ground, pressing so hard on her spine she feared it would snap.

Travis grabbed the bike and threw it a second time against the tree and then a third.

She struggled to draw in a breath, and when Travis started to jump up and down on Starfire, she clenched her eyes shut and fought against the tears welling up.

The death of her beautiful bike seemed to last forever. Ashley had slipped into a fog, a dark tight little ball in her brain.

When she finally unfurled, the weight had lifted from her back, and she no longer heard the sounds of crunching metal.

It had been replaced with a soft pattering of rain.

She opened her eyes.

Her bike lay crumpled on the bushy path.

8

---

*M*ax pushed into the reception area at the Northern Michigan Asylum.

"Hi, my name is Max Wolfenstein. I'm looking for Dr. Lance."

The woman behind the desk, tall and broad-shouldered with close set green eyes, looked up from the book she'd been reading. She set it aside.

"Dr. Lance isn't in today."

"I saw a black van in the employee lot. That doesn't belong to Dr. Lance?" Max asked.

"The hospital owns several of those vans. They're used for transporting patients."

"I see. Does Dr. Lance work with children?"

The woman shook her head. "He works with adults. We don't have children at the hospital anymore, Mr. Wolfenstein. You might be aware the asylum has been closing parts of the facility for the last several years. Our children's unit is no longer open."

"So, there are no kids here at all?"

"None except a few who live with the staff, children of the doctors, that kind of thing."

"I wondered if I might visit Percy Hobbs?"

"I'm afraid that won't be possible," she told him. "Visiting hours are on Sunday."

Max started to argue, but a commotion in the hallway behind them caught her attention.

Two orderlies were struggling with a man wearing state-issued pajamas. He cried and shouted, twisting sideways as the two orderlies attempted to drag him back down the hall.

"Nurse Frances, could you help us here?" one of the orderlies grunted, his face turning red with the effort of keeping the patient from breaking free.

She stood and hurried down the hall, Max forgotten behind her.

Several doors opened off the lobby. Max tried two, locked. On the third he got lucky.

He hurried down a long hall, looking into commons room and peeking through small viewing windows.

He passed a large window into a community room. Max paused and looked through the glass.

A single man sat in a wheelchair, his head bowed and his face slack. A young woman sat beside him, her hand on his. Half a dozen bracelets adorned her wrists, and Max studied her. She looked familiar, but he could only see her from the back. He looked at the white blond hair brushing her shoulders. She was out of place, a teenager, a girl really, comforting an invalid.

"Melanie," he murmured, pushing forward, reaching for the knob of the door.

"Sir, can I help you?" a man's stern voice boomed behind him, and Max turned, startled.

Despite his big voice, the orderly was small, no more than five foot seven with long skinny arms that seemed out of proportion to his short torso.

"Yes, sorry. I'm here to see Percy-" He turned back to the glass and stopped abruptly. The girl no longer sat beside the patient, only an empty wooden chair.

"I see," the orderly eyed him as if searching for identification.

"He's my brother-in-law," Max lied. Max didn't know if Jody had a husband.

The orderly glanced toward the glass, pursing his lips. "Did the nurse on duty mention that we only have visiting hours on Sundays. If you're not here in a professional capacity-"

"Please," Max said, the earnestness in his voice genuine. "Please, I need to see him."

The orderly frowned, looked into the room and sighed.

"Five minutes, sir, but you should understand Percy Hobbs is non-responsive. He doesn't speak. You might think he can see you and hear you, but it's highly unlikely."

"I understand."

Max followed the orderly into the large room, empty except for Percy Hobbs.

He wondered where all the patients were. Had they already released or transferred so many that entire wings of the enormous asylum stood empty?

Max stood in front of the man, aware he'd given no thought to what he'd say if he gained access to him.

"Percy," Max said, but the man remained unmoving.

Max squatted in front of him.

"He's not in there," the orderly explained kindly, waving a hand in front of Percy's glassy brown eyes.

Max surveyed the man, surely younger than fifty, with sandy colored hair mostly gone gray and a saggy, non-responsive expression. His head drooped forward, and he held his hands clasped in his lap, the fingers intertwined.

Max started to look back at Percy's face, but then he paused, peering at his hands. The man was squeezing his hands together, squeezing them so tightly the blood had drained from his knuckles.

Max had to rescue Percy.

The thought overpowered rationality, but his commonsense sense quickly returned in the sound of his brother's voice. *Are you insane, Max? Do you want them to lock you up in here?*

Max sat in the wooden chair and took Percy's hand. The man's eye twitched, but he still didn't look up.

"Do you mind if I have a few minutes alone with him?" Max asked.

The orderly seemed oddly relieved by the request, as if the intimacy of Max holding the man's hand had made him uncomfortable.

"That'd be fine. I'll come back in five minutes." The orderly stood, and to Max's astonishment, he plodded down a hallway and disappeared through a white door.

Don't even think about it, Max. You can't save everyone. This vegetable's going to get you thrown in prison, Jake's voice insisted as Max stood, grabbed the wheelchair's handles, and pushed Percy through the door.

He went out exactly the way he'd come in, praying beneath his breath the nurse would still be assisting the other orderlies. When he burst into the reception area, he halted at the sound of voices. But the sounds receded, and he saw the nurse's chair standing empty.

Turning around, Max shoved the entrance doors open with his hip, hauling Percy's chair backward and into the daylight.

Max's legs shook as he pushed Percy along the paved sidewalk. A wheel hit a crack in the sidewalk and caught. The man lurched forward in his chair, but he didn't fall out. Max reached forward, grabbed the man's shoulder, and settled him back, holding him as Max forced the chair over the bump.

He walked faster, and then he ran.

"Hey, hey you!" a voice shrilled behind him.

RAG DOLL BONES

Max didn't stop.

The voice grew louder. It boomed across the lawn, and Max slowed. He feared if he kept running, a row of orderlies clad in white would suddenly step from the shadows of the buildings to block his path.

He turned to see a man lumbering toward him. The man wore a black coat and black pants. A doctor surely, but then Max noted his disheveled hair, and when his eyes drifted down to the man's feet, he saw slippers.

The man was a yard away when an orderly ran up behind him. The orderly was young, his face full of worry as he grabbed the patient's arm.

"Mr. Bernard, you gave me quite a scare."

Mr. Bernard spun to face the orderly, shaking his head. "I have to go with these men," Mr. Bernard announced, gesturing toward Max and the catatonic patient. "We have an appointment with the judge. Mind yourself, young man. Don't you know who I am?"

Mr. Bernard tried to shake off the orderly's grip, but the young man held tight.

"Sorry, sir," the orderly called to Max as he led Mr. Bernard away, insisting he needed a shower and suit before he could meet with the judge.

Max swallowed the rock in his throat and pushed on, slowing only when he reached his car, which he hadn't driven in weeks. He used it regularly enough on rainy days or to buy groceries in the summer, but this had been an unusual summer.

He'd been opting for his motorcycle because it felt... better somehow, like he'd embarked on a perilous journey and his motorcycle was his trusty sidekick. Without his sidekick he'd never have made it to that moment. He didn't know how, but felt it was true just the same.

And yet when he'd driven to the asylum two hours before,

he'd walked into his garage with barely a thought and climbed behind the wheel of his car.

"Because the keys," he muttered to himself.

After he'd hung up the phone with Abe, the keys to his Toyota had been sitting at his elbow, right there on the kitchen table, though he always hung them on the hook by the door.

39

*a*shley walked through the woods crying, not bothering to stifle her anguish as she pushed the bike, the back rim so bent it barely turned. Her hands trembled, the scrapes on her elbows seeped, and she wanted to curl into a little ball and cry until Grandma Patty appeared with a cup of apple juice and a story about how she'd once lost something she'd treasured too, but somehow it all turned out okay.

Except Grandma Patty was dead, and the bike Ashley had been saving for, for over a year was destroyed, and it wouldn't be okay.

She leaned the bike against a tree and walked toward the raccoon den. She could hold the babies at least. That would be something.

As she moved closer, goosebumps prickled along her arms. She wanted to stop. The den didn't look right. The board that kept the babies from falling out had been ripped away. The gaping black hole into the hut was dark and ominous.

She started to run, stopping a few feet away, her hands going to her mouth.

She could see blood splashed across the interior, blood on the little yellow blanket Sid had brought from home.

"No," she shrieked as her eyes registered the pile of gore and fur.

They no longer looked like raccoons. They'd been crushed, mangled. Protruding from the grisly heap, she saw one tiny black paw.

She stepped back, her head slowly rotating from side to side as if her body couldn't accept what her eyes insisted was true.

She backed into a tree and flopped down, putting her face into the leaves and wailing.

"Noo!" she howled.

The rain, as if God had truly heard her anguish, splattered in fast heavy droplets.

It mingled with her tears and the dirt, and soon she lay in a puddle of muck.

It was all too much, first Starfire and now her raccoons. She wanted to kick and thrash and hurt someone.

Had Travis killed them, or had it been the monster in the woods?

In that moment, the monster didn't scare her. Let him come, she thought. Let them all come. She wanted to punch and tear at the face of whoever had murdered the baby raccoons.

It had been human; she knew that. An animal couldn't have gotten into the tree and ripped the board away.

As she lay crying, her body shaking with the grief and shock of the previous hour, a tiny whimper drifted up from the leaves.

She sat up and perked her ears, for a moment hearing only the falling rain.

It came again, a mewling sound.

She crawled on hands and knees to a thick fern beneath the tree that had held the raccoons. She reached into the leafy plant, searching. Her fingers brushed against something soft and damp.

Peeling back the glossy leaves, she saw him.

Alvin teetered closer to her hands, his little mouth opening as he released another chittering cry.

"Oh, Alvin," she cried, sweeping him up and clutching him against her chest.

He trembled beneath her fingers, and she pressed her face into his sodden fur.

She held him and rocked back as the rain slowed to a drizzle.

"HONEY, ARE YOU AWAKE?"

Ashley opened her eyes. A slant of light snaked through her cracked bedroom doorway.

She started to sit up, but then remembered Alvin tucked close to her beneath the comforter. She reached down and brushed his spine. He wriggled against her hand.

Her mom opened the door all the way. More light poured through.

"Hi, baby," she said. "Can I come in?"

Ashley nodded and used the hand not clutching the raccoon, to rub at her sleepy eyes.

Ashley's mother walked in and sat on the edge of the bed, resting her hand on Ashley's leg.

"I saw the bike," her mom said, her face pinched. "What happened?"

Ashley started to explain, to release an ugly litany of insults against Travis and his friend.

Instead, a gurgling sob rose from her guts. She burst into tears.

Her mother's own pain deepened in the grooves of her forehead.

"Oh, honey," she said, scooting closer and taking Ashley in her arms. "Oh, baby, I'm so sorry. You were so excited about that bike."

Ashley, forgetting she was supposed to keep the raccoon hidden, pulled Alvin out and revealed him to her mother.

"And..." she sputtered between sobs. "Someone killed the raccoons, all of them except this one. Crushed them."

She put the raccoon up to her cheek. He nuzzled his wet little nose against her.

Ashley's mom eyed the creature wearily.

"Where did he come from?" Rebecca asked.

"I have to keep him, Mom," Ashley said, her words blurring through her cries. "I'm all he has."

Ashley's mother stroked her daughter's hair. She looked again at the raccoon and her face softened.

"Shh, it's okay, honey. We don't have to talk about this tonight."

Ashley nodded, continuing to cry onto Alvin's back.

Her mom helped her recline, fluffing the pillow beneath her head.

"I'll be right back," she said.

She disappeared and returned a moment later with a cup of apple juice in Grandma Patty's favorite mug, a little white and red speckled cup with a heart painted on the side.

Ashley sipped the juice as she watched Alvin wobble across the bedspread.

Ashley's mother petted his back with a single finger. "He's tiny," she said.

Ashley nodded, thought of his brothers, and felt a wave of fresh tears course down her face.

"What if I bring in Bernard's old cat bed? The raccoon could sleep in that."

Ashley started to shake her head no.

"He can still sleep on the bed," her mother added quickly. "That way you won't squish him if you roll over."

Ashley blinked at Alvin, and after a moment nodded.

"Okay. But he's staying on the bed."

Rebecca went out and retrieved the tattered blue pet bed that had belonged to their now dead cat, Bernard. Bernard had died when Ashley was eight. She'd built a rock pile on his grave. She and Grandma Patty had painted the rocks in shades of blue and purple. Grandma Patty had even painted mice on a few of the rocks. Ashley had tried to paint her own mice, but they'd turned out like purple blobs with tails.

Ashley lifted Alvin into the cat bed and left her hand curved around his fragile body.

"My lover of wild things," Rebecca murmured, stroking Ashley's hand.

Ashley rolled onto her side, her tears mostly dry now and a trickle of embarrassment at her outburst sneaking in.

Her mom rubbed her back. "Do you want to tell me about the bike?" Rebecca asked.

"In the morning, Mom," she murmured, closing her eyes.

Max carried Percy into his house and laid him on the couch. He sat in the chair across the room, leaving the lamp on, watching and waiting.

At midnight, the man stirred and then again at two followed by twice more in the four o'clock hour. Sometime around dawn, Max dozed off, and he woke to find Percy watching him. His face was drawn and his eyes were bloodshot, but Max knew right away the man was lucid.

Percy looked around. "Where am I?" he asked.

Max sat up, rubbed his eyes, and looked at his watch.

Quarter to nine in the morning. In the center of the floor lay *Heart of Darkness.*

Percy followed Max's gaze. He stared at the book for a long time.

"Have you read it?" Max asked.

Percy tried to laugh, but only a dry croak emerged.

"I used to call it my manifesto, my destiny." He shook his head, his mouth turning down. "My curse more like it."

"Because you traveled to the Amazonian jungle?"

"Because I was a young fool."

"Mr. Hobbs, my name is Max Wolfenstein. I'm a teacher here in Roscommon. Four children have disappeared from my town. Two have been found dead. I need you to tell me your story."

"*I* traveled to Brazil and into the Amazon Rainforest. I was naive, a scientist and a scholar, foolish in my quest for discovery," Percy started, leaning his head back on the couch and closing his eyes.

"Our journey began as three: myself, a French botanist, named Antoine, and David, one of my colleagues from Dartmouth.

The Sanapu lived as a sort of ghost tribe. They were spoken of but rarely seen. When Antoine learned of their miracles regarding plant healing, he insisted we travel deeper into the forest and find them.

Three days into our journey, Antoine fell ill with malaria. He succumbed to the disease before we ever saw a glimpse of the tribe. David, on the other hand, was taken by El Lobizon."

"Spanish for-?"

Percy nodded and picked at his thumbnail.

"El Lobizon is a South American myth of sorts. It's much like our legend of the werewolf. Perhaps our legend arose from theirs. There are a few key differences of course. In the South

American legend, El Lobizon is a curse on the seventh son. If a family produces seven sons, the seventh will be afflicted with this curse. He will turn into a half man, half wolf, and in a state of frenzy he will attack and kill."

"A werewolf?" Max said, remembering Jody Hobbs's words that her brother was a 'very sick man.'

A half smile played on Percy's lips.

"You don't have to believe me, but it's best if you do. If you want to stop it, that is."

Max sucked in a foul breath as if the air in the room had soured. Had he just committed a crime, abducting this man from a mental institution, only to run into yet another dead end? It was worse than a dead end, a madman's boyhood fantasies.

As if in response to his thoughts, a crash sounded in the kitchen.

Percy stood up on wobbly legs, immediately falling back onto the couch.

Max strode into the kitchen, expecting to find police in swat gear with their guns drawn as they readied to apprehend the kidnapper.

Instead, his back door stood wide open, wind and rain blowing in. On the floor, Fruit Loops lay scattered from the welcome mat to his kitchen table.

Max closed and locked the door, not bothering to clean up the mess. He returned to the living room and perched on his chair.

"Okay, tell me," he said.

Percy glanced questioningly at the kitchen, but he continued. "The tribe who took me, they had a special shrine. It was built from wood, and it looked like a ferocious wolf lunging through the air. As I learned more about them, I came to understand that the shrine had been erected for their fallen shaman.

"According to their stories, he'd lived a thousand lives. And unlike most beings, he'd retained the knowledge of every life. Not only was he the healer of their tribe, he was the protector, the warrior. But he did not fight battles. When night fell, he slipped into the forest and turned into El Lobizon. He crept into other tribes and attacked their leaders. He consumed their blood and flesh, adding their knowledge and strength to his own tribe.

"He left instructions for his tribe after his death. The warriors of his tribe ate the shaman's flesh and drank his blood. They boiled his bones for thirteen days to remove the meat. Then they built a statue of El Lobizon, constructed partially from the bones and teeth of their fallen leader.

"Each month, on the full moon, they dismantled the wolf and they built it anew five days later. I asked why they did that, and what I discovered quite chilled me.

"Every full moon, five warriors in the tribe took apart the wolf. The women sewed crude little dolls for each of the warriors. The dolls were a mixture of the shaman's bones and the men's own hair, fingernails, and blood. The men would slice their arms and drip blood onto a seed from the embauba tree - the heart of the doll. That night, they would go into the jungle and defeat their enemies. They turned into El Lobizon, not the same as the shaman himself had, who seemed to have appeared more wolf than man during his shifts. But they ran on all fours and they tore at their enemies with their teeth."

Percy blinked at the floor as if recalling a terrible memory.

"I followed them one night, a fool after his great discovery. I followed them, and I watched them fall upon a tribe of men. They pulled the men from the trees and ripped out their throats. I'd never seen anything like it, Max. They were not merely pretending to be animals. They jumped as if they had the muscular haunches of a jaguar. Their teeth seemed to glow sharp and yellow in the moonlight. They returned home, blood soaked and panting like dogs. They collapsed in a heap and slept. In the morning, I saw the women washing them.

"I lived with them for six months. And then one night, in a moment of madness, I stole teeth and bones from their altar and ran into the forest. I don't remember how I got away. It's a dream, a nightmare perhaps. I stumbled into a group of white men, traders who'd gone into the forest to barter for cocoa. They took me with them."

Max rubbed his temple, considering the man's story.

It was absurd. No sane person would believe it. But his dubiousness was met with a memory. Simon Frank's rotting body, a gash in his throat no knife could make.

"How did you end up in the asylum?" Max asked. He needed the whole story. Maybe then it would make sense.

"Pride," Percy told him, bracing his hands on the couch. "Pride goes before destruction, a haughty spirit before a fall. One of my father's favorite quotes. He was a farmer, a man of the land. American land, naturally, not some heathen's land. He never understood my desire for travel. Neither did I for that matter. How do you explain such a call? A need so powerful it reaches into your chest and takes ahold of your heart until the rhythmic beat sounds only like go-go-go."

Max thought of the man Percy had been the day before, a man imprisoned, not only in an asylum, but also in his own body, held captive by a flurry of drugs meant to sedate and confuse him.

"It was pride that landed me in the Northern Michigan Asylum for the Insane. I had a colleague there who for a long time I had considered a friend. No more, of course," he smirked.

"We roomed together at Dartmouth. Guy Lance was in the top of his class in every subject. I've never met a more brilliant mind. I took him home once during Christmas leave. His father traveled for work. His mother had died young. He would have gone home to Boston to an empty house and a supper prepared by a maid.

"The moment we stepped from the car onto my snowy desolate driveway, I saw his disgust at my meager home. I regretted bringing him with me, but it was too late. He drank and ate with abandon, without prayers or thanks."

Percy sagged back on the couch as if humiliated in the retelling.

"My father pulled me aside later and said, 'that is not a man. He is a snake dressed in silks and golds. He will be your downfall.'"

Percy paused and blinked, chewing his thumbnail. "I get the shivers realizing how right he was. A strange feeling came over me after that trip. Instead of seeing Guy's true nature, an arrogant and selfish man, I grew obsessed with pleasing him, and later, outdoing him. I had to get higher marks, date prettier girls, and go on more grand adventures than he could ever imagine."

Percy sat up again, running his hands over his head as if he had a full head of hair.

He stopped, touching his scalp, running his fingers from brow to spine. "They cut my hair," he murmured. "I had no idea."

He returned his hands to his lap.

"Pride goes before destruction," he murmured a second time. "When I returned from the Amazon, I'd gone half mad. For weeks I sat each night, drinking whiskey and staring at the bones, elated at my escape and wracked with guilt."

"Guilt?" Max asked.

"Guilt for having stolen them. The ghost tribe had taken me in. I'd have died without them. They'd fed and washed me. They had told me secrets they'd told no one. I'd betrayed them, and the queer thing is, even as I floundered through the jungle after I'd stolen the bones, I thought of Guy Lance. I thought, I have finally outdone him! It's mortifying to admit these things. My father is more than turning in his grave. He's probably climbed out and is hitchhiking across the country to put his boot in my ass."

Max tried to laugh, but the image conjured in his mind was not a fantasy, but a nightmare.

"I called Guy several weeks after I'd returned to America. Boy, do I have a story for you, I told him. Mind you, I'd lost my traveling companions. Where was my remorse, my grief? Buried in my pride, in my desperation to beat him once and for all. He came to my house, and I told him the story. We drank a bottle of scotch sitting by the fire. He did not speak. Not a word for three hours. And then I brought out the case and showed him the bones."

"And then?"

"And then he laughed in my face." Percy's mouth hung open after he spoke the words as if he could still hardly believe it. 'Too much ayahuasca with the natives,' he told me. I'd drank so much scotch by then, I could barely stand. Otherwise I might have punched him. I passed out sometime in the night, and when I woke in the morning, Guy Lance and the bones had disappeared."

"He stole them?" Max asked. "What a scoundrel."

"If only that had been the end of it. I should have let the bones go. What kind of legal recourse did I have? Phone the police and tell them this esteemed psychiatrist had swiped the bones I myself had stolen from the Amazon? I confronted him and he had the audacity to say, 'What bones?' as if he had no idea what I spoke of. I began to stalk him. I watched him for days, and that is when I saw the child."

Max sat forward.

"He and another doctor were leading the boy through the

woods behind the asylum. The boy looked terrified. He was crying for his mother. I called the police, and they treated me like a lunatic. Finally, I reached out to Abe Levett. He believed, me, by God, he did. But the article only incensed Lance. He struck back, printing an interview that I had gone to Brazil and lost my mind. I played right into his hands. I took my pistol and I confronted him at the asylum of all places. Fool-fool-fool."

He slapped his palm lightly against his head over and over. "It took the orderlies in that place about two minutes to disarm me and haul me inside."

"They didn't call the police?"

"Oh no, Dr. Lance said he was a dear friend of mine. He told everyone he would hold himself directly responsible for my care. I had no family to speak for me. My sister is across the country and couldn't be bothered. Lance told everyone I was crying out for help. I was admitted that day, and the drugs were administered before I'd even been brought into the building."

"But your sister visited you. Why didn't she sound the alarm?"

"She believed him," Percy said dismissively. "It wasn't her fault. I love Jody, but we've never understood each other. She lives in the same town we grew up in. Owns a farm with her husband. Has five children. She used to send me letters about baking pies and sewing quilts for the church.

"She's like my mother and my father, good, devout, and serving of others. I'm a selfish man. I didn't realize it until I took those bones. But then I did. And I have begun to pay for my pride and selfishness, but it's not over yet. I'm taking them back. Maybe they will let me live, but it's just as likely they will not."

"The ghost tribe?"

Percy nodded.

"I don't understand the purpose of the child?" Max said.

Percy rubbed his jaw. "How about a cup of coffee and a plate of eggs? I have no recollection of when I last ate, but my stomach is telling me it's been days."

Max blanched. "Yeah, sorry."

He stood quickly and slipped into the kitchen, embarrassed he'd kept the man talking and hadn't offered him so much as a glass of water. Maria Wolfenstein would have boxed his ears for such an offense.

41

*T*he phone rang and rang. Ashley listened to it shrill through the quiet house.

Her mother had left for work promising they'd make a plan for the bike that evening.

On the carpet, Alvin slept in a tight little ball. His tiny black hands cradled his face.

Ashley lifted the toast from her plate, nibbled the edge, and then returned it, not hungry. Her heart hurt less than the day before. A numbness had stolen over her. She could see the blue door that led into the garage. The garage where the crumpled remains of Starfire lay.

Several minutes passed, and she heard a pounding on the door.

"Ash? You in there?" Sid's voice drifted through the door.

She didn't answer. She heard him slide the spare key into the lock.

He peeked his head in, looked to the right, and then spotted her.

His eyes widened. "I've called like a zillion times. What's going on?" He walked into the living room and paused when he spotted Alvin. His eyes immediately swept the floor. "You brought him home? What about Simon and Theodore?"

Ashley swallowed, not trusting herself to speak. It all stood there, the grief, the shock of the night before. It stood perched on the edge of a cliff. If she spoke, she would tip forward and disappear into that blackness.

He kicked off his tennis shoes, a habit developed in his own home. Ashley's mom could care less if the kids wore shoes on the carpet. When he sat next to Ashley, he seemed confused, even a little scared.

"Ash, what's wrong? Where are the other raccoons?"

"Dead," she muttered, unable to explain, unwilling to relive it, but forced to just the same.

She saw again the mound of fur and blood.

The vision brought the rage back. She wanted to hit, to hurt, and make them pay - Travis, his cruel friends, and the monster in the woods. All the people who had hurt her. She wanted to hurt them back.

"Did an animal get them?" Sid asked, petting Alvin's back.

Ashley shook her head.

"Someone," she muttered, standing and walking to the garage.

She shoved the door open so hard it smacked into the wall.

Sid followed her. When he saw her bike, he gasped.

Not speaking, he walked into the garage, leaned down, and touched the bent wheel.

"Travis Barron," she told him.

THEY DIDN'T TALK about the bike.

They watched tv and played with Alvin until Shane knocked on her door that evening.

Her mother had appeared briefly around five, changed her clothes, kissed Ashley on the temple, and left for her second job.

"Are we still going?" Shane asked, looking between Ashley and Shane questioningly.

Ashley realized she'd forgotten it was Thursday. It was time to trap the monster.

"Better not," Sid said. "Travis trashed Ashley's new bike," Sid explained.

"No freaking way," Shane said. "Oh man." He shook his head. "I'm really sorry, Ashley."

"It's fine," she said dismissively. "I'll take the old bike. Let's go."

She didn't wait for more questions. She had no interest in retelling the story.

She grabbed the old bike from the garage and climbed on, pedaling onto the road and leaving Sid and Shane hurrying to catch up with her.

Three blocks over, Ashley saw the birds and pointed. "Look."

She stopped in the middle of the street, feeling oddly calm.

"But Ash, it's not a good idea. Starfire is busted and-"

But she didn't wait to hear more. She jumped on the old bike, grinding the pedals until they clicked into gear and flew into the trees.

"Meet me at The Crawford House," she shouted over her shoulder.

The trail was rough, not one any of the kids used due to all the roots. She made noise as she rode, laughing, talking. She wasn't sure when she started to cry, but she noticed the cool wetness on her cheeks when the air hit them.

A sound emerged behind her. She glanced back, expecting to see the creature lumbering through the woods. Instead she spotted Travis Barron, a malicious grin on his face.

"Haven't had enough, spic?" he shouted.

Ashley almost stopped, and she felt her legs slow. She wasn't afraid of Travis. She wanted to fight. She wanted to toss her bike to the side, find a stick, and whack him across the face with all her strength. But beyond Travis, in the shadows of the trees, a white face glimmered. She faced forward and pumped her legs. The fear that hadn't been there seconds before stole over her, tracing the back of her neck like cold fingers.

She shuddered and cursed Travis in her mind. He was going to ruin everything.

Her brain scrambled ahead to the house.

Only one entrance and one exit. If Travis ran in behind her, he'd be trapped inside with the monster. A part of her wanted nothing more than to do just that, but knew she couldn't.

"Fucking Travis," she spit, her feet ramming the pedals.

She hit a root and came down hard, knowing instantly the back tire had gone flat again. Glancing down, she saw the tube breaking loose. It caught, and she had only a second to register what was happening. The bike stopped completely and sent her plunging forward. She leaped to the side, letting the bike fall in the path.

She landed on her feet, but then stumbled forward and pitched onto her hands. Behind her, Travis cursed as he ran over her bike, getting tangled and going down as well.

She didn't pause, but instead jumped up and ran for The Crawford House.

"Poser," she shrieked as she dodged through the trees. She needed Travis to follow her now. If she left him behind, the monster might attack him.

She hated Travis Barron, hated him more than she'd ever hated another human being, and yet she couldn't stomach his picture on the news the following morning. She might not make it, but she had to try.

42

*P*ercy rode in the passenger seat, staring out the window.

"Are you sure you're up for this, Percy?" Max asked for the third or fourth time.

The man looked pale. His eyes were yellow, and when he'd eaten his breakfast his hand shook so badly it had taken him several tries to manage a bite.

Percy turned to face him. "The children you told me about..." His face creased, and he touched a hand to his heart. "It's my fault they're dead. I brought the bones back. I practically gave them to Dr. Lance."

"Do you truly believe he could have fashioned the same dolls the tribe made? And that they'd work? They'd turn kids into the El Lobizon?"

Percy looked away, watching the trees. "I know he could. I described the dolls the tribe used. I gave him everything he needed. He chose children because he thought they'd be less dangerous. He was wrong."

"And I'm meant to believe it's a child then that's killing the kids in Roscommon?"

Percy sighed, rolling the window down and leaning out. When he pulled his head back in, he looked straight ahead as if he didn't want to look Max in the eyes. "It's a child's body, but it is the spirit of El Lobizon."

The drive to Traverse City took an hour. When they turned into the tunnel of trees leading to the towering asylum, Percy stiffened.

"Are you okay?" Max asked.

"Yes. I'm trying to imagine where he would hide the children. There are areas in the hospital that are closed, including an old children's wing. We should go there."

The children's wing occupied a desolate stretch on the ground floor of a large building that had been unoccupied for several years. As issues surrounding institutions came to light, coupled with advances in medication, much of the Northern Michigan Asylum had been closed.

Max pushed on the double doors, but they found them to be locked.

Percy leaned against a brick column. "Let's go around the side of the building."

As they walked the perimeter, they spotted a light shining from a window.

Max and Percy crept closer.

A series of twin beds stood side by side in the space. A rack held boy's clothes. One corner of the room contained children's toys, the kind young kids would play with, but Max also saw the types of things older boys would like as well. He noted three handheld video game players on a table. Teen boys' shoes sat in a neat row by the door.

The door to the room opened, and a man walked in.

Percy flinched, nearly falling onto his back. Max caught him.

"It's him," Percy hissed. "It's Guy Lance." He clutched his chest, his breathing ragged.

"Shh... okay. Breathe. Calm down, okay? I don't think your

body can handle all this excitement. Maybe you better wait in the car," Max said.

Percy stood up taller, dropping his hands to his sides.

"Absolutely not. I make amends for my sins, Max. I will not walk away."

Max sighed, flustered, but he didn't argue. "Where are the kids?"

Percy turned and gazed at the sky. "We're in the waxing moon cycle, still three-quarters full. They're experimenting with the bones. The kids are likely under the spell of the El Lobizon as we speak."

"What does that mean?" Max demanded. "That they're out killing people?"

Percy shook his head. "I certainly hope not. I'm sure they're confined when they transition. I think I know where they'd take them. There's a room in the woods. The day I saw Lance with the child, he was taking the boy in there."

Max and Percy walked into the dense forest behind the Northern Michigan Asylum. It was a moonless night, and the darkness seemed to harbor all the terrors of childhood, monsters and demons and evil witches who ate children. All the horror stories Max had ever heard felt much closer after hearing Percy's unbelievable tale, an impossible tale that made a frightening amount of sense.

They pushed into brush, feeling for the door Percy had described. After a half hour, Max's fear was replaced by frustration.

His mind wandered again and again to the worry that Percy was truly mad and Max had embarked on a futile quest and was wasting precious time.

He walked up to a wall of twisted vines and brush, pushing his hands into the mass.

His expected the tough edges of a berm, but found chilly

emptiness behind the brush. The temperature felt several degrees cooler.

"I think I found it," he said.

Percy ran to where he stood, shoving his flashlight into the darkness and forcing his head through.

Max followed him, shocked as he stepped through the brush into a dark stone tunnel. It was cool and clammy and stank of sulfur.

They'd made it only halfway down the tunnel when they saw the first body. The man, a doctor in a white lab coat, lay face down on the stone floor, a dark pool spiderwebbing out from his neck. Max knew what they'd see if they turned him over, a red gash opening his throat.

In the chamber, they saw four hospital beds with leather straps that had been ripped from the metal frames and lay discarded on the floor. Another doctor sat in a wooden chair, a clipboard on his lap, the white page he'd been writing on saturated in red. His throat lay open.

"They've all escaped," Percy said, touching one of the straps and cringing. "God help us."

"No!" A voice gasped behind them, startling Max and Percy.

Max turned to find Dr. Lance in the dark tunnel, his eyes bulging as he gazed at the dead man on the ground.

"You did this," Percy shrieked.

Lance's head shot up, and he stared disbelievingly at Percy.

"How-"

"How did I escape? How can I form sentences after all the drugs you gave me? Probably wishing you'd performed a lobotomy right now, aren't you, Guy? How could you?" Percy's voice shrilled.

But Dr. Lance didn't seem to understand. His eyes had returned to the doctor on the floor. Blood seeped from the wound at his neck.

Max, too, felt paralyzed by the gruesome scene, unable to think clearly about what must come next.

Lance stepped to one of the beds, he touched a strap. "They couldn't have," he murmured.

"You did this," Percy yelled again, though his accusation had lost some of its power. He stumbled to the wall and braced a hand against the stone.

"Where are the dolls?" Max demanded, finally remembering Percy's explanation. If they dismantled the dolls, the boys would become children again.

Lance didn't speak, he walked to the body of the man in the chair. "Fred?" he whispered, leaning close to the man's ear.

Max felt sick to his stomach. The man's head hung to the side. The gash looked fake, a horror movie prop too revolting to be believed.

"Guy," Percy demanded, his hoarse voice revealing his weakening state. "Where are the dolls? It's the only way to stop them."

Lance glanced up, his eyes registering Percy, and finally, his words. He looked around the room, and his gaze paused on a briefcase sitting on top of a pedestal that held a huge leather-bound book.

"There," Percy said.

Max strode to the case and grabbed it.

The leather suitcase was fastened with a small gold padlock. Max smashed the briefcase against the wall. The second time the clasp broke and fell to the floor. He laid the case down and clicked it open. Inside the case, he saw three objects wrapped in linen.

He unwrapped the first and stared at an ugly doll with yellow teeth poking from its cloth face.

The doll jolted him, and as he gazed at it, a disconcerting sense of déjà vu washed over Max.

"Three dolls and four beds," he whispered. "Where's the fourth doll?" he demanded of Lance.

Lance stepped away from the doctor in the chair. "Six weeks ago, a boy got away," he murmured. "He... he took the doll."

"One of them escaped?" Max demanded.

Lance nodded, walked to the bed and lifted one of the straps. "Vern. His name was Vern."

"Vern Ripley?" Max said. "Where did he go?"

"We suspect he returned to Roscommon."

Max frowned and glanced at the doll in his hand, still unnerved by the sense he'd seen it somewhere before.

"Are you saying that the animal who's killing kids is Vern Ripley?"

The man stared straight ahead. A shudder coursed up his body. "We had two men out there, but..." he opened his palms. "We couldn't track him down."

"You low down dog," Percy huffed, but he barely managed the words, leaning heavily on the wall, finally sinking to the floor.

From the tunnel, a growling emerged, and the doctor's eyes shot wide.

"It's one of them-"

But Dr. Lance didn't have time to complete his thought. The boy lunged from the shadows and shoved the doctor onto his back. His gaunt face sunk into the space beneath the doctor's chin and a spurt of blood burst from the man's neck.

"Stop, now. Get off," Max yelled, grabbing an empty chair and lifting it over his head.

"Don't hit him," Percy called, crawling across the floor to the leather case.

He pulled the dolls from the case and ripped them apart. Hair and bones and tattered cloth piled at his knees.

The boy didn't stop. His hands, the fingernails grown long and yellow, tore at the doctor's face. The boy's own face was a smear of blood from nose to chin. He snarled and shrieked, more animal than human.

When Percy lifted the last doll, the boy stiffened, head swiveling around to where Percy kneeled. He opened his mouth and let out an inhuman howl.

Max still held the chair raised, frozen, unable to bring it down.

The boy leapt from the doctor and ran into the dark tunnel leading back to the woods.

Max heaved the chair away. It hit a wall and splintered.

Percy ripped the doll to pieces.

Max stood in stunned silence, watching the doctor's coat slowly saturate red. He finally willed his legs to move. He ripped off his t-shirt and stuffed it into the wound in Guy Lance's neck.

The doctor stared at him, his mouth opened as if to speak, but nothing emerged. The man's eyes grew distant and then darkened as if a light behind the man's blue irises had blinked out.

Percy stepped to the doctor and pressed two fingers against his wrist. He leaned close to the man's face. "He's dead, Max."

As Max stared at the scattering of hair and bones, all that was left of the disgusting dolls, the memory came to him.

He had ducked beneath the weeping willow after following Ashley Shepherd, and there, on the picnic table, had been the doll, the same kind of doll he'd seen in the case.

"Holy shit," he said, hand going to his mouth. "We have to go, now!"

Percy scrambled across the floor, snatching at the bones and teeth, stuffing them into the briefcase.

"Now," Max shouted, grabbing Percy's arm and wrenching him to his feet.

Percy clutched the case to his chest, and they ran back into the night.

id and Shane had taken another path to The Crawford House. This one was well worn and occasionally marked by a kid's tennis shoe or random spray painted tree, allowing them to ride fast.

Sid tried not to think of Ashley on the opposite side of the woods, crashing through the undergrowth with a monster on her tail.

He had to stop the imaginings right there. Anything more made him want to scream and stamp his feet and rewind the clock three days to when they'd created their stupid plan and take it all back.

But it was too late now. Weird how that happened. One moment you were concocting the most insane scenario, knowing in the back of your mind you'd never go through with it, and in the next moment you were there, five minutes in, which might as well have been a lifetime because you couldn't turn back now.

The only way was forward, forward to The Crawford House, and what if Ashley didn't make it? What then?

Shane pulled ahead, and Sid gasped for breath as he tried to keep pace. At the place the forest grew thick, they jumped off the bikes, not bothering to stash them.

Shane reached The Crawford house first, and Sid skidded into the clearing behind him.

The sky had the glazed red color of a day's end.

"Red sky at night, sailor's delight," he whispered, not sure why the words mattered in that moment, but needing to say them anyway. They weren't sailors, but it still felt like a good omen.

Shane went to the front door and cocked it open. Then he raced all the way to the back where Sid watched him plunge out the window they'd left open, as if doing a trial run. He landed on his feet, wobbled, and then found his balance.

Sid looked at his watch. Seven minutes had passed since Ashley had raced into the woods. He didn't know how long it should have taken her, but definitely no more than ten minutes.

He paced to the front of the house and then to the back again.

Shane had disappeared, and Sid heard a rustling overhead. He looked up to find Shane in a tree.

"Do you see her?" Sid asked, voice catching.

"No."

Shane jumped down, opened his backpack and handed Sid a hammer.

"Get ready to nail the door closed. We won't have much time," Shane said. "We've got to position ourselves so we can see her get here, but still have time to close the window before the monster escapes. You watch from here and yell a warning when she and the monster are in the house, get it? If you yell too soon, the thing might come after you."

Sid stared at Shane, piecing together his words. He glanced at his watch. Twelve minutes had passed.

"Get it?" Shane repeated, and he eyed Sid warily as if he knew Sid would screw up.

Even if everything went perfectly, Sid would somehow be the reason the whole plan failed.

"Yeah, yeah, I've got it. I'm fine," Sid assured him, though he wasn't fine, the situation wasn't fine, and it took all his strength not to plunge into the woods and race for home.

Fifteen minutes had passed when he heard the first crunching of branches, a stampeding through the forest as if a herd of deer were headed their way.

When Ashley broke from the trees, her face was red and her eyes were narrowed on The Crawford house.

"Ash," he called out.

He couldn't help it. His relief at seeing her nearly sent him to his knees.

She glanced sideways. "Travis is behind me," she yelled, but didn't have time for more because she was already pounding up the steps and disappearing into the blackhole at the front of the house.

Travis was seconds behind her, his eyes black and sharp as he took the stairs three at a time.

For a moment, Sid thought it was only them, Ashley and Travis, no monster at all, but then it emerged.

Sid stepped back, heart leaping from his chest into his throat. He held his breath.

The boy, for clearly that's what he'd once been, lurched from the forest. He walked upright a few steps only to fall forward and use his hands. He moved fast. His hair looked grimy and thick with twigs. The skin of his face and arms appeared gray and sore looking. Scratches and welts ran up his arms and over his neck.

The boy crawled up the stairs and slipped into the house.

Two seconds, and then five more, passed, and finally the Sid who wasn't a total bonehead yelled the warning call to Shane.

He ran to the front of the house, pulled the boards hanging loose into place, and started hammering nails into them.

"Stop, wait," Shane yelled, running around the house.

He was waving his arms, but Sid couldn't stop the hammer.

Bam-bam-bam, one nail in. Three to go.

"Sid," Shane shouted, bounding up the steps and ripping the hammer from Sid's hand.

Sid's eyes bulged, and he started to grab for the hammer.

"Something happened to Ashley," Shane shrieked. "She didn't come out. I heard her inside. She screamed."

Sid started to shake his head, to refuse his words, but Shane had stopped paying attention to him. He ripped the boards off and threw them to the side before running into the house.

Sid stood on the porch, frozen. The sticky heat of the day plastered his shirt against his soft body. His breath lay trapped in his lungs, full to bursting, and when he finally exhaled, the Sid who wasn't a coward urged him into the house, whispering in his ear as if he were a little baby.

Come on, Sid. You can do this. Save Ashley, Sid.

But of course, he couldn't do it, not really. But Shane could. Shane could save Ashley and punch Travis and defeat the monster, and afterward they'd all walk home and share a Dr. Pepper. And this time Sid would take a drink.

Except that was the plot for a Halloween special on television. In real life, monsters ripped out kids' throats and left them in the woods to die.

ASHLEY STOOD IN THE CORNER, paralyzed as the monster, who she realized had once been Vern Ripley, attacked Travis.

Vern clawed and bit at Travis's back. The boy had curled into a tiny ball and shrieked for help.

Ashley had made it to the window and had almost jumped through when she'd heard Travis's scream of pain. She could have left him. She almost did.

"Damn you," she spat.

She grabbed the leg of an old chair, jerking and smacking the chair down to break the leg free. She hit the monster in the back.

It howled and turned to face her, its mouth red with Travis's blood. It lunged, grabbed her leg in its teeth and bit down. She screamed, feeling a hot burning as it tore through her skin.

Shane burst into the room, an aluminum baseball bat raised above his head. He swung at the monster.

It released Ashley's leg, and she stumbled back, her ankle oozing.

The monster's hands, curling into claws, grabbed the bat and jerked Shane forward.

Shane let go, but the monster had brought him close enough. It jumped, animal-like, and Shane toppled over. Shane put up his hands, but the monster's face darted around them and bit into the side of Shane's head.

"No," Ashley screamed, grabbing the rest of the broken chair and struggling to stand on one knee as she bashed it into the thing's back. It lifted its head and snarled, jumping onto Ashley.

A rock flew from the hallway and hit the monster in the chest.

The rock bounced off and landed near Ashley's head.

"Come on," Sid screamed. "Come get me."

44

Sid scrambled down the stairs and into the tile room, which had once been used as the embalming chamber. His breath hitched, and he pressed himself to the wall. Across the room, something moved behind a dirty pane of glass. The room contained a small window that looked into another room. As Sid watched, something pressed close to the grimy glass.

Sid saw its sunken face, mud streaked hair hanging limp on its translucent forehead. The eyes in its skull were as black as midnight.

Walking backward, bumping numbly against the wall, Sid opened his mouth and began to mumble.

"No, no, no, please, no, no."

The thing in the window pressed its face closer, its mouth against the glass now, bloody from Shane.

Shane was probably dead. And the thing that had killed him stood only a pane of glass away from Sid.

Sid ran from the room, but he couldn't reach the stairs without facing the monster. He ducked into the room filled with coffins.

Outside, the sun had gone down and soon he'd be surrounded by blackness and trapped in a room of coffins with a child-eating beast.

He cowered behind a coffin as the monster stepped into the room, walking as if he were half dog, using his hands as if they were feet.

Sid crouched and scurried to another coffin and then another until he spotted the open doorway.

He ran for it, the boy monster let out a shriek of rage, but Sid willed his legs up the stairs.

He burst through the front door into the open air, the oncoming night thick with the sound of crickets.

He raced through the trees, thorny branches snatching at his clothes, sweat pouring into his eyes and making them sting.

The monster crashed through the brush behind him. It snarled and sometimes spoke in odd human sounds, yet not.

Sid ran until the stitch in his side felt like a razor blade cutting his abdomen. He'd gotten turned around, though he didn't know when.

Full night had fallen, and the moon was mostly hidden by thick clouds.

His feet hit hard ground, and his toe caught on a rock. He pitched forward and landed on hands and knees. He suddenly knew where he was at: the pit.

Behind him, branches snapped and breath heaved from the boy monster who stalked him through the woods.

Sid looked around wildly, his mind blank for an escape. Could the creature swim?

Sid imagined diving into the black water and watching as the beast followed him in, circled below him, and reached up to grasp his ankle.

He shook his head and plunged forward, coming to the high cliff and looking down for a dizzying moment. He no longer had time to decide.

The monster had broken from the trees, its face white and leering, black eyes shimmering in the moonlight.

Sid turned and crouched, grabbing ahold of the ledge and lowering himself over the side, planting his feet on outcroppings of rock. His heart hammered. His hands felt slick, as if he'd rubbed oil on them, and he knew any moment, he'd lose his hold and begin to fall.

He imagined Stone from his and Ashley's story. Stone, of the cat people with perfect night vision. Stone, who had to descend into the black depths of the deep water to save Sapphire from death.

As he climbed down, his foot swung in, finding open air rather than the rock wall. He'd come to the Witch's Cave.

Painstakingly, he moved sideways, finally wrapping his arm around the rock and stepping onto the ledge of cave. Unable to see, he crawled on hands and knees into the darkness.

As he crept deeper, his legs trembled, his muscles threatening to seize at any moment. When his hands caught something soft and stringy he gasped, jerking his fingers back.

He fumbled with the lighter he'd stolen from his dad's pants pocket and struggled to depress the button.

The orange flame leapt out, offering a halo of light.

He stared at the hairy thing on the ground, his brain piecing the image into something sensical. As it registered, he felt the throb of his bladder. It pinched and then let go. Urine seeped out and soaked his pants.

A mass of pale blonde hair lay piled below him. Dark streaks matted the once light hair. Beneath the hair, he saw the slope of a shoulder. The pale skin was mottled and gray.

Sid didn't move. Shock caused every muscle in his body to firm into concrete. His breath wheezed out from his clenched teeth.

"Oh god, oh god," he whispered, the stones of the cave biting into his knees, the stink of his piss only mild compared to the other smell, the rancid smell of Melanie Dunlop's body.

~

SID HAD LURED the monster away.

Ashley stared into the dark forest where Sid and the thing had disappeared.

Beneath her palms, blood oozed thick and warm from Shane's head. She felt the mush of his ear and the throb of his heartbeat through the pulsing blood. She'd dragged him onto the porch, but he was too heavy.

Her ankle throbbed.

She had to leave him to get help.

It took ages to break from the trees, and when she did, the road lay empty and dark. She limped toward the houses she knew lay several blocks away.

Suddenly, headlights barreled toward her and she paused, gazing at the oncoming car, but unable to move.

The car's brakes screamed as it skidded to a stop. The driver's door opened, and a man jumped out. Only when he stepped into the beam of his headlights, did Ashley recognize Mr. Wolf.

"Ashley?" He took her by the shoulders. "Come on," he said.

To her surprise, he didn't ask what had happened. He scooped her up and deposited her in the backseat.

"You have to help them," Ashley begged, blood filling her sock and soon her tennis shoe.

"Sid and Shane. The monster's after them."

Max and the man in his passenger seat exchanged a worried look.

"Where's the doll, Ashley," Mr. Wolf demanded.

"The doll? What? No! Didn't you hear me? They're hurt. They'll die."

"The only way to stop Vern is to destroy the doll. We have to get to the doll first," he insisted, craning around in his seat.

His words sunk in. The doll they'd found in the coffin.

"It's in my house," she blurted. "But we have to call the police because Shane Savage and Travis Barron are both hurt. They're in The Crawford house."

SID DIDN'T MOVE until he heard the unmistakable sound of something climbing into the cave.

He released the lighter. The darkness immediate and unnerving.

It was coming for him. He would die like Melanie. When his parents went to bed each night his mother would soak her pillow with tears and his father would gaze in sleepless worry at the ceiling above him. But worst of all, he would leave Ashley. He would never see his best friend again.

The thought so jolted him that he stood to his feet, squaring off against the mouth of the cave.

He didn't wait for the monster to come in and devour him.

He barreled forward at full speed and pushed the boy as hard as he could.

The creature howled and reached out its bony hands to grab ahold of Sid, but Sid's own arms and hands were slick with sweat.

The monster plummeted backward into the yawning sky that hovered over the pit below.

The monster shrieked, but his cry was swallowed by the dark water.

*A*shley sat on her front steps, a blanket draped over her shoulders.

Max had shredded the doll on her kitchen table while the other man had carefully collected the bones and teeth and tucked them into his pocket.

They left Ashley to phone the police while Max had raced to The Crawford House to help the boys.

More than an hour passed before he returned, and when his car pulled into her driveway, she jumped to her feet, wincing at the sting in her ankle.

Mr. Wolf stepped from the car. "Shane and Travis have both been taken to the hospital. They're alive," he said.

She nodded, grateful even for Travis's life being saved, but...

"Did you find Sid?" she asked, balling her fists at her sides.

Max's face fell.

"I'm sorry, Ash. I looked and I called for him. There are men searching the woods. We'll find him," Max promised, but his voice sounded hollow, and Ashley knew they hadn't destroyed the doll in time.

If only they'd have known. They could have ended it all the moment they'd found it.

"It's not your fault, Ashley," Max said, as if reading her mind.

Ashley sat back on the step, dropping her head.

How would she live without her best friend?

Max rested a hand on her shoulder, and Ashley leaned into him and started to cry.

"Wait, what's that?" Max asked suddenly, standing up.

She squinted into the darkness trying to place the sound. A rhythmic whoosh grew closer and the unmistakable plink, plink of Spokey Dokeys sliding up and down the spokes of a bicycle.

Ashley shot to her feet, this time the pain in her ankle didn't register as she ran to the end of her driveway.

Sid rode into the beam of a streetlight.

When he saw Ashley, he rode faster. At her driveway, he jumped off and ran to her, throwing his arms around her.

"You're alive," she sputtered, crying as they hugged.

ASHLEY DIDN'T TELL her mother what had transpired.

After Max and Percy sat with Ash and Sid and explained Percy's trip to the Amazon, the doll, and the El Lobizon, they all agreed no one would ever believe them.

Instead the story was quite simple. Travis Barron chased the kids into the house, and an animal had attacked them.

Travis told a different story when he awoke, but it was brushed off by the adults. Travis had a tendency to tell tall tales. And here was another one meant to cast the blame on someone else.

The following day Ashley and Sid sat in Shane's hospital room. Sid played with the stethoscope, pressing it to different places on his chest. "I must be dead because I can't hear a thing," he muttered.

"Not funny," Ash told him, rolling her eyes.

Shane sat in bed, sipping a milkshake. The left half of his head was covered in bandages.

The monster had bitten off part of his ear, and he'd lost a lot of blood.

After Sid and Ashley filled him in on Percy's story, he sat incredulous. "So, he was like a werewolf?" he asked, setting his shake aside. "Do you think he's dead?" he asked Sid.

Sid's face fell. "I don't know. I hope not."

"Me too," Ashley agreed. "But you did the right thing, Sid. He was going to kill you."

Sid nodded.

Shane leaned sideways and scrambled for the remote control on his bedside table. "Look," he blurted, turning up the volume.

A reporter stood in front of Vern Ripley's house. Vern's mother was crying, barely held up by her large husband.

"He came home in the middle of the night. Starved, clearly abused, but alive. Thank you, God, he's alive." She cast her hands to the sky as if sending her words up to the heavens.

"Did he tell you who abducted him?" The reporter asked. "What does he know about his captors?"

Vern's mother shook her head and wept.

Darwin Ripley spoke for her. "He's being treated at the hospital. His doctors believe his memory may come back, but right now." He shrugged. "He doesn't remember a thing. He was soaking wet when we opened the door last night. His shirt was stained with blood. That's all we know."

The segment shifted to the pit. In the distance, yellow tape marked off the cliff that led to the Witch's Cave.

Sid paled and looked away.

Shane lifted the remote and clicked off the television.

"Vern lived," Ashley said.

"And Melanie died," Sid murmured.

"But it's over now," Shane finished. "It's over."

EPILOGUE

*M*ax spotted Percy sitting in the corner of the coffee shop, a map spread from end to end on the table before him.

"Max," he beamed, standing and pulling Max into a hug.

The man looked better, good even. A healthy pink color had replaced his pallor and his hair had grown out an inch. A compass hung from a leather strap around his neck.

"My physician has cleared me for travel. I'm not sure I'll come back this time," Percy announced, gesturing at the map.

Max glanced down and returned his gaze to Percy, surprised.

"Brazil? You're going back?"

Percy nodded.

"I have to return the bones, Max. I won't be at peace until I do. And honestly, I miss the simplicity of life in the Amazon. The new world is a complicated place. Sometimes I think I should have been born in another time."

Max sat and stared at the crisscross of rivers and the dense patches of forest.

"Will they hurt you? For stealing the bones?"

Percy shrugged.

"Nothing compared to what Guy Lance did to me. And here, this is for you."

Percy pulled a leather journal from a canvas bag.

Max opened it and read the first page.

Max saw names listed, including Nicholas Watts, Chris Rowe, Vern Ripley and another boy he'd never heard of, Ferris Maloney.

Max closed the book, disgusted.

"It's all in there. When they took the kids, when they turned them, and a lot of other stuff too. Disturbing stuff." Percy offered.

Max nodded, pushing the book away though he knew he'd have to read it at some point.

But not just then.

Kim's son Nicholas had been found in Kinglsey, a town south of Traverse City, barefoot and confused. There was no one to claim him. His mother had been murdered and his father rotted in jail.

Martha from Ellie's House had called Max and told him.

Without a moment's hesitation, Max had gone to the hospital to retrieve him.

The thought of reading the specifics of the torture Nicholas endured caused a shudder to roll down Max's spine.

"Thank you, Percy," Max said, standing and slipping the journal in his back pocket. "And good luck."

"Can I go?" Nicholas asked Max, some of the shyness of the previous days had dissolved.

Ashley, Sid, and Shane stood at the end of his driveway, their bikes beside them, their faces hopeful.

He grinned at Ashley's bike, offering her a thumbs up.

After she'd told him the story of what Travis had done, Max had gone to Travis's house and demanded his parents pay to fix the bike. Not wanting to attract any more negative attention regarding their son, they'd done just that. Starfire looked as good as new.

Nicholas watched him expectantly.

"Yeah, absolutely. Have fun, guys," Max said, fighting the urge to warn them away from the woods or insist they check back within a couple hours.

Jake sat on his porch drinking a bottle of beer. He waved goodbye to the kids. "Family life looks good on you, Maxy," his brother told him.

Max smiled, still unsure of himself as a parent.

Technically he wasn't a parent. Guardianship papers had only just been filed. It would be months before the court ruled on whether or not Nicholas Watts could stay with him permanently, but in the meantime, this was good enough.

He walked to the chair beside Jake and sat down, lifting his beer and clinking it against his brother's.

Max sighed and rested his head back.

A blue butterfly with black striped wings landed on his outstretched arm. The butterfly paused, flapped its wings several times, and then took flight.

He watched it arc high, catch a breeze, and float down before flying off in the direction the kids had ridden.

Want more Rag Doll Bones? Grab your Bonus Epilogue Here. Send Me the Epilogue!

**Read on for a preview of the next book in the Northern Michigan Asylum Series:
Dark Omen**

DARK OMEN

rologue

T<small>HE</small> N<small>ORTHERN</small> M<small>ICHIGAN</small> Asylum
1966

Greta Claude

"I <small>WON'T!"</small>

Greta woke to the sound of Maribelle's shouts echoing up the stairs.

She blinked at the ceiling and sat up, pulling the blanket to her chin.

"You'll do as I say," their father, Joseph, bellowed.

Greta cringed at the sharp crack that followed and knew Maribelle's cheek was probably throbbing from the impact of Joseph's large hand.

Maribelle screamed and began to cry.

Greta jumped from the bed and raced down the stairs as the front door swung closed.

Through the window, Greta watched her twin sister, Maribelle, disappear into the grassy trail behind their house.

Joseph stood in the kitchen, his hands fisted at his sides. He turned and glared at Greta, and she shrank from his furious gaze.

"Go clean the basement," he snarled. "I'm going after your sister."

He stormed out the door, toward the wooded path that led from the caretaker's house, where they'd lived since birth, into the acres of forests surrounding the Northern Michigan Asylum.

"Don't hurt her," Greta cried out, but her voice was drowned by his heavy footfalls on the porch steps.

When she reached the concrete floor in the basement, the stench of blood and urine overpowered her. Other smells mingled with the odor; smells Greta had learned to associate with death.

Greta pulled her t-shirt over her nose, letting it hang there. She flailed her hand through the darkness, the drawn-out seconds in the black basement causing her heart to crash against her chest as if it too wanted to race back up the stairs and into the daylight.

She found the lightbulb string and yanked, illuminating the blood.

Dark and wet, it lay in a fresh puddle in the center of the floor. The body was gone, but drag marks left the pool and streaked toward the stairs.

Greta looked down and realized she was standing in one of the bloody drag marks. She peeled off her white socks, ruined, and stuffed them into the crumpled garbage bag her father had left.

She grabbed the bucket from the laundry basin and turned on the tap. Rust-colored water spewed into the bucket. She rinsed it and filled it again. The water had the sulfurous odor of rotten eggs, but was preferable to the fluids coating the basement floor.

As she wet a rag and returned to the blood, she hummed "Ring Around the Rosie," a song she and Maribelle liked to sing when they ran through the woods behind the asylum.

Greta sopped up the blood and dipped the rag into the bucket, wringing it and watching the red swirl into the brown water. When the brown water turned red, Greta emptied the bucket and refilled it.

She refilled the bucket five times before the pool of blood was washed away. She swept the bit of remaining water into the drain in the floor.

Greta stuffed the soiled rags into the black plastic bag, her eyes flitting over a single white tennis shoe, the laces stained pink. She tied the bag and then scrubbed her hands with lye soap until they were raw and tingling.

She turned off the light and hurried to her room, to put on a dress before Mrs. Martel, their home-school teacher, arrived.

Maribelle arrived only minutes before Mrs. Martel. She limped into the house with a tear-streaked face.

Greta could see a purple bruise spreading on Maribelle's knee.

"Come on," Greta insisted. "Let's clean you up, quick."

Maribelle cried quietly as Greta sponged off her face and quickly braided her unruly dark hair. She pulled Maribelle's nightgown over her head and cringed at hand-shaped welts on Maribelle's back.

"I hate him," Maribelle whispered. "I hate him so much."

CHAPTER 1

𝒩 ow
June 14ᵗʰ, 1991

BETTE DROVE THROUGH THE EIGHT-FOOT, wrought-iron gates marking the entrance to Eternal Rest, the cemetery where they'd buried her mother eleven years before.

Parking on the grassy shoulder, Bette popped the trunk and stepped from her car.

The cemetery was quiet at four-thirty in the afternoon. The trees watched, large and silent, as Bette pulled out the box that she and Crystal took to their mother's grave every year. It contained the Edgar Allen Poe poetry book they'd take turns reciting from, a handful of photographs, and Bette's letter to their mother. Crystal was bringing the flowers and she'd have her own letter.

Bette knelt in front of the marble headstone, heart shaped and engraved with her mother's name: Joanna Kay Meeks. December 15, 1947 – June 14, 1980. Their father's name, the death date not yet filled in, stood next to Jo's on the headstone, and Bette cringed whenever she saw it.

Bette and Crystal's father had offered to buy plots for his girls when their mother died, but they had both balked. At eleven and thirteen, they were hardly planning their future deaths.

As the minutes ticked by, Bette stood and paced away from the grave. She gazed at the winding road that led through the hilly cemetery, searching for Crystal's distinctive sky-blue Volkswagen Beetle.

Her sister didn't appear.

At five o'clock, irritated, Bette put the box in her trunk and drove to a payphone.

She dialed Crystal's number and left a message before calling her own number, on the chance that Crystal had gotten confused and gone to the house. Bette's machine picked up.

When an hour passed and still no Crystal, Bette drove home and called her sister again.

Crystal's machine picked up.

"Hi, you've missed me. Hopefully I'm on a daring adventure, but if all goes well, I'll eventually make it home to call you back."

"Crystal, it's Bette. Again." Her voice took on the high-pitched notes of early anxiety. "In case you forgot, we have dinner reservations, and we're planting flowers on Mom's grave tonight. You know, like we've done on June fourteenth for the last ten years."

Bette hung up and stared at her clock.

Their dinner reservations were in ten minutes and obviously they wouldn't be making it.

For another twenty minutes, Bette sat at the kitchen table, fuming, and silently willing the door to open and her free-spirited sister to come bouncing through with tales of rescuing a kitten in the road or driving a hitchhiker halfway across the county to make it on time for the birth of his child. Two stories which had actually happened, but never on the anniversary of their mother's death.

Crystal had never forgotten their mother's anniversary, and she'd never missed their yearly ritual.

As Bette tapped her foot and watched the clock, the sense of urgency in her stomach curdled into fear, and she realized that had been the root of her anxiety all along: not frustration that they'd be late to dinner, but fear. The fear crept up her legs and settled in the base of her spine. It clicked its fangs and tapped its sharpened claws. It would gnaw a hole right through her if she didn't do something.

The fear was unwarranted. Crystal was only an hour and a half late, but it had gripped Bette in its talons just the same.

A photo of Crystal and Bette, arm in arm, sat on the bureau next to the kitchen table. The bureau was filled with dishes, things their mother had loved and that Bette, still living in her childhood home, had never been able to part with.

She gazed at the silver-framed photograph. Crystal's red-gold hair hung long and wavy, flowing over each shoulder. Bette's own hair, also long, was stick straight and dark.

"Where are you?" she whispered to the picture.

Unable to sit still another moment, Bette stood and grabbed the phone, dialing her sister again and slamming the phone down when the machine picked up. Next, she called her father, gritting her teeth when his voicemail clicked on.

"Dad, it's Bette. Call me right away."

Bette walked stiffly to her car and climbed behind the wheel.

Though less than two years separated Bette and Crystal, Bette had often felt like a much older sister. She was the practical, sensible one. At twenty-four, she had a serious job as a research assistant for an anthropology professor, and she was well on her way to receiving her doctorate.

Crystal, on the other hand, had spent the first two years after high school traveling the world. She'd finally returned a year before and enrolled at Michigan State University. She worked a series of minimum-wage jobs and refused to do anything out of obligation. She loved to say, *"Should is not in my vocabulary."*

Bette let herself into Crystal's apartment with her spare key, sweeping through the space quickly. Crystal wasn't home, but Bette peeked into every room just the same.

In Crystal's bathroom, she spotted a damp towel and a long t-shirt, probably what Crystal had worn to bed the night before.

A hand-scrawled note was stuck to the vanity mirror.

"The day I met you, a part of me dissolved,
Slipped into the earth and rooted beneath you, grew up inside of you,
You are always with me now. I am always with you."

Bette read the words under her breath.

Weston Meeks hadn't signed his name, but he hadn't needed to.

Bette had heard how the man spoke to her sister.

The professor, who taught poetry at Michigan State University, had swept Crystal off her feet. Despite the age gap, ten years give or take, Crystal had fallen madly, stupidly in love with the man.

"Apparently, the feelings are mutual," Bette said dryly.

A calendar hung in Crystal's kitchen with a few notes scribbled in the small boxes. She didn't post her work schedule and probably didn't record half of her appointments. Crystal simply wasn't a planner.

She had however, noted the anniversary of their mother's death and written: "Evening with Bette."

Except she hadn't shown up, and her apartment was empty.

Bette walked across the hall to apartment four. It belonged to Crystal's friend, Garrett. Bette had only met him once. He was a beautiful gay man who dressed impeccably, and often sat with Crystal in their little apartment courtyard drinking wine and lamenting his latest break-up.

Bette knocked on the door.

She could hear music in the apartment. It sounded like Michael Jackson.

The door swung open and Garett grinned at her. He wore gym shorts and a tank top, wrist and ankle weights adorning his limbs.

"Bette!" he exclaimed. "How are you? I'm just getting my exercise in." He jogged in place, sweat glistening on his tanned face. "No Crystal?" he asked, making a sad face and peeking past her down the hall.

"No, she was supposed to meet me. Have you seen her?" Bette asked.

"Billie Jean!" he gushed. "This is my all-time favorite Michael Jackson song." He snapped his fingers. "I saw her this morning. I think she was going for coffee. We didn't chat long. I was itching to get a meatloaf in the crock-pot. My friend David's coming over tonight, and I'm hoping he'll see how domesticated I can be." He winked at her.

Bette shuffled her feet and glanced back towards Crystal's closed door. "Did she say she had somewhere else to go after getting coffee?"

He wrinkled his brow and shook his head.

"I'm afraid I barely let her get a word in edge-wise — hot date and all."

"All right. Thanks Garret. Tell her to call me if you see her."

"Sure thing, Betts." He grinned, giving her a salute and closing his door.

Bette left the apartment building and stood in the parking lot. Crystal's blue VW Beetle was nowhere in sight.

Bette climbed into her own car and drove to the coffee shop.

Crystal worked at Sacred Grounds part time, mostly on weekends, but she was friends with the other employees and dropped by at least once a day for a cup of coffee or to chat with her friends.

Rick stood at the counter, wiping down the surface. Crystal had told Bette that Rick had an obsession with Nirvana and in particular Kurt Cobain. He'd even grown out and dyed his hair to match the singer's dishwater-blond, uncombed look.

"Hey Bette, how's it going?" he asked.

Bette glanced quickly around at the tables.

"Has Crystal been in?" Bette asked, moving closer to a booth in the corner where a redhead sat with her back to the coffee counter.

The woman laughed and turned sideways. Her laugh was deep and gravelly, not like Crystal's at all, and when she turned Bette realized the woman was well into her fifties.

Rick nodded.

"She came in this morning and had a coffee and one of Minerva's famous butterscotch scones. We've got two left if you're interested." He pointed at the display case showcasing the sugary treats.

Bette's stomach felt like a block of cement.

"No, thanks. About what time was that?"

Rick turned and looked at the Cheshire-cat clock that hung over the trays of variously colored coffee mugs.

"I'd say nine-ish."

"Okay, thanks." Bette started toward the door and then turned back. "Was she alone?"

Rick scratched his stubbly chin and nodded.

"Yeah. Her friend was in here. Um, her name starts with a G. Grace, maybe... But Crystal didn't stay for long."

"Okay, thanks."

Bette walked out to her car and slid behind the wheel.

Grace... Bette searched for the friend in her mind. Someone

that Crystal met at the bookstore, at college, maybe at Hospice House. Impossible to say. Crystal had a thousand friends, and she made them everywhere. Bette often joked that Crystal couldn't get a tank of gas without making a new friend.

Bette drove to The Reader's Retreat, a used bookstore on Pearl Street. She parked and pushed into the dimly lit space, which smelled of coffee, incense, and old books.

The shop's owner, Freddie, had fallen in love with Crystal the moment he'd seen her despite being thirty years her senior, married and with six kids. Theirs was a love affair that existed only in Freddie's mind, and he wasn't afraid to say so. Crystal worked the third weekend of every month at the store in exchange for free books.

Freddie sat in an overstuffed chair; a box of books balanced on the scarred coffee table before him.

"Bette," he said, smiling and blowing a layer of silt off the book in his hand. "If I wasn't just thinking of you not ten minutes ago. Lookie here." He stood and shuffled behind the heavy oak desk where an ancient typewriter sat next to an equally ancient cash register. Freddie's was the only business in Lansing that refused to accept credit cards.

He held up a copy of *On the Origin of Species* by Charles Darwin.

"It's a fourth edition. Impeccably cared for. Look at that binding. Not a single crack."

Bette nodded, barely looking at the book over which she normally would have salivated.

"It's beautiful, Freddie, but I'm looking for Crystal. She was supposed to meet me almost two hours ago and never showed. Has she been in today?"

Freddie stared at her, not believing her lack of reaction to the treasure in his hand. When she continued to wait silently, he set the book on his desk and returned to his chair.

"Not so much as a crimson hair has passed through that door in two weeks. She's been busy with that new flame, I'm sure. A sword to the heart, I might add," he said, clutching his chest as if mortally wounded.

CHAPTER 2

hen

CRYSTAL WATCHED Professor Meeks stride into the auditorium, his smile easy, chatting with a student who followed him like a duckling after its mother.

"Welcome to Poetry 101," he announced, striding to the blackboard behind him. "I'm Professor Meeks, and I'll be the guy trying to look like a beatnik up here at the desk all semester, or so I've been told."

The class laughed.

"Truth be told, had I been born in the age of the beatniks, I would surely have joined them. Instead, I've been blessed with the lot of you."

He started to go through the syllabus outlining the poetry they'd focus on that semester.

Meeks seemed to be in his early thirties. His sandy brown hair brushed his shoulders, and a neatly trimmed beard covered the lower half of his face. He was handsome and looked the part of a shaggy poet. Crystal imagined him sitting at a scratched wooden desk drinking scotch and pouring his soul into a tattered notebook before collapsing into bed, exhausted.

He'd have only a shred of passion left for teaching, but he'd stretch and warp it until he could cast a luminous veil over every student in the room.

He wore dark jeans and a t-shirt covered with a wrinkled-looking blazer. As he spoke, his hands flew nearly as fast as his lips, and the students in the room watched him, rapt.

Crystal had read both of Professor Meeks' poetry chapbooks, crying during each as she'd sat at her favorite coffee shop listening to Christmas music and missing her mother. Poetry and memories of her mother walked hand in hand in Crystal's life. The poetry could be unrelated, about seagulls or lemons, and still she'd find the words curving into the shape of her mother's smile or softening like her hands.

Meeks wrote about abandonment, fear, travel and love. It was the love poems that had struck her like a bell deep in her ribs. The reverberation continued for days after she'd read them. She'd been excited to meet the man who'd put the heart's longings, the sheer magnitude of them, onto a one-dimensional page.

When his eyes fell upon Crystal, he paused, his sentence cut in half, the silence stretching out long and empty.

He ducked his head, breaking the stare, and chuckled.

"Sorry folks, lost my train of thought there."

As the lecture continued, Professor Meeks kept his gaze averted. Whenever he drifted toward the right side of the stadium seats where Crystal sat, he'd pause as if realizing his mistake and shift his eyes left.

When class ended, Crystal made her way to the front of the room.

Up close, she saw thick dark lashes fringed the professor's blue eyes.

"Professor," she said.

He glanced away from the boy he'd been talking to, and his smile faltered as if he'd been struck silent for a second time as he stared at her.

The student glanced at Crystal as well and then back at the professor.

"I'm just nervous," the boy said, tugging on the collar of his gray polo shirt. "I've never read any of my poems out loud. My girlfriend says Open Mic Night is the perfect time to share, but... " He grimaced as if the mere suggestion brought him physical pain. "I'm sick at the thought of it."

The professor smiled and put a hand on the boy's arm.

"Forget the crowd, Ben," Meeks said. "Choose one person. Better yet, bring your best friend or your girlfriend. Bring the person you can read the poem to and mean every word. Read to them and only them."

Ben swallowed a big shaky breath and nodded.

"Okay," he said. "Bring one friend. Thanks, Professor."

He nodded and headed from the room, continuing to mumble the advice to himself.

"Hi," Meeks said, returning his gaze to Crystal. "And you are?"

"Crystal Childs."

She held out her hand, though it seemed an awkward thing to do suddenly.

He grinned and shook it.

"Lovely to meet you, Crystal Childs."

Their hands lingered together, warmth coursing from his hand into hers. She gazed at him, their eyes, like their hands, lingering overlong.

He forced his eyes away as if with great effort and stared down at the desk where he shuffled papers together. "Are you looking forward to Poetry 101?"

She heard him trying to sound casual, forcing an ease that

didn't flow into his limbs. He looked stiff, awkward, as if he suddenly wasn't sure what to do with his body.

"I've been excited to start this class for weeks," she confessed. "I read *Musings in the Morning Light* and *Long Drives.*"

He studied her, as if surprised by the admission.

"I must admit, it's rare that a student reads my work before the semester starts. I try not to force my own poetry on my classes. My goal is to teach you the greats."

"It was…" she murmured, "great." And it had been. She thought of the poem titled *Her*, a long list of words that described a mother present in the flesh, but never in the heart.

He took a step back as if the space between them had grown too small, though it hadn't changed.

"Thank you. I've been writing poetry for twenty years, and I still stammer when someone comments on my work. That's the beauty of it, though. The vulnerability. Of course, your experience of my poetry has nothing to do with me at all."

Crystal smiled and nodded, studying the fine bones beneath his large, long-fingered hands.

"That's why I'm drawn to poetry. It evokes something different in us all," she murmured.

"Exactly," he agreed, reaching to grab a planner on his desk.

His hand brushed Crystal's, and she shivered. The contact moved between them like an electric current. Soft and enveloping, as if someone had thrown a sheet, warm from the dryer, over top of them. For an instant they were together beneath that shroud, tucked safely, solidly, and then the door banged open and a girl, probably a freshman judging from her frazzled expression and the campus map clutched in her hand, burst in.

"I'm sorry. Is this Poetry 101?" she squeaked.

Professor Meeks blinked, took another step away from Crystal, and nodded.

"Yes, you're in the right place. Grab a seat wherever," he told her.

He returned his gaze to Crystal and now he didn't break away from her eyes.

"I have to…" he gestured at his notes as if in explanation.

"Yeah, absolutely. I'm sorry to have kept you, Professor Meeks."

"Wes," he told her, reaching out as she turned and touching her wrist.

He looked surprised that he'd offered the word, his name, to a student he'd only just met.

"Thank you, Wes," she said and left.

She paused at the confused student who peered at the two hundred seats in the room as if her seat choice was the first question on the exam, and she was bound to fail.

Crystal pointed to the upper back section.

"They dim the lights for slides. You're practically invisible up there," Crystal told the girl, who gave her a timid smile.

"Thank you," she whispered, clutching her map and hurrying up the stairs.

As Crystal slipped into the hallway, she glanced back and saw Wes watching her.

Enjoying Dark Omen? Grab the completed novel in eBook, audio-book or paperback.

Get Dark Omen Now

ALSO BY J.R. ERICKSON

Read the Other Books in the Northern Michigan Asylum Series

Some Can See

Calling Back the Dead

Ashes Beneath Her

Dead Stream Curse

Rag Doll Bones

Dark Omen

Let Her Rest

Bitter Ground

Don't Miss the Troubled Spirits Series - where paranormal mysteries and true crime meet.

Troubled Spirits Series

ACKNOWLEDGMENTS

Thank you to all the people who helped to make this book, and the series, a reality. Special thanks to my husband, Kyle, my parents and in-laws for all their support in my writing journey. Thank you to Rena Hoberman for the beautiful covers. Thank you to the editor of this book, Kristie. Thank you to my beta readers and advanced readers. Thank you to all of you who have read the series. You bring the books to life.

ABOUT THE AUTHOR

J.R. Erickson, also known as Jacki Riegle, is an indie author who writes stories that weave together the threads of fantasy and reality. She is the author of the Northern Michigan Asylum Series as well the urban fantasy series: Born of Shadows. The Northern Michigan Asylum Series is inspired by the real Northern Michigan Asylum, a sprawling mental institution in Traverse City, Michigan that closed in 1989. Though the setting for her novel is real, the characters and story are very much fiction.

Jacki was born and raised near Mason, Michigan, but she wandered to the north in her mid-twenties, and she has never looked back. These days, Jacki passes the time in the Traverse City area with her excavator husband, her wild little boy, and her three kitties: Floki, Beast and Mamoo.

To find out more about J.R. Erickson, visit her website at www.jrericksonauthor.com.

Made in United States
Troutdale, OR
02/28/2024

18062147R10207